Sunset's Dawn

Glyn L. Hughes

PublishAmerica
Baltimore

First printing

ISBN: 1-4137-6317-0
PUBLISHED BY PUBLISHAMERICA, LLLP
www.publishamerica.com
Baltimore

Printed in the United States of America

dedicated to "dad"

Contents

Chapter 1
The Onus of Intentions

"Often it is said among those who lay a claim to wisdom that…
'Precious is the joy that brings its ease from suffering to the soul above
all riches and blessed indeed are those who have possession.'… but
apparent they are also, standing proud in peril, only to be plundered."

The stiffening breeze forced through in gusts, confusing its
disturbance of the early evening air, striking chill upon exposed and
naked flesh as flames flapped noisy their complaint whilst yet dancing
harmony's indulgences, seductive to the tune.

Beyond the burning, away across the valley the people came,
beckoned in from fields and forests so to gather in the city as they
always had on nights like these. To pay their homage and to witness
highest deeds, to be a part of sacred acts and nearer to their gods.

Ishtaac watched with curious interest the snaked procession
hugging saliently the contours of the land. Men, women and children
rolling in on an advancing human tide to flood the pavings of
Zamanque-quetan from neighbouring hillsides in an ocean wash both

docile and indifferent as only subjects can…and somewhere out of sight a lonely bird's screech pierced the night with thoughts betraying sudden of the unseen, mindful watcher.

The Plaza below was beginning to jostle around the footing of the royal threshold as many voices splashed upon its wall of steps, a foaming spray of distant and contagious conversation. Behind and all around vexation's priesthood ushered forth a company of servants, royal hand maids, dressed alike in flowing, stainless white and too, the counsel in traditional storm's mourn red. The former's giggling murmur to excite a squall that swept discourteous the incumbent palace terrace and lend press to fracture in the patient reservation of neglected, reverent aged, whose then testing unto utterance would invoke immediate sombre silence once more to befall.

The massing crowd was choking now the very air from within the capital itself. Their waiting, a simple product of intended reinforcement and hierarchical stature handed out from high above descending from the justified unto the lowly undeserved, a ritual in itself.

And then at last they came, remote and wrapped in arrogance, challenging defiant, the king's own personal guard preceded. Hand-picked, fell and strong, proud men, the very elite, chosen with intent from all his loyal host, magnificently dressed inspiring of an awe imposed with regal finery, wearing dominant the honour of their ceremonial breast plates gifted down, of bone and finest turquoise. They asked for nothing but desired all and never met refusal.

By practised means unyielding, penetrative forward staring gazes of attention brought them to their marks without the shame of downward glance as for themselves alone they ordered to positions of internal rank on either side the royal throne, raised above the windswept cluttered courtyard purged aloof atop a high stepped, moral tier. A seat from which to view a kingdom, a seat by which a kingdom also may perceive its king, whose heralded arrival on the platform prompted then the customary wave of exclamation, forcing audible submission into one collective gasp. Resolute and patient Tomakal-Zaqual awaited restoration, until his flock were once again subdued whence only the impertinent draught would boldly dare defy him, thrashing out its ridicule in flames that fought and wrestled for their freedom snared within the limitations of the hallowed vessel standing firm restriction's duty, as indeed were all.

Two spans wide and shallow were its gently sloping sides and chest height from the floor. Fashioned from the hardened rock revered in title, Firestone, whose polished surface threw a fiery glow that scorched surrounding walls, creating of observant faces, amber-shadowed demons with its eerie flickered glare, spilling forth a heat, that those behind, downwind, had wisely learnt to meekly stand and bear.

That tall, familiar shape emerged to view alongside Ishtaac gazing off impassively ahead undaunted as regally the multitude of light and dark green plumage that adorned him blustered vibrant its distraction on the ever changing air. Looking out across his world, he well accepted their commitment and imbibed of blind obedience whilst relishing the dominant hand that he possessed. He was their power, they shared his growing strength, unquestioned, irreproachable and omnipotent. Opposition fled or fell before his might…and so they came.

Tomakal-Zaqual moved on with cumbrous solemnity to take his elevated place that commoners may see their worth and that he may gift to them the wonder of his being and so watch repeatedly with satisfaction the responsive tidal surges fabricated rightly by encouraged motion, as with a simple raising of his hand compelled another single drawn-out, self-fulfilling sigh.

Above the burning glare, shielded to his comfort by the handiwork of cunning palace craftsmen, he savoured the occasion and took his ease to survey the clear and starlit night, from the magnificence of his earthly kingdom to the Ceiba overhead, gloriously majestic its trailing, milky white. Thence to let attention fall with ponderance drawn towards convergence on the distant, untransceeding boundary of horizons where gods and men dwelt closest, and yet still remained at bay. Where between the mountain peaks of Aclan had himself awakened their beloved, celestial hunter, where the Quauchen's reverent Holy Order chose their dwelling place and where also grim discomfort overcame his eyesight there to scorn endurance of a moment.

Turning away he glared unseeing down upon the assemblage as darkened thoughts of envy gnawed his mind, to shift withdrawal from his unsettling and so place considerations onto other matters, for to once again experience simple pleasure, however manufactured. An innumerably well attended feast of reverence was awaiting him this night, all else must take its turn and suffer his discretion.

Each present, within themselves, regarded also the ever turning heavens and stood undulating patient as the Quetzal tail in flight, in unison, reflectively together. Then finally from within the thick, stone fabric of the palace, came the expectant, rising commotion of long-awaited protestation to meet untimely, gawping death's habitual greeting. But louder tolled the deeper note, blown resonant through shell for quelling of disquiet, swiftly drowning all intrusion fearful, to wrench a muted lull.

Onto the stage, a spectacle for subject's witness, suspended between unyielding guards the limp, defeated body of another in the long procession of humiliation's leaders came as dragged exposed and naked to his final resting place before them. Unforgiving and remorseless were they long accustomed to accept the spoils of victory on offer, and cold the watchfulness was mirrored in that polished stone of old.

The press of tensest intrigue carried murmuring on the breeze awakened him, their sacrifice, to die again one lasting time eternal, to play his part as had and would, the others, in assuming helplessness complete. He was the first this night, and justly so the pain for his endurance would be catalyst enough to bear him to his sacred haven. There remained no longer any thought of questioning past services to rue or search for some forgiveness nor even a reward from futile struggle, but rather was a humbled preparation there adopted to embrace instead, the fate with welcomed ease. The single choice that reinforced the remnants of a pride, no sense a victim or a victor only what must soon and surely be. The fleeting pass of agony to which his body would succumb at this, the sad conclusion of his days would thus be the only testament to ever having lived at all. Traditional and complete was the denial of the vanquished, with all recordings of a failed existence cleansed to the extreme, where even the most stubborn imprint of a vile and bloody death in eyes that saw would lose its clarity before the night was done…well indeed were Tomakal-Zaqual's schooled audience acquainted with this theatre and over acted scene.

Blood throbbed coarse within the victim's ears and thundered starkly honed through senses clear and brittle. Conflicting inner turmoil saw arousal on the last, of chaos borne from terrified renouncements which would wrestle through disgrace for honoured calm…whence into view the dark and dreadful shadow that foretold his end appeared slowly to disturb.

Plainly robed and likewise hooded, the harnessed, storming cloud of sombre menace drifted ominous across the floor. The face unseen, ignored the desperate plight at hand, lacking both the pity and respectful grace to afford even the slightest of acknowledgements, but there, would steal attention to absorb, his stature thus enforced. Came the Raven to its carrion. For so was known by those who feared his name throughout the lands, a figure that numbered if not all, then far too many to conceive. Dark was the bleakest soul beneath the matching raiment, dark also were his deeds. Evil to exceed repellent, the highest of Chanestii priesthood, rebelled within his own remodelling of the ancient Quauchen creed. Positionings of power attained by only but selected few, the station of a lifetime from which was granted no retiring end, such were the paths that had defined them. Advisors also to the king and guardians of much declared as secret. Whispered rumours in darkened corners where men are brave and drunken tongues hang loose held sway that this particular beast was cast among them from the heavens by the very gods themselves to feast upon the corn. A malignance personified surpassing every measure and cruel beyond the lusting were his traits, insatiable his relishing of every other's pain. Rashkulcan only to the king himself and Ishtaac Maluk, his longest known accomplice, High lord, the title in the hands of those few souls that dared. Gnarled grotesquely in appearance although unchanged since any, their first encounter could recall, or indeed despite the wish, could utterly forget.

The figure approached whilst cautious throwing back for drama's glee the cowl that would conceal his foul and bearded visage, to reveal a bared and shaven head, painted at the fore in the custom of the ancient wise. Dotted swirls, anaemic round the eyes, on background blues of lost soul darkness, truly suited for a night god's viewing of its feed.

Sinewed straining arms flung out unleashed to either side with sudden rigid spasm there to freeze upon a stricken pose of frightening challenges whose cries impaled resounding…and in one clenched and knotted fist was held obsidian in the dagger's form reflective of occasion and high office displayed as such for all with eyes to see, bewilderingly ornate and keen, but worn through constant usage. In the other, brandished firm, the Polcan staff of serpents writhed, carved coiled and twisted from the tree of life, headed sinister with fiery God's stone, burnished to a deep perfection, blackly smooth with sleekness to beguile, fulfilled a destiny once more and fell as stayed at ritual's bid snug lodged inside the designated slot provided near unshod feet without the need for sighting. Releasing only then but haltingly his grip for nothing more than tasted musing's sake, the sceptre stood alone, aright obediently, as every other noble did, allowing for his work.

He demanded of the gods to hearken to his call, that they may grant him time enough to last a new born's reach for manhood undeterred, a generation of their sacred cycles…a term of one Katun.

Remote, the vigilance of heaven crept and turned relentless, unresponsive to his words, uncaring of desire toward each layman's thus deceived interpretation.

Once proud, the tribal leader knew now with a horror fully realised the Raven's interest come as dire consequences swept insightful visions through him. Both terrible and cold gleamed merciless, the blackest eyes beholding with a clarity uncompromised, his fear. The harsh severity of features offered no compassion either to his pleas. Undeserved, his begging also floundered flat refused upon the inner ring of bared and swollen foreheads, deformed, inhuman characteristics of a monstrous people seeking always to increase their volume of awareness. Learned sound in wicked arts they would observe duress from either hand but stood unmoving nonetheless as merely faithful in attendance of despising's vilest, master.

Panic for the preservation of hereafter's essence seized the offering at its very being. Clutching feverishly his throat he struggled now to breathe and squirmed, unmasked by fright upon the altar of demise, though not for death itself the source of doom's despair, henceforth perceived was unavoidable damnation.

The Raven's bony hand lay claw like down across a sweat-soaked brow for fixing tremble to submission with a strength beyond the prayer where pleasure watched and knew true meaning of an impotent conclusion as thin lips moistened in anticipation, welcoming due tally.

Ishtaac watched his lordship's form at work from rapt concealment nigh the throne as he had done on countless times before but noted for the first with mild surprise the outline struggle in its bid to gain required mastery of its chore. Where too defeated as the warrior was came framed a vision of that same face cheated, wrung taut furious with some hampering affront afforded by his body's willing not to easily succumb.

Teeth bared, snarled contempt portrayed the difficulty Rashkulcan encountered in trying to grapple free the precious organ from internal chaos, whilst benumbed to mock contrastingly the victim seemed immune towards intrusion, sunk as mercifully spared the reawakening of ordeal. Only could he take his role as witness to the scene, denying, disbelieving even of the nausea that filled his anxious sight. Then suddenly without intention, convulsions forced his breathing torn and rasping shallow empty, as a hollow failure sucked its hoarseness through both punctured lungs. So began the vague onsetting that would herald in the final wrack to overwhelm from rising deep within his chest though now stayed strange removed, astonished furthermore to find himself forced upright gracing momentarily bought freedom from the Raven's icy grasp.

Looking placid and confused upon the faces of the gathering, he eyed with fascination the curious interest of expiring. Thoughts to flee invaded from subconscious reason, tear down the steps and speed away to flight through crowded streets and on unto his homeland, to where a cherished family once would wait upon return across the distant mountains. An escape lay bare before him simply for the taking, his mind was clear, his wherewithal intact. Instinctively considering the options he turned as fast he could to know just why the Raven had released him and how fortune's sudden strike had somehow been delivered.

Rashkulcan's pitiless eyes ignored him as again he avid fed upon attentiveness and blister parched the thirsting of a crowd. Arms aloft the dagger dripped its glint in tightly fisted, knuckled hand and indistinct within the other pulsed removed another life's possession clenched, was finally hailed as precious on command. Warm the plundered wetness fell from hand to floor to form an oily pool that ran in trickles lost beneath the hemline of his robe…and flickering lustrously for apprehension's sway, the blade shone vibrant with desire itself unveiled, imbibed from blood's let scarlet glare.

Deeply rooted and inescapable swelled the burning sense engulfing, surging upward from below as crowded clamour stormed the bastions of the victim's mind where then serenity gave way to screaming madness and a thrilling of the horde. The Raven turned and looked to scoff distasteful of another ending, sneering scorn to form at either edges of a harsh, embittered mouth as the skeletal hand in charge brought forth to show a sight no living host should ever view. The pulsating death throes of its own dear ripped and ragged heart torn brutally exhumed for naught but witness to enjoy and held alone for torment's humoured sake before its dying eyes forever not to close. Nothing but a token jest of one man's inner strength extinguished, glistening clean not withered fragile, less decay and age both delicate and new, it offered little purpose to either owner since deceased or recently accrued…although had granted to the donor deep, insightful wisdom that none could ever share. It was thus that Rashkulcan bestowed his blessing on the world.

"A new Katun has now begun!" Rashkulcan proclaimed aloud that each may hear his judgement.

A fanfare played instinctive on the moment drawn through conch shells droned across the valley, marking for the land the promise of another era, expectantly more fertile than the last.

Celebration commenced to rant tumultuous in its manner immediately upon the understanding of announcement.

"Ahaucan decrees it!" Rashkulcan hailed high again above accomplished adulation and with relish would enjoy such fine occasion, nurturing thoughts of things to be, whence came complete his reign of soul dominion, due rewarded…and so with custom now fulfilled and other pressing deeds required, receded then to contemplate in private his design, retreating thus towards the darkness siding Ishtaac's forced distraction for to smile his grimmest smile perverse with satisfaction. The way was led then for the many now to follow. More ritual death would stain exacted in the aftermath, continuing throughout the night beneath the name and spirit of a god's unwholesome, meagre gratitude. A unifying bond between a man and his presumption of a deity.

Condemned to fate beyond the marrow's toil, subdued the dead procession filed its lingered snake without a tail to see, unto the restless hands of serpent priesthood and the clumsy young but willing acolytes their callow torture to dispense.

The king, raised idly above the carnage, having gifted the masses with his presence, soon grew weary of the ceremonial slaughtering of those already dead. It was become a chore of diminished interest now the eve had brought its guarantee. He returned then, consumed by arrogance towards his quarters to prepare receival of the feast that lay in readiness within the confines of his palace. The Raven followed on and one by one invited dignitaries, the hand maids and all other personal servants trailed thereafter from that place of orchestrated butchery, for pressed events to unfold in their absence.

Spent and worthless, people flowed as rivulets and deltas down into the boiling morass far below to pass unnoticed even, for the most, amidst the rejoicing of great merriment and effluence of drink.

Ishtaac watched the deathly frightened faces lining past pathetic in their silence to a preordained and certain end. Sad to behold was the bewilderment of infants clinging joyless to their loved ones, sad also the impotence of parents to protect.

Escaped, he pondered morbid on a time, briefly either real or imagined but maybe long ago while schooling at the fane, before the plague of human serpents writhed upon the land. When no blood needed to be shed anointing names to thankless gods. No price then, to forfeit for the harvest, excepting that of sweat produced by seasonal labour. When Chaac had sent the rains, he had done so freely through a once believed and boundless adoration of the people on his land. Nowadays however, as royalty and priesthood had become nigh indistinguishable through mutual contention to appease more grandiose and pompous needs, insatiable was grown the appetite for increasingly larger palaces and temples, boastful of the obvious prosperity removed and careful stowed within, though outwardly displaying evermore their brash and complicated facades as evidence fit only for one's envy to behold. And this, before him, was the melancholy price so dearly being paid in crops of flesh extracted from remote and foreign fields…but well and in deep contrast Zamanque-quetan had come to know that sanctioned poverty oft stalks and close, the lavish spoils of wealth.

Ishtaac's musing's led recalled the first dour showings of such consequence, on a day when ancient pious gates were closed to spare the sensitivities of their overseeing visitors, the High Order, from the offensiveness attributed to the amassing, beggared horde without. Never before had this occurred beyond the set agenda. A precedent which began a curt withdrawal and so to distancing from lesser men. The ragged old and young alike, the thin and dirty grey, children amongst the tired, squalid number also, with their hungry, hopeful eyes, crushed or crushing to gain entry. The bedraggled dregs of conquest had arrived upon their very doorstep with only one place left to go.

So came the royal command to cleanse the city streets and raise itself in eminence, high above the heads of each entitled crude and servile, setting those of worthy disposition further yet apart but closer to the realm of gods whilst marginalising others to exist on tendered sewage.

The High Order came again that spring unbidden, unannounced and hence believed as undermined by what they saw befalling...for with them followed new demands to curb presumption's tasteless progress.

Outraged at this interference, Tomakal-Zaqual took counsel granting Rashkulcan the priesthood reins that he desired, breaking with tradition and dispelling outside influence. The gatherings had then commenced and blood was let aplenty bathing city stone that summer in a sickening, deathly red...and the people showed themselves obedient to the cause there entertaining his ambition. The spirit was the god's affair but the heart was man's concern.

With borders widened in due course to feed the ranks and forced, accommodate expected confrontation, old allies floundered to comply on new arrangements, frequent made in absence. And the towering length of shadowed edifice reached always in the grasping...further outward to consume. The court and lineage of the king matured ever stronger and with them hand in hand a-merry dancing to the frenzied fervour of destruction thrived the priesthood all around. Scholars and architects became more akin to soldiers and as used to reeking death about them. Temples stood as fortresses upon the masses that had built them...and every day he watched as Rashkulcan grew increasingly, the spectral power, to becoming the demonic symbol of a human misery incarnate, feeding from the carcasses of new spent life along the way.

Grotesque and sinister was he now, his sallow, sunken corpselike features, defined and honed to their extreme. The aroma of decay enveloped him complete, preceding wheresoever he might tread and befitting always, would this acrid mantle seem.

But to the fore, it was Tomakal-Zaqual of recent, who concerned Ishtaac's discomfiture the most, as, upon too often an occasion he would turn unwelcome interest his direction. Persistent questioning had created a disagreeable predicament, for emerging was that natural bane of man and with it firmly shackled the disquieting one's hindsight felt towards the irretrievable slip of every faded season, where would find itself anew a value in an old concern, intensely so it was when life paused fearful near its end but even moreso was this plight to him full understood a peril when those in askance were themselves known fearful kings.

The once awed respect that came to he, acquired from the youthful almost always slowly turned to sullen, bitter envy honed in search along the hopeless path for desperate explanations. He had none, the gods revealed little of their secrets to him. Despite the unwanted standing that he held and regardless of suspicions, he simply had no knowledge to impart. Only that of internal politics, necessarily acquired, without which he would have earned himself a rather more prostrate position long ago, he felt. The retarded advancing of his years was as much obscure to him as it was to any other, he could only offer humble solace then to those who sought it at their last, and the ungrateful line awaiting that particular task he knew moreover, trailed forlorn as endless. So wherever possible these days he busied himself with the tuition of the minors, declining with evermore frequency, the company of his peers, and indeed in recent years had reduced his roles to little more than supervisory, though still he chose to wear the esteemed jade necklace of his office and the leather binding headband of the wise. Inserted regularly at right angles with cut and polished segments of the sacred guiding stone, he sensed alignment lost, incomplete somehow, when called abroad without.

Rashkulcan was at best disinterested in the mortality of men, refusing all approaches to discuss the matter and as such provided absolutely nothing in the way of assisstance for Ishtaac's increasingly unbalanced welfare and concern as regards the king, despite their sharing of mysterious longevity.

Foresighted life span he assumed to be the reason behind his naming, Ishtaac Maluk, gifted or the gifted one, a subtlety that could see interpretations meaning either but which in addition was taken from an exclusive tongue he also shared apparently alone with Rashkulcan, for no other whom they knew could use it. In common too, was the characteristic facial hair about the neck and jaw line, waywardly unkempt Rashkulcan saw fit to wear it, trim and neatly close was Ishtaac's choice of fashion.

Never having known a parent's presence, Ishtaac often paused to wonder whether they too could be still alive somewhere, and if so where exactly that somewhere might be. Always there had been just Rashkulcan to bully and misguide him, as a brother would.

He had however, gleaned that some time long ago, together they were found abandoned, or as Rashkulcan had since decided, delivered near the outskirt dwellings, though why at such an early age…there simply was no answer. Indeed Ishtaac's curiosity had raised many questions which seldom found reply but further to nigh fruitless, lonely siftings several things had quietly been disclosed to him along the turning of the years and through a small succession of those principals who had chosen his acquaintance, though none in recent times. One of which, that he, or at least his name was mentioned in the Vuhmartra, the sacred and most holy of all Chanestii recordings, a presentation to the city order from their highland Quauchen brethren, though little more than but a single copied chapter of a comprehensive understanding which in their realm, was held as close and secret. Never had he, or ever would he have, the privilege of reading it first hand, that honour being reserved solely for the high priest of the day and of course the king himself, should his whim command it. It told of all things pertaining to the Chanestii histories before they came across the mountains. Of the great journey, their struggle through the plains and the inspired deeds of noble men. It had given them governable laws to order and to shape their lives around but furthermore professed to know of things preceding transpiration…or so it was the held belief. As the mantra would proclaim. 'As was declared, so shall it be.' The first above all things learnt on entering into holy service.

Once, when scarce more than a child, Ishtaac had found himself free of supervision and had allowed the infrequent spirit of adventuring to guide him. Thus forsaking his errand near the deepest vaults of the temple where light itself, to him it seemed, was fearful of trespass, he chanced to gaze upon the very chamber that was said to house this Quauchen gifting and so had bravely dared the anger of already wrathful masters. But whereas such a misdemeanour then would merit certain repercussions, these days, with the current system of intolerance such transgression would almost certainly exceed the call for measured punishment and bring instead blood's fatal wastage. A predictably unquenchable solution devaluing itself with every over frequent act. To the point, where, as this evening sadly demonstrated, no one seemed to care or even notice any longer to whom or why the slaughter had occurred just as long as it continued. A faceless procession of souls were simply required to avert the dissatisfaction of the gods…a subtle twisting perhaps but one that went unquestioned. The priests had said so. Rashkulcan had said so. That was enough. 'As was declared, so shall it be.' But as blood fell upon blood not yet even dried, the circumstances remained unaltered. Chaac delayed the rains and disease among the poor was commonplace. The Quauchen watched aloofly from afar biding on a time of their own choosing and the harvests feeding them were doomed to wither insufficient. Who next then to the altar? Indifference may well begin to ask some questions of its own…awkward, probing questions.

Ishtaac watched morosely as the last of the victims received her fate screaming and kicking to a despised, dishonourable death, as if the struggle in itself was nothing more than an attempt to merely gain a recognition for her passing. He felt he owed them that much, whilst again he listened to those dying echoes haunt the enclosure for a moment's grace before their fading on the night's uncaring draughts as nothing, blown away to some forgotten and eternal namelessness. She also, as had her kindred gone before, found the mutest ending, rudely slain amid the inconsideration of routine. One last heart still beating, coldly torn from sanctuary within its living corpse slumped thrown mundanely to the grisly heap behind those righteous executioners whilst what was left protested limply to its rolling from the altar for then casting down upon the steps, there thudding used and empty to the sodden mound beneath.

The plaza carried on the thrill of the occasion, spirits high regardless of the blood-soaked mire it drank in, or the fetid company it kept. And stark morn's light would see the scavengers a-shuffled come to scour the slack jawed human waste, to set about their gruesome labour, to take their pickings and survive. A ghoulish, welcome ignorance had spread across the land and Ishtaac watched appalled as deafened by his silence.

Still there was an order, vaguely discernible, but clearly felt, however temporary or delicately balanced. The people had, at least, their reasons for what went on. Whether to believe or not came down to personal intuition, if one had the mind, with the determining view, as often is the case, largely depending on which side of the king's fenced borders you relied.

Ishtaac stared from atop the palace trying to avert disgust, out again across the valley realm to the serrated mountain ridges stabbing, blackly jagged at the stars, sighed and so retreated to the haven safety of his thoughts.

There also was another time, still stalking from remembered distant childhood, one whose tendrilled entrails even now would serve political intentions. A brief period of grave unsettling depicted nowhere in any form but verbal and then in hushed and fearful tones. A term known only as 'the vanishings', bereft of all forewarning, when entire communities would somehow disappear overnight without defining reason, leaving not the slightest living trace, but deeply scarring no less every mind throughout their world with cause to live beneath mistrusting darkness, ware as frightened for themselves and for their own.

It affected mainly the areas over the mountains to the north initially but had slowly crept a southward reach from where the holy order dwelt, reticent and isolated in their sacred lands, hidden from the interests of the most inquisitive of kings and prying thieves. The events were to occur repeatedly over numerous seasons before suddenly concluding without the need apparently, for adverse intervention.

Many of the sceptical, led primarily by Rashkulcan often proclaimed misgivings, declaring that the High Order themselves were to blame and had sanctioned those displacements, or at least contributed in some clandestine form, acting more than likely somewhere at the root of such affliction. It was they, he claimed, who had stated during the time of the vanishings that the gods were voicing their displeasure on the reluctancy of frugal offerings and had thus sent Camazotz himself to quench their yearning for the blood of life. And in this manner and many more besides divisions were so seeded, and habitual, reinforced between the peoples and the Quauchen order with old trusting nigh become extinguished and resultant orders shaped divergent henceforth on to canter.

Thus the Quauchen, condemned with high suspicion, functioned largely to their own devices, ignored to practice on the edges of the realms…but here, especially was it so in Tomakal-Zaqual's firm reign. His provision met with but the basic needs, whence came they gathered merely now three times each year for tribune much resented, under strictest order and only then on those occasions where the king was not required to spill before them either royal blood or precious seed. Usefully this restriction segregated to cohere a vital sense of bonding which, together with the unpredictable, unsolved nature and constant reminders of prior disappearances with the ever-present lurking fear that it bore, had allowed Rashkulcan his recent interpretation of the feathered serpent, Kukulcan's religion, incorporating fully each macabre desire. Desires the High Lord and his priests were gladly eager to fulfil, developing the required skills of argument, justification and efficiency which saw the churning out of bloodied spectacle that was the ritual of today. Unite against a cunning foe or die unknown, misplaced forever. An evolving society of promise thus reverting, or indeed would plough its natural furrow in progression through full circle to barbaric origins whilst questing on the privilege that benefit but few.

Perhaps he witnessed then the birth of civilisation new emerging before his very eyes and in its place one sadly beat as fated to demise. Doomed from swaddling birth by man's inherent greed and self-possession. Presuming for to start again no less as seemingly afresh but wholly flawed unsound instead at festered root and on a scale far worse.

Ishtaac let out a resigned sigh, the chill night air and death's aromatic presence sat there ill upon him. He had never got accustomed to performing the duty himself, despite the frequency with which he was called upon to do so, and had therefore taken it upon himself from early days to learn and gain techniques sufficient in their swiftness and clinical enough in application to dispense a life with least remorse and panoply. Deft was he become with bladed cold obsidian clenched reluctant paired in either hand.

Now finally, was his allotted time to escape the ghastly scene, and burdened with his reservations Ishtaac passed inside to join the feast.

The required fasting oft preceding such occasion had by now leant pain beyond the hunger regardless of an eyesight being overfed, to depths where issues of morality he deemed, could wait until much later to then ease digestion's fullest fathom on intact, and grateful stomach. And however much that thought might be displeasing, the rich luxuriant fragrances would bring a welcome change to this.

Descending along the corridors, a route dim lit but known to him, he followed the enchanting lure of Jasmine scent's sweet wafting thickly to entwine, with simmered conversation's music drifting echoes pleasantly midst draught free harmony and time....On into the great hall where the banquet was already under way, to platters laden with the spoils of their expansion and the good, collective harvesting of another's land and labour.

The troubled sea of costumed finery that met his gazing there writhed overshadowed only by the abstract coloured, bountiful displays of polished shellfish, swollen fruit and vegetables to bulk the choicest meats available and lain for those now in attendance duly gorging to assuage themselves upon.

All but the guards and Rashkulcan spoke freely with abandon.

An area set aside, as previously requested, harboured with his seat a company of some of the thankfully, more docile acolytes. Oblivious to his arrival they ate earnestly their fare whilst all around, the crowded tables of the vast and lofty hall embraced the passages of food and drink from one site to another, from vessel to vessel and from hand to heaving mouth. Chatter like the river's flow, swirled long to linger in secluded corners, eddied over him and came again resounding from the hard stone walls of his surroundings. And in the air hung scented wood smoke, mingled with the spiced and roasted succulence brought frequently to hails of heartfelt cheer. He considered as contrasted then, the homage paid, with salivated gasps of wonderous acclamation towards the flesh so patiently prepared and placed triumphantly in offering on each table whence comparing to the value of some other lives cast squandered, violated and discarded, their only worthwhile further use to dress the scene outside with such a hideous facade....Silent and with frowned observant eyes, he took some fruit and ate.

Eventually the banquet would unwind in wandered clutches to a tired, bleary-eyed and fractured clung affair adhered only in the private pockets of discovered friendships whose worthless speech remained, through drunken loyalty as thinly parched beneath the prowess of a dwindling stamina, until the early, empty resonance of hollow dawn's infringement. Ishtaac retired to his quarters shortly after Rashkulcan had taken leave. He had felt the glower of disapproval cast upon him and so thought it wise to do as was expected and, although weary in a sense, it was not he knew, a fatigue to be bathed consoled by mere sleep alone. Indeed very seldom did he ever feel the need for casual slumber, rather using instead, the peacefulness afforded by those lonely, partial hours for insightful contemplation, to study or for simple, unimpeded walking, and when the night enshrouded clear and bright he might indulge all three together with another of his interests, the exploration of the stars.

A strange affinity would stir within him whenever he gazed to ponder upon the complexities and mystery of their being never to encounter boredom in the lustre of their company. Although frequently there were occasions when the emotion of an undeserved denial overwhelmed, through his being blinded to those stingily withheld predictions that most others stoutly claimed were plainly there abundant, seeing only on his part the constellations' images and the routine cyclic paths of glazed celestial traversing. Nevertheless despite this and although himself an erudite priest, Ishtaac privately conceded that he felt, by way of contradiction less religious in those awe-struck instances than at any other moment, ceremonial or otherwise, being quickly lost regardless whilst descending far removed from anything and everything that might occur elsewhere.

The remainder of the night ebbed swiftly, and now in this early morning, blanching, twilight period he watched the arrival of the ragged, human infestation. Creeping their way stealthily through the fallen living to the sacrificial scattering piled about the palace steps. Ishtaac saw them busily set about their ghoulish, sickly operation with revulsion, stripping away, as intact as possible, the tanning hide to satisfy their unsophisticated needs and dragging with them to their lairs all manner of dismembered carrion portable enough to feed whatever other yearning purpose they saw fit…he dared not picture. It was vile business, a poor existence that held attraction solely for the base. Their number consisting only of the desperate, the incoherent, rambling insane, the dim-witted and those most prone to spontaneous bouts of inexplicable uproar lacking any pious reason. The scum of man not yet worth the killing.

Oddly, or maybe not, they were non religious in their outlook on the whole and resisted whatever feeble attempts had been made to approach and educate them in more civilised fashions. They dwelt downwind and largely out of sight a mere stone's throw from the outskirts of the city, among the nearby forests that would hide their ugly feature, where few dared venture and where the suffocating stench and dangerous interest of emboldened wildlife might well strangle one to death. Where Jaguars, Ocelots and other demons serpentine both large and lethal small would often visit under stars, fearless of man's cultivated taste but fonder still it seemed of children folk. Where flourished also the vermin, crows and vultures and anything else that crept and crawled or flew, their driven hunger to appease. Wits then sharpened by the ravenous, civilised encroachment, each had slowly overcome inherent fears…and habitat's decreasing, forced now not just hands but teeth and claws to join the fray…and the flies…the black, swirling, droning clouds of flies. Horrible swarms that clogged the mouth and nose, at worst in drier spells.

There had been many difficult issues to resolve as regards the area of this grim but necessary work. The advantage of their activities were only too obvious by the end of the morning after, but the arguments had raged internally nonetheless for years. The priests resented them as an abhorrence reflecting poorly on their status as being the most affluential city in the realm lacking in solution to alternate system or even proper will and deemed it bound to effect their longer term prosperity, furthermore seeing themselves as slighted when Tomakal-Zaqual ignored their pleas providing such ignoble creatures ample sympathy to practice. For he, within the limits of his wisdom, understood that his streets needed to be cleansed occasionally and that it was the natural order of the unslain vanquished to seek survival wherever they might, but moreover because he cared nothing for the whimsical dislikes of common priest or subject, scoffing openly at naive worries for protecting wealth he saw already as secured. His future plans for greatness lay not in the compliance of successful trading or the luring of good will but rather in the careful, calculated swelling of his borders and the gradual, if possible, undetectable erosion of the Quauchen grip upon his ever-expanding populace, besides, so long as they rid themselves before he woke he saw no reason to concern himself.

Ishtaac was aware that there were other differences arising also, ones that might make the clergy appear considerably less than perfect in the eyes of Tomakal-Zaqual. They vined around the palace in a claustrophobic latticework to snare as lame on gently murmured implications made to gnaw a kingly paranoia, especially after private periods among the influence of courtiers. That whilst he had but one abode, albeit mighty to behold and in fact to date it still maintained its rightful position as the city's most majestic centrepiece, Rashkulcan and his most trusted, a referred status that the king's opinion oft had voiced itself in dubious tone as regards to whether such an individual actually existed, had their choice of several. Certainly they were more conservative testaments of office at present, but nevertheless they were to be found indulging in the sweeter quarters of Zamanque-quetan where fruit and flowers grew from soil untainted…and making matters worse yet still, he knew that there were plans for even more to come. Ishtaac observed this conflict from afar not wishing to involve himself with the beginnings of it and certainly not wanting to be in attendance at the end…more than likely his, he presumed.

One fortuitous coincidence that had aided the growth of the city however, regardless of politics or pride's inevitable intervention, lay in the fact that a serviceable quarry of good stone was to be found close at hand. Which made transportation of the massive blocks required a much less daunting proposition. In days gone by, Ishtaac could recall begrudging teams of humble, parish men hauling almost from their knees in semi-ordered lines, their excess burdens pained to carry, as priests of higher worth gazed down to find small entertainment in those who struggled by beneath, succumbing to their undulation's falling over with the heavy stones much needed…small stones by today's comparison. When citizens themselves were forced or less decisively coerced to improve religious stature and each king's inherited residing. Such unsavoury methods, employed upon so many needed subjects, could and often would no less result as compensated in curt sovereignties, which this one knew full well and therefore sought from early days diversity in other ways to execute the chores.

At that time the outer lands were settled mainly into scattered villages and farmsteads, idle, comfortably slow, uninspired with poor communication and smaller yield to benefit from. A bygone languid, tired tempo abrupted in permission to continue, adjusted on to where once the city's own perspired over questioned labours, both menial and dangerous, and further then improved of sorts to finding now a granted privilege, whose duty oversaw and worked the able, recently defeated through the sodden blood mires of their oft demising predecessors. Where ever since was rightly commonplace that unfamiliar faces should be heard to curse in tongues unknown amid the lengthening, mournful, shadows of a stranger's modern doom, blame's anguish to deny. A new arrangement bent to sap a lesser's worth instead, for ruthless purchase of the goals so yearned for by their glorious rulers.

Tonight would see its unforgiving glare pass wry about the second of imposed festivities. The climax to the ritual of their union. The High Order were due to arrive as near the culmination of each cycle as their call allowed and with them they would bear their precious charge which aptly was entitled, the harmonics key. The one key. Created of two. Fundamental to this most revered of ceremonial occasion, performed in turn, by every leader of their governed world as simple token gesture of commitment.

The act of symbolically adjoining the two halves was perceived reflective of the harmony existing between, and essential to, the kingdoms' thriving and would again take place before the public's gathering. Bringing them together before the people was thus assumed the indication that all was stable in their world and would, through union, surely stay as such. A spiritual guardianship made fast, free to be the individual but strongly wholesome within their collective brotherhood. The link between man upon his ignorant meanderings along the servile roads of life and the unmoved wisdom of the gods.

The key was said by the priests to be a very real and practical device that could unlock a pathway to the heavens along which the ancient Quauchen were understood to enjoy direct acquaintance with divinity, the master…and it was through this act that they were granted their unique perception, enlightenment they would, at times, bestow. It was, then, the physical representation that led to the source of all knowledge, both known and yet to be revealed. Permitting gracious insights to ensure correct, the timing of the planting, and of harvesting, the utilisation of the hardest ground, as in the thin aired, upland regions where a myriad canals and water courses stored the warmth of daylight sunshine to release again at night allowing for the crops to yield where once the savage frost bit hard, of the positioning and the nature of the stars, and all the secret understandings held secure, untold, on their behalf.

Guarded ideas, the king long thought them, hidden solely to preserve a despised, concealing order whilst protecting from the rise of wit's ambitious leaders, with the whole event deliberation and there, artful by design. A manufactured ploy to publicly demean and demonstrate dominion over all the realms. His realm included. Serving merely to humiliate before the watchful conscience of his subjects, graphically reinforcing their dependence on the Quauchen…and so he had grown to dislike this particular ritual with condemnation undisguised and a special kind of loathing.

Tomakal-Zaqual was a proud man who saw no advantage in maintaining the elevated status of the High Order at his expense, his own priests caused him strife enough. Indeed the very idea infected his mind, opening fissures of disgust where wept the sores of malice. Thus his musings frequent bled to compensate and spice the pleasure he could gain by ridding himself of suckling parasites that drained and fed upon him, brooding also on the deepest delving outcome of forced acquisition of the key, believing other heads must bend their inclinations likewise but stagnated strife compelled, as too was he, to wait and stay their eager hands until more advantageous times presented, for fear of misjudging dear a will that might cold galvanise against them should the one attempt bring either failure or success. Each result presented similar problems.

The ruler with such an instrument at his disposal would doubtless stand alone there always, whilst alive, a focus for adversaries to plot collectively against, one of Tomakal-Zaqual's many sound and self-protective reasons to quietly reduce the influence and number of his opposition, but that one ruler unsuccessful in his bid, would doubtless quickly flounder, weakened to destruction, impotent beyond the beggar's salvage.

Although firm in a domestic capacity, Tomakal-Zaqual's standing in the wider vastness was for now, contained. Outside the parameters of his own convenient land, interference was, at best, to be seen as being strained and under the tension of increasing sufferance, with each expansive practice duly frowned on from behind the thinnest veil of diminished tolerance, to the point whereby a keen resistance to abide his agricultural projects and most other policies of reclamation, showed itself exposed and raw, all along new borders. The ignorant simply did not, or refused to, understand the growing responsibilities he was having to endure on their behalf in order to sustain the advancing of the realm...and if the difficulties of this situation saw no improvement, Tomakal-Zaqual felt that soon he would be forced to embark on new, more widespread undertakings and completely reconsider any previous promising of compensation.

He saw clearly too, the twisted irony that as he sought to grow so he needed more than ever the full and unconditional support of faithful, close around him. But they in turn would need to know then that the gods were on his side and that they were destined not to be cast adrift and forfeit because of his ideals. Such doubt could be reaffirmed though, constantly if necessary, if only he were to take charge of but one small detail. Therefore he deemed it not only his ambition but his rightful duty also to protect the key from every other leader whom he knew, made plans to steal it. He thought to keep his treasure in the palace or better yet would build another, a grand and special placement purely for its housing. Where all would come and pay their rightful homage…and accordingly, would grant respect, to he, Tomakal-Zaqual. Then he would truly be the king of kings and worthy of the company of gods.

Rashkulcan was in full agreement, they had spoke often of the merits and was known to openly fuel this particular vanity….But were he to act upon these thoughts….Whether the link to the gods was real or not, unless the power behind the key did not transcend with swiftness to his hand but was found instead to loiter, whilst accusingly proclaimed as stolen, then his guardianship at best would surely be in question and his strength presented fragile, ripened only for contesting. The land could then be seen, through clumsy, unfit leadership to be in jeopardy, with him reviled as radical and henceforth held at fault. The charge alone could carry gravest consequence, if unprepared, and well he knew that these would be the weapons planted in the minds of every unenlightened, coupled to the inevitable threat that the High Order would evoke in withdrawing favour from the gods, forever to forsake them. Also, he saw these reasons as sufficient to internal, nurture undesirably contagious misgivings of a great betrayal even among his own people, strong enough perhaps to incur the blame for each day's mundane failing that befell them in their new found disassociation, ultimately bringing downfall by attrition. He would require quick successes to rally and cohere his own on the first of those most crucial steps to attaining full supremacy. To avert their doubting of himself and allow, once sound, his open calling for a different order there extinguishing all notions of a weak deception…but his patience, as the years grew stretched and sorely taut about him.

Ishtaac had spent the day browsing the strings and charts in the stuffy, airless, vaults of the temple and was by now very much in need of breathing a relative freshness once again. He strolled down into the city as he often did, to an old, familiar place and sat himself upon the grass beneath the trees that lined the western avenue to watch the procession of recent apprehensions, trudging weary by, through shadow's probe before the setting sun. The walking dead, soulless eyes unseeing, blinded by despair. Cowered bodies, trailing limbs fatigued and spiritually eroded, a linear void of care. Their fiercely ordered ranks stretched, winding up towards the temple and then from sight around the rear. The origins of the sequence traipsed, lost somewhere among the municipal buildings where those of any passing value had been selected first to work instead, their passage to an afterlife. All around the wide plaza they were ignored, a commonness of sight that had turned their suffering invisible to any but the guards. Only they paid them due attention when required, in the form of harsh and brutal, sharp correction…but this collected currency was almost spent already and there was seldom any protest.

Ishtaac shook his head miserably, tonight the grandest slaughter would commence. The second but most important night of their festivities would take its place, although the venue would be altered. This time it was the Rashkulcan's address that would provide them temporary lodgings until untimely, came dispatching to beliefs.

Built opposing the palace, quite aptly Ishtaac had thought on numerous occasions, it was sited directly across the main square. The most efficient abattoir of all the highest places it stood plainly tiered to seven lofty levels, maturing grandly on the diminished shells of each its many predecessors, reaching high above the other central buildings, dominated only by the royal residence itself. Better equipped for its grisly purpose than the palace, there were exceeding by five the altars put to service, and much required owing to the added workload evermore demanded.

Ishtaac sighed and stretched his legs, thinking it regrettable that so many were to stain the symmetrical beauty of his once fine city in such a costly manner, and that spring the season's choice for rebirth should soon witness such demise on so singularly human a scale and likewise be corrupted in this way.

The tree-lined avenues that criss-crossed Zamanque-quetan were but one of few allowances of natural intrusion. Rivers and streams as plundered lives of men, also ran designed incumbent to the clever will of overseeing architects delight. Channelled through their neatly ordered strictures as canals they graced the radiating roadways, swirling by beneath seductive carved and ornate bridges, built on whims of mere fancy, off conveyed from trickling to the gush, then splashing on their merry way without reluctance over weirs to purposes ingenious and intriguing to the eye. A foaming sparkle of cascades in effervescence trilled to cleanse the mindful spirit with its warbling for denial of unspoken, inner guilt. Reflecting in the ponds and lakes the beauty of the heavens themselves displayed on earth, in man's domain, abducted without loss.

At least that was how he liked to remember it, these latter days the rivulets tended to ooze and heave a boiled obscene, slow and sickly, pink blush red the majority of time.

Rising uncomfortably to ignore such images of discontent Ishtaac set off aimlessly instead, struggling to lose himself in any other concern, only to find himself, despite accustomed numbness, inescapably aware and utterly confuted. Shying shameful from the face of melancholy provocation was more commonly his wont and rarely was he ever roused to lend a voice objecting with compassion but had simply learnt to blindly drift along conviction's tide obedient and chaste.

Borne absently upon the allure of drawing currents however, he had stumbled on the marketplace and managed his distraction in the recent influx of outsiders whose added welcome sparked a fevered trading far above the normal fervour.

Diversely coloured fabrics offered by the visitors shone interwoven in the gold of fading sunset. Their secrets, revealing tales of distant, unheard yarns captured skilfully, if one chose to look, within the cloth itself, holding the viewer tantalised, with charm and dazzling confusion. Of faith and aspirations concealed within the making.

Consumables in ripe abundance potatoes, maize and forest leaves in baskets at their masticating sellers' feet, crowded the narrow pathways and forced attention downward for fear of spilling out their precious load. Potent drinks alongside strange and curious pots of burning scents proposed to put one at one's ease with varying degrees of swiftness through their effortless consumption, and wondrous aromatic spices that could regalise the plainest dishes, filled late afternoon's receding with a perfumed air of newness and an expectation to be treasured.

Ishtaac enjoyed the market and often came to listen to the charged, excitable exchanges, to quietly observe the vibrant, dashing traders and the music of their speech. Dealing animated, confined beneath the claustrophobic intimacy of their blustered, multicoloured overlays caught billowing as the summer water meadow sweeps its flowers clean on warm and sheltered breezes. Conjuring up a unique atmosphere of sight and taste and scenting, a privateness to nurse and tuck one's tired cares away.

Unfortunately, today scant freedom was more limited, soon he would be required to perform his most detested, binding chore of office at the ceremony this evening and protocol demanded that good time be spent in preparation for the coming of the High Order…forever would be nice. Though in honesty it was they themselves who had uttered first dissension to amounts spent in their name. A restriction Rashkulcan was quick to crush, for the ritual he saw increasingly as his and the old High Order ought to reassess their place within or simply not present themselves he was eavesdropped counselling his king…merely send the key alone and all else could be done, was known his advocation.

More often these days, Ishtaac would quell inherent fears and dream of his escaping, to roam in distant lands released from kings and Rashkulcan, and flee imprisonment from there, within the rooted cage of his concern…from bars that kept him bound and flightless, which came nonetheless eroding, weakened further every day by the salted tears that unified his own with those of unknown children who cried their wilting innocent departures in every place misfortune forced his eyesight's look.

Reluctantly with dreaded obligations weighing heavily upon him, Ishtaac turned away from the enchanting scenes of respite, reservedly encouraged by more fruitful speculation and began his ramble along one of the many secluded alleyways.

In the relative silence he sensed himself enveloped, isolated now and vulnerable thus consequently walked to counter, hastening through the pressing elevation that surrounded. High, red clay, brick buildings which provided constantly a dampened shading offered also opportunities for undesirables to ply their trade, and was therefore better to maintain he knew, an air of swiftness in such districts, for had learnt by past mistake. His directness would at least afford the idle boned assailant with a moving target to assault. Soon however, he found himself, unmolested, once again out among the open spaces only to be confronted by all the misery and hopelessness that remained the human chain.

Following upward to the skyline on the racing burn of sunset's chase he considered the progressiveness of more recent structures, where to his dismay, after recent shady confines, saw his gaining a familiar consolation in their presence....The temple especially, where he frequently resided with its altars painstakingly sited to the accordance of a universal harmony within its uppermost courtyard. Each dedicated to Tonatiuhchan, the residence of the sun, the after life hallowed land, where entrance waits assured for every one of those expired, either on their cold, remorseless surface or any heated field of battle. A paradise of curious pairing, Ishtaac believed since it proposed the conundrum of continued, cyclic malevolence between the victor and the vanquished, contested on a celestial battlefield with the triumphant claiming defeated souls again as spoils. Suggesting to him, the plausibility of being dispatched once more, to, if not returned, he knew not where.

The floor space immediately behind each one had a retractable wooden cover from which no one ever had emerged. These hatches would be removed this night to accommodate, revealing the black, remorseless, empty drop unto the holding pits below, where the carcasses were stored until those hungry allocated could remove them. A labyrinth of gullies lay there also, designed in channels to represent the sacred patterns of divinity, cut deeply in the polish of the paving stone's grim lustre, keen to carry off the blood for spewing freely from the mouths of gods as torrents at the outmost edges of the temple. A sickly cascade that spilt its tumbling to the redirected rivers and canals below. Furthermore this most soberly deviceful of enclosures, was surrounded on three sides and formed a rising arc stepped in tiers upon which to stand and meet the rising sun. A viewing gallery, the arms of which embraced wholeheartedly the vain atrocities composed within its eager welcome.

The priesthood was indeed very proud of this developed system of a necessary carnage and Rashkulcan specifically. Ishtaac compared it to the single altar buildings of the not so distant past and exhaled deeply with regretful sorrow and a downcast shaking of his head. The attraction of the newest planning being all too evident amid these more, or rather less constructive times.

The summoning conch brought the city's holy fellowship together from whatever task detained them. Its resonant vibration emanated from the temple's peak to browbeat Ishtaac hasten on his way. Already he had overstayed and would doubtless, face the penalty tomorrow. He sped across the busy plaza passing by unnoticed, the threatening heads of two stone serpentine creations grafted there as sentinels afoot the pyramidal imposition, fashioned with an impact to enhance in towering, charismatic forms of rattling reptiles at the strike. The writhing undulations of their twisted bodies scaled the vertical to each their detailed warning tailpiece, flanking either side the central stairway crawling on a graceless beauty to adorn its frontal aspect with a calculated menace.

Some of the younger and more fearful hurtled past, racing upwards, pressed towards the vacuum of their designated places. Ishtaac stepped out shortly after, neatly in their wake, amongst his waiting brethren already amassed along the tiers and approached his mark to side the nearest altar unprepared but nonetheless quite present. With effort he refrained displaying desperate need to regain misplaced air and too, avoided accusation's withered stares aimed in his direction, choosing instead to feign a curious peering to the cavity agape beside his shuffling feet, and in so doing managed there to harness something of an inner sense of rectitude whilst filtering quietly his breathing to a pretence of composure.

Only the barest minimum of torch light was being employed at this early stage of the ritual prompting Ishtaac's forceful nonchalance to turn attentions upward once again and take his opportunity of cloudless skies above. Tonight the stars would stir in greatest numbers, through their reasons born of either sympathy or morbid spectacle, he decided not on motive, but the moon, already silver pale lit clear and looked upon the rise with favourable mystique, blunt weary optimism thought....They waited.

The arrangement of the terraces meant that it was less exposed than atop the palace, having a more secluded, personal quality where the draught intruded less. A theatre of shame standing stained with unseen guilt preparing for devouring whole, the harrowed crop of further blameless.

Rashkulcan, deliberately unhurried, emerged slowly between the stacked, segmented tails, his weight borne heavily upon his snake's head staff. At the summit of his climb he lingered briefly on collective rein, his laboured breathing hidden sound beneath the heavy robes he wore to full concealment. Assistants on either hand offered dutiful attention but were promptly found denied of favour, receiving merely the annoyed curt motion of dismissal that was naturally his custom. It was only then that Rashkulcan continued on his way.

Ponderously the Raven neared Ishtaac, but on passing suddenly ceased his progress, hovering to reside prolonged, intense, unsettling moments in a brooding, frontal challenging of any weakness calling for exposure. One suppressed perhaps, resigned to lurking deep inside the primordial consciousness of prey, considering, no doubt, some detrimental form of crude address in keeping with his way. Ishtaac however, remained outwardly impassive although internally he squirmed intimidated to endure regardless, the expectant, delving search, whence in return stood asking naught of his superior. Eventually Rashkulcan decided to resume his stalking prowl once more leaving each to gauge within himself the measure of their triumph.

Several moments later the anticipated runner bounded clumsily to sight, stumbling over the upper threshold of the temple steps without due reverence or its premise, fully naked to the glare of the arena and the discord of its covey. Rashkulcan spun around at speed to face him with agility that gave more lean to warning than any mere caution gifted from the tongue could ever match. Never was approach made through such conduct, quickly from behind, even those of a naturally wayward gait took pains to announce throat's clearing introduction first and those with prudence and affinity towards their life would hail position meekly from afar, with preference through another. Nevertheless he bade the runner near with a tolerance rare witnessed and listened as, bowed through gasping breath, the messenger proceeded to relate his tidings.

The High Order were arrived and sought prospective audience with their remote Chanestii brotherhood. Rashkulcan consented and returned the man then called upon his own to go inform the king. Two young men on cue, dashed enthusiastically in practised manner from the lofty courtyard about their long appointed errand, vanishing to the clenching grasp of night with acute and youthful haste. Rashkulcan, escorted by advisors returned to the edge of the platform and looked down upon the city faithful, icily removed to witness the arrivals as they came. Petrifying gazed a while, his gnarled demeanour as a fossil tree left proud alone where ages past a forest stood on desolate horizon, then gave to wave his hand with but a snatch of invocation. A subtle gesture aimed at those who watched abiding, tirelessly vigilant along the outer wall. At this signal the upper terracing stark flooded with the brandished firelight of a hundred flaring torches, formed to eyes observing from their lowly station, as a single lofty beacon, burning brightly high above their ken and brought to them with flourish from beyond the hand of invite.

Ishtaac also could, from placing near the steps, stare down into the excited midst of those now gathered in the plaza below. Where inhabitants and visitors alike again were crowding close together as they had the previous night. Except this evening, there emerged from the confusion of the horde a clearing pathway cleft among them, created and sustained by palace guards, as too a swell of vast excitement rolled in through their number heralding the first suggestion of a sighting.

Over many kingdoms was their trail obscured, a wake whose source failed truly into folklore by the bearing of their treasured charge, a momentary gifting to the people. Unhindered or deferred in any way they would continue steadfastly that journey in the sedate and tranquil guise that was their usual pleasure. Transferring through the land the one known key, proffering equilibrium and strength through solid unity. 'As was declared, so shall it be.'

Firelight amber lit, the sacred snake meandered forward in procession through the throng with less, it seemed, attending than in previous years. One cycle's inconsistency that Ishtaac later mused upon, as first impairing otherwise the flawlessness of jewelled ceremony, although for now he paid no further heed. Instead his attention bent across the masses out toward the palace seeking the appearance of the king…but there only absence and serenity did reign without undue commotion…calm expectancy prevailed with neither sign nor indication of his coming. The High Order continued on their reverent passage for the moment, noticeably unmet. On indeed, until arrival at the footing of the temple steps, and still there came no movement from the king's abode. Something was amiss. Ishtaac could sense it and so too could every other present. The High Order answered only to the gods and yet, here for all to know, they suffered the display of being subjected to endurance on the mere trifling of regal whims. Anxious moments followed. Never before had such audaciousness occurred. Ishtaac was intrigued. Rashkulcan shifted uncomfortably, his shadow blackened torment struck a visible impatience on the coldest stone of scrolling snakes, as brittleness was tested to its limits.

Notaries flocked around like crows to carrion, encircling their master, testily flapping to distraction with the flighty nervousness of their disquiet. Then at last to gift relief the audible sigh of a collective strained release, proclaimed long overdue, his highness' approach.

From the embarrassed silence a murmur rose to cheer and greatest clamour. The people parted of their own accord before their unborne king, whose footsteps wandered easily allowing for a steady forward saunter. Greeting willingly he paused for often to accept in readiness the adorant delay of those particular subjects whom he stopped to acknowledge along the shameless, swaggered touring of his way.

The High Order for their part remained peacefully untouched by the gravity of the gesture, resolved to linger on in patience for his welcome.

Painfully slow wound the progress of the king and his entourage until eventually they gained, without complaint, the diminished Quauchen order's standing firm beneath the elevated judgement and unsettled temple glare. Without a spoken word or recognition of any forthright kind they climbed the steps together, whilst whispering conjecture, on anticipated tiers dried through plaintive hand wrung woe and ultimately ceased.

Rashkulcan straightened markedly, taking up his usual posture of superior nobility as Tomakal-Zaqual made entrance heading a surly column of select elite who moved on haughtily to preordained positions. The High Order filed in alongside dressed to contrast simply, in uneventful robing blanched but for the narrow black and crimson banding sited at the hem, travel stained and bound around the waist with humble twine, concealing everything about them but exposed and shaven heads. Little was there to distinguish any one from any other. No outward sign of wealth nor indication of a rank. The one that led was merely, at the time, the one who walked in front.

Rashkulcan thus welcomed each in turn with formal full embrace and led them to their allocations, dispersed affront the ranks and before the large stone altars. Their number being less than usual was more apparent now, giving rise to uncomfortable discernments of a slighting nature whence noticeable gaps of absence appeared at the extremities of their arc.

Ishtaac scanned the faces curious to determine features, but only age appeared to differentiate and single one out from his brethren. This eldest whom he pondered on caught his eye and held his stare with knowing ease. Both then, proceeded to invade the other's distant privacy, though neither was exposed …and then the old man smiled traversing full the bounds of his expectancy. Never before had Ishtaac seen a smile adorn the usual stern, grim faces of the Quauchen Order and so received it with disquiet almost to the point of sound disturbance. Not a happy smile, but one born rather of an understanding where the owner relishes possession of some purposefully undisclosed, but all the more required information.

Unintentionally frowning in response, Ishtaac directed his attention away to where Rashkulcan was daring in his converse with the king, displaying clear agitation under the restraint of preventing his displeasure toward the evening's conduct. Tomakal-Zaqual himself though seemed at ease and unconcerned, expressing the emotion openly by nonchalantly taking up his station at the altar nearest Ishtaac, leaving as he did so, the void of curt disinterest gaping obviously between them.

Rashkulcan glowered angrily after his king's revealing impudence and moved to stand before the row of tolerant, overseeing holy men before there making the accustomed requisition for production of the key. For gifted freely was the way, unquestioned. 'As was declared, so must it be.' The completion of the mantra. He was ignored completely and in unison further enraging Rashkulcan's suppression of ill-temper. Each of the order denied him as a whole staring on oblivious to the night, unmoved as mere spectators to the ritual.

Turning away, the king spat upon the sacred ground, a solitary figure never more so riled to face his subjects from despised religious steps, to stand before them bold defiant in the insolence of flaring silhouette. He coughed distracted and fidgeted impatiently, feeling the eyes of all the host upon him, watching for the fracture of deliberation's slow reduction. The offence cut deeply to his fragile core as quietly he considered of his options. Loyal guards there were in plenty, situated round the temple's penned arena and thoughts were justly bent to use them, ending finally that biding, foreseen moment there and then, causing too, an end to this perpetual charade and so command deliverance of his key from the clutches of provisional bearers. If in fact they had the item with them. His suspicion was that they had not, having grown concerned of him from cowardice in hiding, watching fretful with a woman's scheming whilst his hand unknowingly had strengthened, and that the entire proceeding furthermore could be construed on this occasion, naught but ploy elaborate enough to try allegiance to tradition. If this was so, they played a deadly game.

The populace beneath was shifting restless to the testing of their king. He would rather be slain than fail himself before their eyes, bent to kneel before a lowly, outcast priesthood.

A tautness seized him as he settled matters in his mind. They could offer only small resistance to he, Tomakal-Zaqual, paraded arrogance there deemed…but as if the gods played toying to their entertainment's daring jest, exceeding all perception's mortal skill, at that exact same thwarting moment his plans fell interrupted on the suscitated hiss of Rashkulcan as the designated keepers made their offerings known by stepping hesitantly forward. Hastily they were ushered before Tomakal-Zaqual to whom they dutifully submitted their components parts and with unceremonious swiftness, from them were they snatched to holding tightly, with possession resolute in royal hands.

Night black as the sky without a distant star's illumination, created from the godstone, gifted flaring through the heavens. Born of ill-omen. Harbouring weight beyond expectancy of eyed dimension. Fashioned not by the hand of any earthbound craftsman, or so the legends told. Two kindred discs dwelt sited at the end of each a shafted piece, locked together face-to-face, inscribed with echoes of the Sun and of the moon uniting, forming forged, a central hub. And from this hub stood forth across the bond a single flange, discreet but of mysterious, usable proportion. The shafts thus emanated either side the centre…and along each their length at random distances and radially located, with a variance about more limited circumference, spurred the lesser, activating pivotal protrusions.

The whole of the object measured little less than half a stout man's forearm when complete, as now it was, and more, whilst in this state the bearer found created too, the strangest resonation, soft vibrations venting from an unknown source contained within. A privileged flowing to the world without through likewise, privileged touching which, outside the Quauchen Holy Order only kings had come to know.

Odd, thought Tomakal-Zaqual that the key should be named in plural when only the one note had he ever heard on both of his occasions. The mainstay of society as known, the pathway to the gods, fastened as a partnership within his eager grasping. And in awe he gazed upon it, driven more than ever previous to hence foster as his own.

The outer lying face of either disc had too, their series of engaging images compiled to hem the shanks, though these he saw defying him elusively as cryptic and thus beyond his care...but still the king took time delaying evermore to glance and ponder, sensing wonderment as stirred anew, enflamed with flickering eyed intent whilst drawing to the recall, momentarily, that past inspiring time whence he had held the key before.

Aware of envy's, crushed anticipation ringing in his ears, Tomakal-Zaqual smiled inwardly, sniffed to clear perplexing, and then raised for public view, deserved desires, extending all theatrics to his triumph.

Tension shattered, the crowd roared full approval like the breakers crashing in upon the coast. Relentless was their overwhelming in resolve collectively, for harbouring will suffice to overcome the sternest obstacle in given time, bringing even the loftiest of mountains to humility along their partisan, coercive, crumbling shore...and with such purpose galvanised behind him, he himself would see accomplished, every aspiration dreamt in lucid night.

As if called in covert summons his manic eyed to bulging stare fell sharply on intense concerns, heard mutely echoing from Rashkulcan's bare held composure. Spurted flashes of conspired recognition passed between them, and all the while did Ishtaac, watching, silent note.

And on command despondent captives fell among them, cast in from the awfulness of their confinement to the open breathing freedom of their last...from whence commenced the jubilation of a joyous slaughter. Life poured ceaseless from the reservoir of deep, expendable humanity while grateful audience gave thanks for personal sparing and a unity of sorts throughout their shadowed land.

The king's taste lingered on the edge of famished sight nourished by seduction close, before reluctant yielding on advice and ceding to the sway. Handing back the pieces he then rounded angrily on heel without disguise and pride, for felt as compromised, to strut away, towards his palace refuge place considering now, a sordid obligation awkward filled.

Filing from the hideous mess undaunted, Tomakal-Zaqual came followed by the Holy Order and advisors seeking also to review the remnants of the evening from the comfort of the royal house and there exempt, pass time among the pleasure of selected womenfolk.

Rashkulcan remained a while, enjoyed the kill and ate his fill with ugly relish, satisfying wantonly the obscene soiling of distorted needs on preference to pursue them later at his leisure. Ishtaac though, continued to deliver his repulsive deeds of pity after even Rashkulcan retired, enduring to perform allotted tasks with empty, heartfelt dread. Bound sorely by the bitterest of commitments he would stay until his wearied limbs could act with clemency no longer, regretfully resigning to abandon poorer wretches yet to come to a barbarous drawn out termination in the cumbrous hands of lesser men, finally trudging off exhausted to desert that high enclosure spent and spiritually dead.

His frozen heart drummed icily the mournful march of guilt...and his ears, relieved, turned all denied to distant deafness far removing from vociferation's tapestry of those undead who still could further harry him.

Retreating inside the protective shell of duty unconvinced, he went to seek his solace in the drink pots readily available on those stalls about the central city, a welcome detour from his route towards the palace and an opportunity to halt and somehow bathe what thoughts he could in apparitions of refreshment. To cleanse away the blinding horror of a vivid, unrelenting memory in water running still untainted by the shamefulness above, while knowing soon that it, like every other thing that entered Zamanque-quetan, would find, by far, the task too difficult to leave without impairment to its fundamental traits.

Drinking from both jug and offered pot Ishtaac meandered his way through the company of revellers who perhaps indulged their jubilation overmuch he thought, but then no dismal doubt were full aware that situations very easily might alter for their worse.

Presently and without his really noticing, Ishtaac stumbled on the grandiose foundations of the palace where overhead could hear the king's musicians playing out their whispered melancholy intonations. A capturing release of summer draught, the music drifted peacefully upon him, steadying to soothe with sombre, mellowed colour, the frenzy of imaginings, and there he chose to sit a while, removed and quietly adrift but clinging always to the timbre. Away from the distracting chaos of the feast he could, whilst here at least, best savour of their captured mood. Thus he pulled his bloodstained cloaking fast about him, harnessed in the darkness and obscured his presence from the occasional pry of passers-by, escaping further still within a snatched but precious moment of elusive solitude, and was a time content to simply hide…but all too soon and unexpectedly, with deep regret the music ceased abruptly, dropped curtailing with a rudeness, the enchantment of its deft melodic weave.

Attention bent to skyward in complaint, Ishtaac saw the knot of a disturbance spewing from the topmost step. At first mere jostled silhouetting clouding in the night and then the Holy Order clarified his disbelief…projecting haste and disarray, descension's wings swooped hurried down to swamp him. With an air of unseemly anxiousness they advanced at speed appearing angered by some inhospitality incurred. It was customary for them to remain throughout the evening, to leave then on resumption of their southward journey at the sun's first greeting of the day. Until now and without exception, this had always been the way.

Steps clattered to the bustled sound of scattering feet as the Quauchen elbowed noisy past, surrounded by an entourage of flustered palace dignitaries. Many protesting at, others apologising for, some previous protocol infringement. From the confusion he learnt that Tomakal-Zaqual had managed to upset the feast by excluding his honoured guests from dining at the regally esteemed high table, reducing them to sit among the ranks in a dispersed, belittling casualness, deliberately implanting reputation shoulder to repulsive shoulder amid the comparatively ordinary of the realm. Enflaming unhinged matters moreso by his gifting answer to their displeased whines, whence stating even for the gathering's deaf to hear that should they wish to continue accepting charitable benevolence and dine at his expense, then they would do so at his arrangement or face losing contribution altogether. Then in choicest phrase where none were spared embarrassment, likened their order to a nest of parasites existing solely on the labours and the graciousness of others…a point very much contested through denial from all the palace aides right now. He had furthermore attempted to enrage proceedings by concluding that their insolence and lack of gratitude was henceforth to be found unwelcome in his palace, but by that time he was calling after only the most tardy of their somewhat lively group.

It seemed to Ishtaac, an irredeemable situation and one best left alone at present. The priests and royal staff clearly worked in vain, with their efforts only succeeding to infuriate the Order at every reinforcement.

Revelry died almost instantly among those close at hand on hearing the commotion, each stopping to enjoy with intrigue the unfolding of the conflict, where an interested silence spreading from the privileged individual granted seedings of encouragement in others for a likewise conduct.

Casting eyes upon the awesome spectacle of the royal household emptying of its venerable with haste and lost decorum, many were themselves inspired to follow suit and swarmed as they, spilling off in all directions to informing any that they knew not in attendance of the news that had befallen and choosing also, in their furtive wisdom, to be as far removed from an unpredictably dangerous king as politeness might allow, but rather more the inclination prayed, before their absence could be noticed. Ishtaac could not however bring himself to remain in ignorance much longer, seated so far from upheaval and decided therefore, though forever after he would regard it a most unwisely reached decision, to swim against the fleeing tide and climb his way instead, up and onto the palace courtyard for a closer, personal viewing.

Inside the banquet hall, Ishtaac saw the trappings of the feast lain scattered and abandoned. Two Sentinel guards looked out across the meal remains from beside the main internal doorway at the far end of the room, speechless and without regard awash on sterile faces depicting firm, that all was well in keeping. Ishtaac thought to enter, when the raised emotional voices he recognised as Tomakal-Zaqual and Rashkulcan, came locked in heated disagreement, bursting through to sudden revelation, heedless of any that might intrusive, linger nearby, and so stepped lightly backward to the veiling of the shadows undetected.

He knew the king to be wilful and arrogant in determining his ways, and the clearness of his thoughts against the High Order were there and set in stone but under Rashkulcan's skilled counsel and diplomacy, had thus far, always managed to avoid such confrontations, at least on such a public scale. Rashkulcan was a vengeful, spite driven man who worked in devious ways also but was never blinded rash by the immediate for sacrificing truer gain and barely raised his voice in anger. On this occasion however, neither listened to the other for fear of stalling in their argument thus falling prey to the other's sure conviction. However, despite the virile nature of their dispute only the guards and Ishtaac had the displeasure of hearing the exchange.

Tomakal-Zaqual was adamant in his stance to call upon his most entrusted watch, apprehend the Quauchen plague and forcibly return them for completion of the feast, expressing loudly too his wishes to relieve them of their valued content. Such disclosed offensiveness Rashkulcan thought madness and declared as much. Which did little for Tomakal-Zaqual's infuriated disposition. To consider him a madman alone, in privacy of thought was one thing, to suggest it, was an act, for others, tantamount to begging execution.

Rashkulcan sighed and carefully withdrew the remark. The king accepted the indiscretion and continued casting his aspersions on the Quauchen Order and their worth to his society branding of them an expense that he could ill-afford. Rashkulcan argued that their presence was an important catalyst at this particular juncture and so, worthy of preserving until he saw the time as right. Unless of course, Tomakal-Zaqual was prepared to set his kingdom far aside for standing on its own.

"The knowledge that they grant consolidates our people through belief and allows us all to thrive," Rashkulcan stated, his eyes flitting around, now mindful to make clear his loyalty to any ear that might perhaps be listening.

"…and I shall release it," Tomakal-Zaqual reasoned, " not introduce it in the whimsical manner that they dispense, but freely without the reservation. " He proceeded justifying his requirement.

"But they are many and strongly forged in will. Have we the might to succeed in outright conflict?" Rashkulcan whispered privately barely on the edge of even Ishtaac's noted hearing.

"When I have the key at my disposal, every other kingdom soon enough will bow beneath my praised advantage. Then…I shall have the strength I need."

"But there will be little time for such a vigorous transference of allegiance before we are descended on."

"Then I must hope that there is time enough."

"Hope? Design is more reliable an ally." Rashkulcan sneered away whatever was remaining of a smile.

"Then inform me of your counsel. For it is clear to me that you possess ideas of your own concerning this particular matter but be swift in your delivery. I have plans to set in motion."

Their exchange acquired then the hushed air of conspiracy, difficult to discern with any confidence or distinction. Ishtaac retreated warily away across the open courtyard, vulnerable as chaff exposed to rampant breezes. He could see the pair advancing still towards him, emerging from the brightly floodlit hall utterly engaged in devious fabrication of audacious, awful scheming with their eyes held fast intently to his blessing, as each assessed the truthfulness proclaimed, to sway the other's thoughts. Backing abruptly onto the unseen lifted dais of the royal throne's plinth base, his muted gasp betrayed the root sensation of subconscious pause now punctuating fretfully their guarded conversation but yet managed artfully to scramble coy atop the seat before his prying was uncovered…a treasonable offence that bore the stiffest of eternal of penalties.

Alone, ensnared within the pressing silence, breathing raced to panic trespassed only by a heartbeat pounding death-knell's toll as every nerve end trembled to the calling of alarm, his mind an overflowing storm drain of confusion, producing explanations to implausible excuses in a muddled preparation to emit upon demand…though nothing was to surface clear or gain his satisfaction. Ishtaac crouched concealed as he was able adhered perversely to the whispering's encroach, from the rasping of a serpent's tasting to the barely audible level of his strained and throbbing earshot.

"We cannot endure as we have, I am forced to agree, but I must take issue I feel, with the direct manner in which you propose to achieve your aims. As you must surely know, were this undisguised course of action to be taken....Then I cannot utterly convince myself of a popular reaction going in your favour, or see clearly each eventual contingency that might dreadfully occur. On the one hand, a success immediate and total could plausibly be expected and in the short term the majority of the people may initially applaud your strong, decisiveness in wresting back the produce of their labours...but were events to err this night or indeed let us say, for example, in the future as when the rivers dry...which they may well do at any time henceforth. Then to these events you may be assured, as consequence of hindsight, your name will duly be associated and a measured degree of condemnation must then doubtless be presumed to follow."

"Are you saying then that I cannot prosper even standing key in hand upon a rout?"

"No...but there are alternatives that ought unsettle the populace less so."

"I shall deal with any disquiet when and where or even if, it should arise. Always I have assumed total responsibility for my people's welfare, it is in their interest that I must have this key, and moreover it will be in my possession before the rising. I pledge it in the presence of all that claim ability to hear, be they man, beast or god. I will not suffer disparagement nor tolerate another plunder of my harvests from these insufferable vermin and if they choose to live in their reclusion never to return, then so be it but ask naught of me, I say....and furthermore demand that you, Rashkulcan, bear witness and recall my words with clarity."

"I forget little, Tomakal-Zaqual, as you know." Rashkulcan reminded giving a deliberate show whence again looking carefully around for secret listeners. He saw that the king ought well succeed in his ambition, but knew also that in failure...there would be no option other than to accept full liability for a situation of his making. Alone if possible. A fortuitous outcome that deserved the most pleasant of deliberations. One thing was a surety however...whether the bid succeeded or not, once the attempt was made the High Order would be returning to Zamanque-quetan in one capacity or another. It was imperative therefore, he decided, to maintain from now an outward distancing towards these events, in the short term anyway, and keep his actual involvement limited, in readiness for a disagreeable eventuality…but if Tomakal-Zaqual was in the larger scheme of things…fortunate, then it would be simply a matter of biding time until the most sacred item in the land passed rightfully to him. A time that he, Rashkulcan would have the luxury of choosing. Rashkulcan's lips split to the thinnest guileful smile forcing him to turn his visage downward to avert the king's awareness, and with a slow, deliberate nodding of his head he feigned to ponder the importance of the words about to be unveiled. "Seizing it by force," He began "…here in the city, for all to witness leaves little to manipulate for our advantage…but supposing the High Order were to be, shall we say…set upon…waylaid beneath the forest bough, unseen, as might conceivably befall on rare occasion…"

"Not to the Quauchen! Never has such a thing transpired, it is better that they litter openly my streets as gaping dead for all to know my will…or perhaps remain as hostage…but yield they must as testament to my ruling unopposed." Tomakal-Zaqual's pride interrupted without restraint.

"…and the key was to go missing. Temporarily, may we suppose," Rashkulcan continued, ignoring the king's arrogant display. "A vagrant band of mercenaries perhaps, strayed from lands afar and thus unaware of whom they had assailed."

"Ah, then that would fall direct as my responsibility to have failed in guarding them whilst plying shuffled vagrancy within my borders. Showing me at fault in either way. But still, I repeat, none have ever before stalked to accost your cursed High Order." The king reiterated unconvinced.

"Quite so."

"Strength," Tomakal-Zaqual nodded, agreeing with himself, "….must be shown in this affair."

"Listen further, I entreat…" Rashkulcan found himself burdened with an inbred regal obstinacy now thriving on aloofness, "…the entire situation together with this old and stagnant regime, can only be redeemed by your retrieving the key from these most terrible of fictitious bandits…am I right? If you ever have the desire or need to redeem it, that is."

"….and if none escape to tell a different tale…" Tomakal-Zaqual was begging haste to see the dawning of some merit.

"Exactly. You would have the key and although be perceived at fault, an honest mistake that could easily occur to any other guardian, be seen also as hence championing the cause of reclamation one might say. Orchestrating the hunt. Tracking them down to far flung fields, no man spared…frontiers advanced maybe…? I'm sure you know the sort of subterfuge and pretence…." He waved his hand dismissingly. "For as long as you wish you can appear to be working hardest for the union's sake until their collective will is either stretched beyond its patience or finally subdued through the reinforcement of your manipulating…new allegiances. You know the politics as well as I. Regardless, it shall grant us time enough to measure fully the substance of our people and that of all the other tribes who rank for now, as neighbours. Ask questions of true leanings and create safer…more personal alliances within those already established…but if things should go ultimately awry and we have erred in careful judgement….Then we may have to contemplate eventually relinquishing the key…one day. Until maybe another opportunity presents itself. It will however, have provided time for consideration and might give us…er you, that is," he corrected quickly to encourage Tomakal-Zaqual's approval, "a valuable insight into the object's working substance and then consequently better gauge of its potential."

"When the key is in my hand, forever it will remain so."

Tomakal-Zaqual's inflexion rose to dangerous levels. Ishtaac flinched, hidden in the shadows above curtailing discourse, and through the paranoid insecurity of a delicate position felt that vented rage directed towards none other than himself.

"Think what you say, sire," Rashkulcan cautioned and gave a spurious, furtive look around. "I counsel to take the key that is true, but to hold obscure for a while and then decide a path. At least keep open your options on this most complicated matter. I urge you." The king considered the advice as if pained at first to do so until forceful calming to a seething placid hemmed him once again. Ishtaac felt contrastingly, that as their tension tangibly receded, concern for the Quauchen's welfare and for that of the land in general stoked suppression's long fuelled furnace angrily combusting into flame within him.

"Roving outlaws you say?" Tomakal-Zaqual was rubbing his chin in a visual portrayal of a thoughtful game's reflection. "It will be suspicious," he conceded.

"Suspicious perhaps, but not obvious. There will be room to manoeuvre…and further I advise, that once, whenever the time is adjudged correct to make known that you have the key…"

"Ah! Then I will say that it is too perilous and foolhardy to permit such an importance out into the world at large again at the mercy of any thieving mendicant who wishes to make scurrilous their claim upon it." He interrupted once more, adding, "And I will declare to build a fortress here. Secure from all intrusion where other kings will come to pay their dues, and there too shall be improvement to the ceremony of unison, conducted with the key remaining always in my hand's custodial pleasure. The pathway to the gods must begin right here. And I will truly become the king that I deserve to be. And you, Rashkulcan, will keep the spirit of my people buoyant and forevermore as righteously contented."

"Quite so sire." Rashkulcan allowed himself his driest smile of satisfaction.

"And when I have achieved my strength in full. What then for the rest of the High order? What shall be done with them, I wonder?"

"Their link to the gods denied. Their access to that knowledge severed, the following they enjoy must surely then extinguish. They may seek to gain our favour….Be reminded there is much still that they might offer."

"Even to us?"

"Even unto us, for we shall be the New High Order," Rashkulcan affirmed.

"They may before such a time, take arms against us….Gathering sympathy where division only is expected."

"That is why delay in their response must be to our advantage. Do you now see the relevance of my counsel?"

"Know you exactly where they dwell?" The king felt no need to be subjected to the ordeal of supplying answers and Rashkulcan presumed as much.

"No man does."

"Whatever or whoever you are, Rashkulcan, you are no ordinary man. You age in spirit only. Of that I am envious and hide no shame in declaration. How is it so? How may I also achieve this? May I find a similar favour biding with the Quauchen and the key? I ask."

"I know not," he lied.

"Then I opt to believe I might, but now I must leave as my destiny slips so hurriedly away. Will you come?"

"No, I cannot sire…and must question if you feel my services in this pursuit are truly relevant. Is it not better that I remain to uphold the falsehood of your presence here? It may after all serve to avoid suspicious implications later."

"Very well. When next we meet I shall be the richer…and mark my words, by far," Tomakal-Zaqual concluded.

Together they moved back inside. Ishtaac heard the king calling to his guards as they went. He squirmed uncomfortably imagining a world with Tomakal-Zaqual as its unchallenged leader. The incalculable perishing that would follow was beyond the nauseous but even that would pale to mere tragedy when Rashkulcan's direction uncontested, took control. He decided at that dire moment, upon the kingdom's very throne itself, to warn the Quauchen personally of the fate awaiting them this night.

Reaching down tentatively with his foot, he began to carefully ease himself from the protection of that highest seating, when the sound of hurried, padding footfalls brought him swiftly to retraction. A palace guard jogged by, within a lethal spear's thrust reach of him. Ishtaac held constricted breath until disturbance passed from hearing and continued to remain thereafter for an age it seemed before resuming his descent to creep away amid the cloaking safety of the night.

The king strode purposefully along the palace corridors towards his private quarters banishing his household staff before him as he found them, and soon his footsteps all alone would echo harsh throughout its lower regions. He would change his attire more according to concealment whilst his personal bodyguard collected dutiful without, awaiting his command. Ten they came in total, loyal and devoted, age long friends willing to submit their lives to Tomakal-Zaqual's disposal. Discreet they brought with them the hunting bows and spears as had prior been requested, bringing also scant provisions although ample to sustain the briefest hunt. As yet their understanding was at best determined vague, their requirements uncertain.

Whispering guardedly amongst themselves they waited, guessing the nature of their unexpected call. Sparks of excitement flashed between them, and then the king emerged. Grim with serious consternation etching deeply of his brow. He spoke quickly, but hushed with meaning was his tone.

"Tonight, my friends, a great deed beckons us. We must act wisely but also we must act with speed. Keep faithful with your king and put aside all private fears, for the higher good and fastness of your realm. For intentions long unseen have moved upon us whilst we slumbered freely with our loved ones. Dark forces that appear in cunning guise to fool our recognition, walked among these palace walls this very night. Thus the time has come for us to seize back the initiative and wrest while still we may, our destiny from malicious minds who seek further to control our ways. Subtle have they been, eroding the foundations of our jewelled, just rewards. This…." He stopped cautiously looking in either direction along the flaring, black and amber passageway. "This was, believe me, as unpleasant to dare consider as it was to watch unfold before my disbelieving eyes. Some of you I know, were present, some of you were not. But trust me when I say that the Quauchen Order are moving, as I speak, against us in their hearts, to rid us from their world. They have plotted our downfall from afar and now they seek to implement the commencement of their plan upon this sacred night of nights. But through these artful dealings they have thrown unwittingly seditious seeds to find maturity in malcontent," Tomakal-Zaqual professed with added mood to emphasize regret.

"I believe this to the true, I too have sensed their betrayal and was present at their slighting."

The king acknowledged his captain's loyalty and then continued, "They bring forth division and chaos, disorder where previous there was none. Opening fissures in our ranks for the rising tide to breach and benefit who other but themselves, this craven enemy whose tools in place now function in their absence. We must stand firm and stand tonight. It was declared and so too, shall it be. I, your king, proclaim it. Why else would they persist in hiding truths from us? We have no alternative but apply completion to this abhorrency of movement...." punctuating his methodic rise in temper, needlessly he spat, "....before it is too late and their will, infested widespread. We must prevent all further passage of this harmonics key, so that I, Tomakal-Zaqual, can impart the understandings they conceal, divulging hitherto defended wisdom to the usage of the people, our people. Then will we, together, banish the Order from our land never again to steal their cursed existence from our toil filled stores and plunder. Indeed from the very mouths of our own dear, hungry children. Too long have they suckled on tradition, gorging to create this present barrenness we suffer. For accountability to these and many other crimes as yet to be perceived I insist the time is ripe to undertake courageous preparation for our offspring's futures. Do not cower from the difficulty within your soul nor delay the moment troubled by a sense of misplaced duty. With contempt deliberate we have been misled, subjected to the art of their misguidance. I urge you, in your hearts, to vanquish age old fears and superstitions which have bound our hands as impotent together, and follow my lead instead, the new lead, to the forest. To make correct the past and all those further wrongs to be imposed, and so behave as men, men of families hence swelled with pride and there perform fulfilling parts in truly honoured deeds, deeds worthy of their song. But come! We must be gone! Time is not our luxury to squander," he rallied.

Waving his arm motioning them to follow where he would the king strode off along the confinement of the dimly lit corridor passing into darkness and then out quietly, absorbing to the night by secret ways little known and seldom ever trod.

The guard thought not to discuss the issue but instead to take their lead and give entirely to the king, their trust, above all else. Leaving at his side, experienced hunters all, they left the city quarters, slipping quietly to the forest shroud and sped along the much used trail that welcomed commerce to their bosom from the south but which now provided the assistance to escape for their believed betrayers.

Twisting wide on damp soaked earth, well passed of recent days, descent would take them to the river. The moon shone pale above the treetops, a silver grey admonishment that peered occasionally through the branches lending little light to see by, but tonight the darkness was their friend, stealth their means and swiftly they proceeded. Silent was their aim determined and inspired, their fealty certain.

Ishtaac's tense foreboding played demands on sight and limb and set his heart to beat as does the humming bird's in hovered flight. He pushed himself as hard as daring could allow negotiating deftly of the perils on this ill-maintained and over wielded, nigh diminished trail as its awkward snake, without a smoothness or fluidity, coiled around and down the mountain through the trees to skirt the rocky, moss furred outcrops whilst then running dread and brittle at the top of sharp ravines. Creatures real or fearfully imagined leered to pounce from every shadow, their attendance pressing only for to drive his urgency along. At times he caught, when paused for breath, the drumming press of guardsmen pulsing in his ears or mind, but held no inclination to define. Back and forth, ever downward deeper to the valley's bilge he chased the distant, brethren priesthood. Down upon the river rush to where the track unwound, straighter now he gave small praise for dimmest forecast, neath a vaulted avenue eclipsed and sombrous that would harbour still its unseen danger either side. Fleet and fast he raced along beside the river course. Ahead to where he knew a ford to be, a crossing wide and shallow. Cold and quick the water swept...and on the other bank, the road the holy men must take and where he thought to meet them.

It was then he pictured his approach. The greeting faces of surprise and panic as he came to bear, without due warning, suddenly upon them. The first of many, bearing malice, doubtless in their eyes and he too far away to whisper his intention. Conceivably a prelude causing scatter, grounding plans to flounder and himself condemned as equally exposed. Pausing then a moment of consideration and jogging slowly to a halt, he chanced himself inquiry through the margin's hedge of vegetation, lush with frightening and deceit.

Crouched for cautious observation through the overhanging branches of the river's tree-lined shore Ishtaac there could see the moonlit, sparkled crossing, flashing white with bursting foam, but more, along the fringe of darkness hesitantly dead ahead, appeared the vague and distant silhouetting of the Quauchen order seeking unperturbed escape. Conflicting madness rose again with thought to overwhelm emitting calls aloud, in hailing of his coming in an instance of revealing, a foolish word unguarded that would certainly betray him. Somehow salvaged though, his silence kept he knew in time, their path along that furthest bank, reverted back his way thus far before it turned again and climbed away to lose itself among the rare, trod ways that ran in deltas to the mountains.

It was, alas as he had feared, much too late to near before they entered in the water and by the time of his arrival they then ought be nigh across or far enough at least to never hear his cries above the churned crescendo running at their feet, where then his showing from concealment in the open would inform them of pursuit and as unto himself foretold, compel expectancy of bolting.

Upon a sigh, as would the desperate man with little other option, he resolved to stunt his route and creep past dread of poisonous intrusion, wary down beneath the broad, engulfing leaves' consumption, to the final, steep edged terror of the rapid current's writhing.

A fallen tree enlaced of vine, lay roots exposed but top submerged below the murky surface tempting wryly, arid passage only for short distance. Ishtaac took his grip and found it to be wanting as the creeper came away in grasping hand, resembling some angry, serpentine creation. A thousand, tearing fingers relinquishing sequentially their hold hissed menace at the trespass from old slumber to evoke head spun, sensations of a swooning threat to topple. Struggling on regardless of the folly, he fought against the branches' blinding whip and got astride to begin his straddled way along the awkward twisted, length with legs up to the thigh now dangled, quickly losing feeling, overlong immersed in treason's icy waters.

The trunk rose, swayed and fell resentful under the efforts of his striving and would soon prevent advancing in this manner, and so mustering whatever courage Ishtaac held, he contradicted loyal instinct plunging scored with gained abrasions and a painful grimace deep up to his chest's constriction. Fighting brave for air, through lungs he found could only there expend with breath he nevertheless, though slowly, after many frightful moments came to conquering the first, small, sucking bursts of his survival and to calm the gagging choke of reeling senses torturing his mind. Thus without delay, as best he could, Ishtaac began commencement of the dismal crossing.

The cloth he wore, now laden stiff and heavy, weighed the burden of a stifled headway, whence thrashed and flailed he swam persistently in the expensive style that only novices know how, which effected drifting ever further down the river course but bore him all the same, towards his goal.

Prey to the current and in this wayward fashion he maintained a gradual progress, until eventually, shivering profusely, under open, starlit sky he saw the welcome features of deliverance approaching.

Bushes and plants presented themselves in a confusion of potential opportunities with some more favoured and attainable than others. And as the bank rose steep in places also on this side, so he changed his route to match…to where priorities espied the most accessible of respites, sparsely free from barb and tearing hindrance.

His body ached for leniency, was tired and suffered limbs having long since given in to numbness but on he fought, and clawing, kicked his way towards it, reaching out in desperation when at the last he knew that even thought itself was gullet drained and spent. Surging short then sinking in despair to scorn the blackest humour of a worn and timely rhythm he converged on where his straining taloned hands could chance the thick, unyielding stalk of but a single plant's particular salvation, and with gods, he deemed, upon his side, substantial would it prove, enough to bear his weight. Ishtaac dragged the resistance of his bulk in close across the shale, afraid of tearing free a fragile holding from its roots. And daring neither tug nor flounder but with utmost care came rolling out, released again embraced of land, to lay a while preserved from drowning, enveloped by his saturation and blessed divinely with a scant ability remaining still to refrain from voicing cursed ill-fortune.

Any liberation purchased by his labour was however, well he knew, only to be relished in the moments of another time, dusty shelved and lost for now intact somewhere, maturing to revive perhaps whilst at one's ease revised sublime on unsuspecting days, conjured from the stale disordered recesses of memory, and so would push himself along once more to stumble ragged motion.

Rising sodden to his knees, he scrambled for the path, where again was felt the urgent need to sit and take the briefest instance for appraising full, the wretchedness of his condition. Ishtaac trembled uncontrollably breathing in through short and hollow bursts…but fate uncompromised awaited, the future of his land lay in the balance with he the only worthwhile weight to tip the scale correctly. Loping off bedraggled in the direction of the shallows, he made surprising speed, stamping life and warmth along the pathway back to senseless feet.

Through the trees he saw and heard above the crushing din, profusion's ford approach. The swirling cascades of the torrent, splashed and rushed incessant, growing ever louder over every jarring footfall. Then just ahead and to his left the trees depleted sparse, revealing both himself to all and they at last, to he. Ishtaac staggered into view and looked upon with sudden shock, the unsurprised expression of the old and smiling priest in whom earlier that night had found a personal contact.

Onward, recklessly to convolution's valley floor plunged Tomakal-Zaqual accompanied by his loyal guards. Trusting obligation's guide they bound profoundly down towards their kingdom's calling slid upon a trampled track, crushed merciless along its fringes, littered with shard's scattered debris from the inexhaustive pass of overladen pilgrims. The river's course grew loud and well received, enshrouding any careless sound they may have made in haste allowing them the grace for lesser caution. The clatter of bow on spear and swiftly pounding feet, all lost to the eddying roll of thunderous tumult and the rock strewn hammered uproar. Tomakal-Zaqual pulled them to a halt and peered steadily along a trail of shade, tranquility beneath an interlacing canopy of dappled starlight, where shadowed fronds of fern and leafy bough wove fibrous latticework to make celestial patchwork of the ground, and up ahead the only narrow thread they knew the key must cross by.

But for themselves, only the river stirred their conscience, heaving on its seaward run, glinting with its sparkled, surface ripples simmered to the boil. The king gathered tightly in his breathing and surveyed as best he could, much that went before him then chose to lead the race once more away through night's black air, crisp and thin until at last they came upon the nearside bank to look across from privileged cover, out to where the Quauchen stood, engaged as herded to the gathering, lowly and attentive.

Motionless, the Order listened, a spectral congregation adhered intently to an unseen preacher's sermon. A mysterious overseeing that caused them each good reason for concern.

The soldiers stayed themselves among the rush's stems to make complete their plans, preparing both the heart and soul for dulled suspension of their feeling. To slay the unarmed layman absent of the battle, brought a redefining shame to bear, even on the craven art of the assassin. Nevertheless, for the welfare of the realm and on the asking of their king they would willingly endure such compromise, but never was it spoken of again beyond this night, although at present, each there in attendance leant to whispering reserve on circumstance as freely as he might.

"What plan have you sire?" The captain dared to nudge a recognition from his king.

Tomakal-Zaqual broke from his scanning of events and searched his trusted sternly before responding without doubt. "When they have moved sufficient distance from the river," he began, "we will cross to gain the other side. From there we must divide ourselves into two parties. You will take charge of six of those among us…at your own selecting…and will flank the priests inland, pass them by unseen and reach appropriate positions for a favourable encounter. I, and those who remain, will follow along the path close behind and await the sound of your assault. Choose well….” he advised. “…there must be none to go astray.”

“Assault?” the captain questioned himself, putting grim thought's definition into sound with the resigned nod of acceptance. It was now bitterly clear to him that it was going to be he and he alone who would be the first in all their history to assail a member of the sacred order. “Could we not demand it under threat of force?” he asked, already fearful of the answer.

“They would undoubtedly refuse or scatter to our losing the initiative. It is regretful….but the painful decision I have made is for the protection of our people and our custom. Deplorable yes, but still we must fulfil the plan this way, decisively and clean. We must ensure attainment of this precious charge but also we must leave no trace of ever having been here on this night.”

The captain saluted solemnly but was reluctant in agreement. “Who among them bears the key?”

“I know only that the two parts are always borne separately amidst their rank, so when a piece is rendered forth waste no time in looking further from the same,” he instructed, “and be wary also of any attempt to discard this item to the river or indeed, elsewhere.”

“And when they fail to return across the Aclans? Will our lives not then be under greater threat?” The captain shifted uneasily his eyes flitting constantly from his king unto the Quauchen.

“Be assured, I readily assume full responsibility hereafter concerning this affair, for all reprisals…and the politics entailed. Remember only that none escape. It cannot be considered.” Tomakal-Zaqual's words came ponderously deliberate and grave with etched sincerity as an awareness of the group's complete attention settled ill upon him. The riverside clamour became uncomfortably stark and overbearing, where moments previous it had been absorbed unnoticed. Rancid teeth befouled in blackmail ground their dire incriminations across the gravel bedded spoil of rasped and scraping crispness as the chill wind scythed, spurned bitter on the tongue of highest treason to and fro throughout the margin's reed beds with a whispered, wagging accusation rife within its keenness.

And he accursed with knowledge bowed as humble, falling into silence, alone to stand and overlook the threshold of his reckoning. The truest nature of the deed to execute too fully realised, and the burden of conspiracy not lightened by their number.

The captain straightened pledging his commitment to the king. His comrades instinctively did likewise forming circular to convey the traditional salutation.

"May I counsel, sire, that you remain here inconspicuous whilst your orders are accomplished? For should unlikely error manifest...it would, I feel, be beneficial that your presence in this place pass off unknown."

The others nodded their approval. Tomakal-Zaqual considered the captain's words then shrugged dismissive. "There will be no mistakes," he declined, simply.

Eventually the Quauchen melted slowly to remoteness, away and lost behind the trees that lined the distant roadway. Tomakal-Zaqual when satisfied, gave then the awaited signal and cautious, one by one they each began emergence, sinister from hiding. Gathered low, yet still exposed, they waded through the piercing bite of crystal mountain run off stealing smoothly up to claim the narrow track unnoticed. The king now motioned to his captain, who, along with his selected men, disappeared to the undergrowth as ordered, and so did beckon those remaining few to follow likewise, stealthy in his wake.

The captain's guile and cunning were already ample inspiration for the many odes and images among Zamanque-quetan's artistic idle, thus it was with silent ease that he and his elite dissolved into the night to pace as hunched along the lonely jaguar trail, long worn to clearance by the timeless passage of a patient, solitary hunter that often stalked unknown, the partial scent of man.

Their cloistered way cut straight and true, providing vantage points with cover for the pouncing but the road it prowled wound often here and there expensively, accommodating accurate the contours of the land but more precisely to the whims of human straying. Inevitably then, it was not long before the sacred order's progress had been matched, surpassing too their roaming, undetected.

Soon, the captain hunter stood alone and proud, to view the path assessing best his company's deployment. Behind came the Quauchen order ignorant of fate, someway distant and beyond the range of hearing so was felt no need, as yet, for haste to dash deduction. Ahead among the gloom of early morning's night time glow, he noticed that the track turned sharply, skirt an outcrop, loop and then return upon itself once more, rising steeply in so doing on an inclination towards the tree-lined hillside shielding well his sighting of the of dawn, the lower section being overshadowed by its own continuation many clear, seductive bowshot yards. A place where insight knew the Quauchen's vulnerability would stand to be sufficient to perform successfully his allocation's deadly task. Without delay but gestures soundless for his men's pursuit, decidedly he trotted on for preparation of the killing site.

"Err...God's favour." Ishtaac managed, startled by the suddenness of his own appearance.

The old man nodded shallow his acknowledgement, whilst observing stoic, Ishtaac's disposition. "And returned," he replied in custom.

Ishtaac cold and wet, dripped and shivered resolute before him, composing order from a broth of scrambled thoughts. "I am Ishtaac...Maluk..." he announced haltingly. It seemed as good an introduction as any he could muster.

"We know," said the old man. His voice spoke softly without concern. "You are wet, Ishtaac," he added, looking him over and remarking on the obvious.

Ishtaac's pardon fell upon himself and felt obliged to offer an excuse. "I had need to swim across the river," he complained.

"You would find it less troublesome to cross here, as have we." The old priest turned slowly, indicating with a steady, outstretched arm to sweep the river's flux behind him. "See, the water here has little depth and affords one almost effortless transference from this shore to the other." He smiled, his face ascending to a wrinkled mass arising honest from the corners of his mouth to twinkled eyes and onward, ploughed across his forehead, there contrasting sharply with the sheened reflection of his baldness.

"I must speak with you urgently. Terrible events may fast unfold this night....and have therefore come to warn you, I am certain of assassins who ensue," Ishtaac offered, agitated by the press of his impatience.

"We know," the priest replied unmoved.

Silent, his companions added nothing of support or intervention. They too seemed neither concerned nor surprised by Ishtaac's presence there. Though he afflicted, glanced incessantly above their heads across the lure of moonlit dappled water to the peril, skulking close, obscured to sight beyond and edged each passing moment nervously to offer finally his hand in consternation's hope of hastening along.

Eventually encouraged from the river's wash, they flowed ashore unhurried as the winsome mist will haunt the twilight hollows at the wax and waning of the count, and on the bank with upturned gaze placated stood content to bear discourtesy, when harsh his words were spoke.

"Know you also then of the great risk that I assume in bringing you this caution?" Ishtaac snapped indignantly.

"We do." The old man paused with the expression of one who is trying to recollect elusive, dimly, faded memories, head cocked to one peculiar side and listening to the peaceful workings of his mind. "Walk with us a while," he prompted "....that we may speak of your distress."

Ishtaac found himself wondering whether they fully grasped the gravity of their dilemma. "But you have so very little time at your disposal, I implore...." He besought their realisation to afford his earnestness some credit.

"Time...." the old man considered as he strolled serenely unaffected by projected sacrifice. "....is too precious to be of any consequence to just one man. You especially should be aware of this, Ishtaac Maluk," he responded, with the look of sheltered wisdom leant towards correction. "Ask of time to the stars and moon, the mountains and the rivers or of the seasons even, upon which mankind exudes the need to measure its passing and its presence by, if you hold good patience for their answer. Not squandered on such curiosities are we, as yet…our faith…in time, suffices."

"Though likewise, time afforded could be seen as more the individual's tool, its fashion sharpened by our own brief witness…but I have not come here to discuss the finer points of differing philosophy. You…" Ishtaac declared, "..are the guardians of the one key. The key to all claimed knowledge. A gift granted unto you from the very gods themselves." He spoke rhetorically.

The old man simply stared with a bemused expression smugly on his face although his eyes urged Ishtaac to continue, and so he did.

"A worthwhile object in itself there is no doubt…but as most will readily agree, the significance behind the key is its real value, that fragile spiritual binding which has unified us all, regardless of our histories or determinations. Tomakal-Zaqual has revealed designs to seize control of this endowment for himself. His purpose tonight is to take from you, forcibly if necessary, this most treasured asset and use it to procure dominion over the entire land and, if within his power, forge his own links to the gods. Dispensing with the people's need for your, or any other order, excepting that of Rashkulcan's along the way, I do honestly suspect. Already as we stand here now I sense his grip around us tighten."

"Why though, do you seek to advise us of Tomakal-Zaqual's intentions? Are we not the High Order…and do we not profess to our seeing much of that concealed, with adequate conviction? I see your faith in us assuredly lacking Ishtaac." The old man maintained his pleasant visage. "But tell us as a mere aside, that we may learn directly from the spirit of your diction why you yourself would not find profit through association with this infantile establishment. It might do much to ease the troubled hearts of my companions."

A look of exasperation enflamed Ishtaac's clear unease as his eyes rolled skyward searching for an explanation. "I seek only to retrieve lost, bygone days, and uphold once more the stableness of old…" he began, incensed at first before relenting to more measured utterance, "…when men were free, the rivers ran untainted and the earth fed wholesomely from Chaac's dependable donation. I believe that the only way to stem a tidal sweep of pointless blood loss is to prevent Tomakal-Zaqual from obtaining the potency that you posses. Take it back to your temples. Guard it. Never bring it forth again, for if it should be taken by his hand then I fear that much may find itself misshapen even further, completely lost to any recall and repairing. Listen and trust me when I say I have no covert yearning nor a use in founding power for myself. My lack of political position will give credence to these words and is public enough for everyone with eyes to see. This is no ploy nor darkened scheme by which to waylay or deceive you for his ends. I am nothing more than sadly too aware of my grown impotence to merely reassure." Ishtaac impressed desperately, reading only calm detachment on the old impassive face and blew hard in exhalation at his floundering on the sure unyielding and dispassionate wall of even tempered mildness.

The priest then frowned, knowing well the unsettling his demeanour had provoked and so, at length responded with the reason for their converse on this day. "It is not Tomakal-Zaqual who truly concerns us, but that which lies obscured within the shadow that he casts. The king belongs and is bound here also, as indeed are we, and his age will pass in course. Hastened, should ever he achieve the ambition he so foolishly regards as his, by he who labours indistinct behind. It is, I fear, upon such little understanding that you must now accept your bearing part of this, the only sacred key, the guardianship and thus entwined, its burdening, to keep secure throughout the difficult days that known to us, ensue." He reached inside his robe and produced a small hide bag with a securing drawstring attached and handed this together with its contents over to Ishtaac. "The light of the land is extinguished with this last concession," he said as he surrendered finally, his care. "And an opportunity for dormant healing drifts upon us all. You are long lived, Ishtaac Maluk, as is Rashkulcan, you are sons of distant lands. It is written as clearly as our encounter was foreseen."

Ishtaac rapidly dispelled flawed expectation of the situation and glimpsed instead inside the pouch to stare in wonder on the item nestled snugly there within. Never before had he held such honour in possession, never before had he experienced its sensation at first hand.

Where weight within his trembling grasp belied by far the diminutive proportion that his eye perceived. His glance intrigued, drew wonderous then on the inscriptions for a moment before returning it to hidden safety, searching through his disbelief with narrowed eyes for the answers to a thousand fleeting questions. "I glean naught in depth or detail from the stars that choose to hide their secrets from my observation…unlike most others who would openly profess to…and freely do I make confession. I see nothing either that approaches in their movements. Why then charge this thing to me and not to those with gifted sight?" Ishtaac queried.

"Because it was declared," came the old priest's staid reply.

"But I dare not…" Ishtaac saw no safeguard's warrant offered by his hands only his misguiding failure to a nation.

"The insight," interruption faltered his disquietude to heel, "…that has been provided cannot be understood by mere individuals. It is much moreso than can singularly be perceived, and lies more within collective nature, built on sharing and compliance. This and more the key has taught us. Greed alone will not suffice nor will it prosper long. Hence our motivation for the gradual introduction of its larger worth. Your presence here, upon these shores gave prompt to anguish once and greatly, strange, but apt it also seems, that now we ask the usage of your life's endurance.

"I can impart few words alas, for your assistance…but will say that while mankind remains in shackles, tethered to the world the key will not be reunited. It is on this and knowledge more profound that we give unto you the task in part as keeper. For neither Tomakal-Zaqual, Rashkulcan nor you, Ishtaac Maluk, will partake of this responsibility alone, although we feel it wise that you specifically reside in solitude and hold your whereabouts unknown…until such time as you are needed. Seek shelter from the flashing, storm of man on beast that rages unseen in the east and soon arrives engulfing all, but harbour with you also, added words foresighted and of caution. You are not immortal and may fall victim as might any other. Your days however numerous, have nonetheless been counted as have ours, as indeed have all things that exist, so cursed or gifted be informed that when next you stand upon this soil with key at hand those days remaining are but few. Use them wisely, and beware the Raven in the land where once we trod. Remember too, that we have seen just one predicted facet. There are many more and this revealing, though bestowed in all good faith, can possibly mislead in truth, as part the subtle mystery in the cunning of life's story." The old man looked up meekly holding Ishtaac with a pensive interest for a moment then came to rest his eyesight humble on the waterlogged condition of his sandals. "And now…our task is nigh complete." He smiled thinly with an air of regret, let out a melancholy sigh and stared through eyes that cared, reflectively towards the heavens up above and to the river and the flora all about.

Imperceptibly premoved the Quauchen ambled past their faces deep concealed once more within the hooded apparel, and whence so passing by, the elder priest would touch them each upon the shoulder in a sombre recognition of unspoken, predetermined duty.

"I cannot remain with you. The king and his men are abroad. I urge you now to scatter to the forest. One man alone may return at least to issue warning and prepare your order for the worst," Ishtaac tried in vain.

"We have prepared long enough, Ishtaac Maluk. Concern yourself no longer with our welfare but go now as you will and keep you well. One day you must return."

"Return?" Ishtaac wondered. "Have I to return to the city before my absence is discovered?" He sought some confirmation for his hope then suddenly assessed the old man's truer meaning.

"I fear that may not be possible…but as you wish." He waved Ishtaac away. "As was declared, so shall it be."

Watching as the Order trailed away, Ishtaac held reflectively concession's purse in hand there lacking confidence through brittleness though would recall in grateful time, a line of scripture more than once heard mention. '…and should one let release by accident to falling it would neither shatter nor betray the slightest trace of poor reception.' It gave little comfort for either.

"Therein lies greater durability than you believe, Ishtaac Maluk." The old man gave him an encouraging, sympathetic smile and turned to follow unabashed, his brethren on shared paths towards fate's welcoming reception. Before he left though Ishtaac strained to hear the elder's gentle murmur, "I believe the time now to be correct for you to…" but it trailed away to nothingness.

Ahead of them a sudden disarray and clamour shook diversion from his words. Cries distraught of torment heralded commotion and a sanguine blur of shadowed movement rustled through the thickets in the distant, heaving foreground.

Ishtaac spun nervously around to gauge more fully of the danger…but the old priest at his side remained as ever calm, unmoved and placid.

Challenging calls rang out along the track. Of heroism never once to be acclaimed in song or verse nor even to be witnessed, mere chaff upon the gusting breeze of high ambition's inspiration…and behind so Ishtaac heard from whence already they had come, the sound of thudded, racing feet approaching with intent.

"Go now…" the old man urged with unaccustomed press, "….to the river."

The lead of brothers staggered, groping blindly back toward them into view, pierced many times with rigid bow shot as pulsating blood in far reached spurts, arced freely from the neck and upper torso whilst his features drenched obscure, congealed beneath a savage, gaping head wound. Forlorn the young man tried in helpless vain to stem the ebbing flood. Stunned, bemused and frightened, still he came to seek an aid, aware no less beyond all hope, of his presenting naught but honour's violation sprawling useless to the muddied trail before them. Lifeless evermore to lay as worthy manhood cheaply spent.

Ishtaac crouched and drew his daggers in an instant as two burly palace guards, enraged befitting cornered boars, emerged in flight from nowhere, knocking clear both he and simultaneous, the elder to the ground whose head cracked crisply at impacting on a large protruding rock before then sounding out a long and sickly moan. Instinctive, Ishtaac plied befouled momentum spun and slashed with expert aim to fell assault in unison and ere the blinking of a nervous eye. One sank heavily atop the fallen body of the holy man, turned to glare with dead man's sight and mouthed bewilderment of endings unforeseen. Ishtaac watched him slowly fade remorseless, empty as the void, removed inside and coldly unashamed of numb indifference…and with his body's last convulsion rolled releasement from the priest's embrace to light a face exposed to violent forfeit undeserved, yet holding still, tranquilities that blessed his passing life, with eyes that saw no more laid gently closed as tenderly as if in peaceful slumber.

Repulsive, suffering wails of pain and terror echoed through the forest nearing with a panic. Thrashing undergrowth burst forth to life as half seen figures charging, falling, fled or chased, came heedlessly stampeding back towards the river. Arrows hissed and stung the air pursuing in their wake, some clattered dryly through the branches where a prospered welfare told they missed but many more would find their mark with woeful cries of unmet fortune to persist.

Without a pause for breath, another guardsman came on reckless, roaring through his own ferocity, murderous spear seized in hand and poised a moment from its strike. Hesitation too expensive for design, Ishtaac launched on nothing more than trusted intuition, long life's loyal dagger sped on fear, slicing true and coursed at will it seemed, towards intended target, making good the distance in a single, fevered heartbeat. Spear's threat dropped from unclenched, tensely splaying fingers, harmless to the ground beside his feet, a frightened look of due regret paid visit to a shocked visage whilst dreaded comprehension of impending fate's conclusion with all its destinies cut short, swept to overwhelm before then twisting to a snarled and vengeful yearning ugly to behold.

Ishtaac watched him grab confused and vaguely at the blade lodged fast within him falling backwards in the process, slumping heavy to the floor. His body thumped defeat as promptly as the shouted hails of providence and merit greeted grim a sordid triumph over aim, whence obscene with self-appraisal, grotesquely steeped in festered arrogance, came tardily approaching from the distance, Tomakal-Zaqual for barking loud, his murderous orders.

Ishtaac cast his sight then on the dagger…his dagger, irrefutable evidence of his presence there that day, and dared himself delay to watch the stricken soldier clasping tightly to release again, in clawing spasms strained about familiar implications carved upon the handle. And all around the accusations mounted as defiantly, the carcass writhed and kicked refusals, coiling and contorting loathsome to relinquish life so easily. In groans and spitting protestations forcibly emitted then, he saw attempts perhaps to draw and focus more attention on the act…thus it was that Ishtaac gave concession, knowing far too late all hope for its retrieval gone, his only recourse now, was past assigned in destiny no less, accept his charge and flee.

Chancing but a single, backward glare of saddened disapproval to the dying wretch, left spewing forth its contents to the dirt he opted for a nearby scratch of thicket, crawling off to claim the river's refuge, thinking lonely thoughts of far away…with selfishness escaped, the scream and smell of slaughtered death surrounding him again.

Ishtaac heard the soldiers meet along the trail behind him, drawn together by their comrade's plight and heard too, of their pledge to recompense all those they found at fault. Dragged among them two less favoured not already dead, hung limp between an unscathed might, their stifled protests to release but rancorous resentment. Tomakal-Zaqual arrived soon after, less able to comply these days, and meet the rigorous terms of battle, recognised at once and then removed exponent's dagger, uncaring that the guard passed on whilst cursing bitterly the malice of his king's withdrawal.

"To whom have you betrayed me?" he demanded of the Quauchen kneeling at his feet.

Stubbornly refusing him an answer, they chose instead to stare their last upon the earth.

"What part does that damned excretion Maluk take among your ill-conceived designs? Answer me!"

Tomakal-Zaqual held Ishtaac's blade to pressing firm its blood let at the throat of one whilst prising nothing but mere satisfaction's failure from the other.

"Tell me the whereabouts of the key and I may spare your brother's life. Who among your servile order bears it on this day?" he hissed menacingly, his eyes red raw with fury scarce contained as spit escaped his teeth.

Both young acolytes remained unspoken as Tomakal-Zaqual applied his threat, spouting warm a sudden crimson spray across the face of his companion, forceful turned, to view the horror gushing from whatever life remained, as water spills from shattered pot, without directed form or hindrance. Trembling through mastery of fear, he watched defenceless as the body sagged without complaining, forward to the ground.

"Search him!" the king commanded, gripped by thwarted madness, shaking as he pointed Ishtaac's blood-soaked blade towards the empty corpse. "And him. Search all of them…and remember, none alive!" Then with insolence and swiftness slashed the other's throat impassive, killing thus, the last of Quauchen holy men to ever tread that realm with peace upon his heart.

Offering no resistance to demise, he rendered forth upon his fall, a part of that which Tomakal-Zaqual so dearly sought. Descending with its old custodian, to imbibe of fouled congealing mud, the purchased item sodden rolled its costly revelation from beneath a crumpled robe, and fickle, nudged impartial rest against another warder's boot.

Glancing down at the onset of success the king's delusion toyed aloof, delighted with fruition's dreamt imaginings. Now that the sacred piece was his, he could do whatever he saw fit… refuse it even, deny himself the pleasure and prolong the savoured humour of the moment… if he so wished. A choice until that moment utterly forbidden, to he and every other previous individual's claim. Nevertheless, inhaling deeply to suppress the unseemly show of his excitement, Tomakal-Zaqual, eyes devious and furtive, quickly gathered up his prize.

"Bring me the other part!" he called. "I will have them both!"

The guard proceeded brutally to carry out the order, divesting all the bodies of their modesty, but little did they find. Such was the relationship between the Quauchen order and physical possessions. Several mis-founded exclamations merely brought a darker depth to Tomakal-Zaqual's frustrated rage.

"Maluk!" he bellowed, manic to the corners of his kingdom when at last a realisation of denial's worst had overcome him. "I will find you!

71

You know this to be true! There is no escaping me! Come forth now and you will be spared. To that I promise! Stay hidden from me and I shall hunt you down. This also I will swear to! Do you hear me? Never will you find your pardon from this reckoning of mine! Do you hear me?" he repeated, venting his anger wildly causing each of those who heard to turn as shy for fear of their lives.

"Search the area. Now! Find any trace of him and I will reward you greatly. I am standing here your king, the victim of deceit!" He proclaimed with seething, "Bring me the head of Ishtaac Maluk. You!" and pointed at his captain busy rifling through the fabrics piled and strewn discarded. "Organise the concealing of these bodies and ensure that none can ever be discovered. Burn the cloth! Then follow me down river to the coast if necessary. Take two men to aid you. You!" Indications fell upon another of his guard who shuffled nervously close by. "Return to Zamanque-quetan and inform Rashkulcan alone, in private of Maluk's treachery. Search his quarters. Let all know whoever would lend haven to that rank, accursed rat's bile forfeit's swiftly with their lives, wherever they may stand but give them not a reason! You and you, search upriver for any recognition of his passing and send word to me if labours prove availing. The rest of you will come with me. Go! Now!" He shoved his men impatiently, dispersing them in all directions. "I will not be rendered impotent nor ever shall be stolen from!"

Tomakal-Zaqual, followed by his soldiers, sped off back towards the ford. On arrival there he sent a further two across with orders to pursue the trail towards the mountains far beyond and then continued on his way downstream.

For many fruitless leagues Tomakal-Zaqual and faithful company alike scoured the forest for signs of Ishtaac's flight. Occasionally the squalling in the treetops, or a rustling midst the bushes would startle them to hopeful, spend inquiry, but always without prosper and resulting only in the slowing of their progress. A distant half seen shadow here or there…but nothing to redeem them. Darkness turned to light and daytimes came once more and slipped away again and so the king's ambition was resisted, the scent turned dry to dust and Ishtaac vanished from the world. Cold atop the mountains west where barren salt wastes lie, to brood a solitude complete above the valleys of the condor. Where too, tormented wails long left behind resounded years within in his mind and roused him often from his daydream with the shifting of discomfort.

Chapter 2
Shant-lei

Likened are the ways and paths that guide to triumph or disaster, their potentials to deceive.

The washed up lifeless figure lay heavy in the sand, mortified in solitary grasping, oblivious to the coastal breezes that rippled gently through its sun-bleached, matted hair as shoreline's crested waves lapped salt on blistered, burnt and unshod feet. Around and in its hand the scattered remnants of a makeshift craft, reed constructed once with care, now strewn about and broken…as above the gulls encircled with suspicion in their cry, hanging on the air to eye the ragged man below, keenly mindful of a knot of children cautiously approaching, courageous in collective spirit, to arrival at a distance safe enough to prod.

Intrigued and concentrated grubby faces stared intently searching with impressed alarm for the merest hint of any threat or movement. Gathering close, they saw the wealth of rampant sores both fresh and raw on arms exposed and weather broken features. And beneath the knife edged, rigid crease of clustered garb the glistening promise of reward for each, a moment's further daring. A necklace of the finest jade called unto them with quality alluring, magnificent begged its glisten in the sunshine's rays to tempting each yet closer.

The oldest and largest of the children, a dark-haired, round-faced boy of thickest set proportion, produced a driftwood stick and thought to demonstrate his nerve by closing in sufficiently to poke at the inertness and thereby gain approval from his comrades. Tentative and fragile, he reached out barely to the touch but alas, on wavering to overbalance he opted only then to lunge a final, throwing stab, released the stick and fled. His small companions instinctively did likewise and chased along the beach a way until regarding far enough removed to dare the over shoulder glance of satisfied escape. Whereupon relieved, excited laughter would ensue on seeing thus the form unaltered at its resting. After a brief discussion they came again, drawn along on prospect of the jewellery and that macabre sense of curiosity inherent from an early age. This time bolder and direct, to where the stick lay settled in the sand. The boy reclaimed his branch and began to nudge once more for reassurance, enough for self-convincing. When achieved, he cast aside his tool and stretched out bravely, open fingered, mouth agape and dry with trembling, focussed dread.

Before the noonday sun, a chilling cloud passed by that moment, casting shadow raced upon the sand to suddenly engulfing as beset with sinister's sense of stealthy crept up loneliness for darkening his deed, and yet disturbing him much further was the far off conversation dwindled fearful now to stress his isolation. Almost though within his grasp he narrowed splaying fingers, delicate towards a daring clench but to his horror found the once thought corpse came stirred alive and groaned beneath his gaze.

The boy had frozen shocked with rigid terror panicking his mind. He sought to flee but found no movement there conveyed to firmly rooted legs. He thought to scream for aid but no utterance could he master, instead a strangled, choking gurgled sound was issued feeble from inside. He saw the body lurch and cough before him and felt its retching spasm rising up too quick upon his startled outstretched hand. A moment then elapsed enduring of the longest life itself it seemed, now trapped as stunned and caught through lonely greed. A lesson learnt, a private promise made, he stumbled backward to the ground, released at last to run though knew not why and cared much less to where. Frantically scurrying to a crabbing gait, he scuttled away quicker than really, he could scramble. To the haven of his mocking friends who watched the exploit from afar.

A grain-encrusted eye flickered peering out upon an unfamiliar world. It blinked and strained on heaving, whence the saline bitter sap convulsed emittance for to acrid taste once more. Trapped within a tidal swell of rolling consciousness, the figure struggled on the ebb and flow of understanding, cramped again upon the numbness of his stricken being and knew not even who he was in that confounding moment. He wasn't dead yet, his brain repeated. Alas not quite dead yet. Then felt the writhing agony of life surge unrepentant through him, heard his moan and tried to move…anywhere would be escape…anywhere. Thus unsteady on the easy give of sand, he raised his head the slightest for to view the world anew.

The sound of gull and surf behind and overhead would offer little to his bearing so there awhile remained to lie, alive but somehow glad, remembering a journey. Of relentless silent solitude, adrift and aimless in an endless void of blue and of the heartless tormenting imposed beneath the blinding glare of cruel sun. His only respite, that of freezing in the long, cold grip of night where even old, familiar stars had lost their worthy lustre. Deserted and abandoned was that empty place, with only gods there for acquaintance.

An eternal oneness, he and they for always bounding westward on the faithfulness of guiding stone's direction…and on enduring ordeal's testing finally accomplished, was he thus rewarded or condemned with suffered life returning?

He sniffed the accursed ocean's scenting, fainter and the better for its distance and found small cheer once again…but then as awful clarity invaded, with its desperate sense of loss to overwhelm was forced to put his hand reluctantly to stiffened movement in an effort to locate and hold again, the leather bag forever tied about his waist.

Once satisfied he crushed against its painful content and smiled relieved, despite the ache for still he had the key and that would be enough, he thought…enough for now at least. For while he had the key or rather this particular part, so were Tomakal-Zaqual and Rashkulcan to stand deprived, restricted in the world.

The world… he thought, a word assuming strange and hitherto unknown proportions, unmatched by even his long years of formal learning. Nothing of the lands and folk of his encountering since his taking flight from them were known to him nor even held the vaguest title in that native tongue he once regarded commonplace and therefore used by all….but as for having found his safety in remoteness? He knew the leagues proposed small hindrance in the quest for this belonging, they would come, for certain…one day, they would come.

Through great taxation of an ailing will he raised himself against the shifting sands, completing to his knees, and with head awash, embroiled within the motion of the sea ingrained upon his balance, Ishtaac swooned to fall continuous, being caught surprisingly upon the last however, by a stabilising unseen grip that seized and grappled with his weight.

Odd, shrill, nasal voices confused his hearing, fast and incoherent they suggested haste, projecting grave concerns distraught, although contained within, a rare politeness easily defined. Lifted and supported upright, he was guided thus across the labour of the beach's heavy compromise followed by excited babbling children, piping all around, their avid interest to disclose.

Catching just some bleary-sighted glimpses of reed-woven, wide-brimmed hats, Ishtaac could only surmise that his bearers were smaller in stature than he but held fair strength unlike a child, though probably as innocent and kindly, he imagined wryly or else they would have left him there to die. Under a combined and orchestrated effort, they brought and dragged him stumbling to a dwelling perched upon the dune and took him in to shelter for to lend attention to his wounds. And it was there inside, sat formless on the solitary bed, he saw his helpers clearly for the first.

Lean, bent and stunted humble folk, were tanned with weathered wisdom worn, but pleasantly on aged faces despite the obviousness of hardship. A matrimony, he deduced in private, of enduring partnership and no mistake, their devotion as apparent as was the poverty they lived in.

Stark and cramped the single roomed abode appeared to be, but those who dwelt therein had gladly offered free to gift the meagerness of their constrictions upon such wayward, needy stranger as was he, without it seemed, a pause for even thinking of refusal, nevertheless their afforded generous welcoming was poorly received. Ashamedly then it was that Ishtaac sought for hidden motives, embracing close the leather pouch protectively, and through defensiveness, instinctively assumed a fearsome glare. The guiding stone, the jade, his key and solitary blade the only remnants of a previous life somewhere, spent once upon another time and now perhaps unreachable beyond the lonely sea. If the gods themselves had chosen not to take these treasures from him then none assuredly would.

The old lady looked up from deformed and stooping posture to smile a worn-toothed, warming reassurance and placed her delicate touch meekly on his arm. Ishtaac reeled at her affection, unused to such intrusion. Thus she shied away with frightened hurt, to the ready comfort of her husband who took her gently with embrace and led her downcast form across the cabin to where the cooking area lay. Ishtaac watched, presuming of their whispered conversation, remorseful for his unbecoming manner to those unworthy of such treatment, but with reluctance, soon conceded to his bedding down and graced the tortured sleep where one's delirious sweat through turmoil's candid reckoning unveils a striving's real intent whence secrets are revealed.

Unheard or seen and undeterred, the woman occupied her time preparing from the frugal for their guest, and on awakening was then presented with the thin but nonetheless substantial product of her labour.

A broth of grit, wild grain and herbs with fish and rooted vegetables unknown to him was consumed immediately with uncouth, hearty relish to his utmost satisfaction and a comforting where Ishtaac felt agreed that if any could suffice and feast on kindness as a dish, then his present host could fill a starving man thrice over. The gratitude he now declared with genuine thankfulness was equally appreciated. The dulled rejection in her tired eyes, defeated through the years of crippling life's endeavour, shone with a marvellous expectancy akin to scampish youth once more…and both were pleased sincerely.

Outside the shack the air was vibrant and alive to the chattering excitement of children investigating the details and the nature of discovery. Each with their particular version of recent, past events to honour the occasion, seeking fervently, conveyance to surpass the efforts of their rivals. Ishtaac listened quietly, reminiscent of a temple far away and long ago where the youngest acolytes who came each spring to be taught and raised toward the service would so congregate outside the imposition of a consequential structure with anticipation of a future life within. He considered the pathways of the innocent and the guiding hands it meets along the way then sighed with mixed emotions, stretching weak his lifeless limbs, for there would sense his presence both reflective of the tired ancient and indeed the new-found also.

Ishtaac remembered little of the sunlit breezy days that followed, excepting the continual assistance of his guardians and the apparently endless ration of the fish grained soup that made up almost to entirety, their diet. Gradually his strength and wherewithal returned and coupled with the release from stiffened movement, he embarked upon the dogged route to convalescence.

Frequently the children came to play the energetic games of youth along the shoreline near their abode and as often he would watch their frolicking whilst standing in attendance of the old man whence repairing daily damage to his fishing net, and in that time became curiously aware of the absence of an inter-mediating generation between the youngest and the elderly. Neither with them nor wandering alone had there appeared any of parental age, however, owing to the lofted barriers of communication, though sufficient for his basic needs, Ishtaac found himself prevented from dispelling of his intrigue to any reasonable degree. In fact, he met constantly with a noticeable reluctance to accommodate enquiries and was usually deferred away, in a polite and friendly fashion, on to other matters deemed more pressing for the day. He did however manage to discover through depictions in the stick drawn sand, that he was no longer cast upon the beach of one of the innumerable islands littering that accursed sea, but had instead struck fortune on the outer reaches of a mainland. A land the couple referred to in their awkwardly demanding tongue as Chung Guo, when eventually he had arrived through stricken laughter unto voice interpretation as correct enough to stay their ready humour.

For the moment, but with an ever-watchful seaward eye, Ishtaac saw no immediate threat of danger or sensed detection from pursuit, and so ambled leisurely his road's ease to recovery, leaving the hospitality of the little home to embark on ever further reaching explorations into a foreign land habitually each morn'. On one such ordinary day he came returned whence seeking solace from his hunger, to fraught and anxious faces rushing eagerly to greet him consumed with urgencies unknown, and so encountered there a deluge of confusion inspired by hurried speech exceeding mild perplexing. The couple argued incessantly over something plainly regarding him, though what was said as yet, remained an incoherent mystery. It was during this fevered exchange he noticed, in the distance, hailing on the southward surf, an oncoming storm of activity ahead the kicking up of billowed sand…this then he would take as rooting their concern.

Argumentation ceased as both looked on with nervousness to where Ishtaac's gaze was fixed. Rumour had preceded this arrival but as to who or whatever they might be, he found again his knowledge wanting, so enthralled, he watched instead awaiting the approach with curiosity unmoved.

Land roaming beasts clearly, but taller even than the sacred men, reflective on their part as is the sun upon the stillest water. Magnificent in finery beguiling to the eye, brilliant hues of verdant green, latesky blue and the luscious regal reds that chilled with thoughts of new spent blood. They gradually emerged as two not one alone but bound in skillful harmony. Man atop the beast, the master and the mastered coupled as a species new. The mind of man astride the speed and power of large and wilful creatures…or had the power of the animal indeed so harnessed in the mind of man? 'Seek shelter from the flashing storm of man on beast that rages unseen in the east…' Ishtaac pondered the potential for directional mistake and doubted it applied, the Quauchen tongue had never slipped before…and on that inherent trait his entire world relied.

The old woman tugged irritably at the sleeve she had painstakingly repaired for him, in attempt to drag Ishtaac from their notice to the dark seclusion of the hovel nearby. Absently he resisted her intentions, his imagination stirred and coloured by events, for they, he judged, as yet were too remote to be of trouble to his thought.

Shielding his eyes from the coastal glare, Ishtaac peered eagerly regardless, oblivious to any other interference and for this reason he was come upon unwarned…but for the whine of aged pleadings at his side he may have heard his downfall stalking.

From across the dunes, inland, on foot they stole. A flashing brilliance with the sound of whipped wind tearing through the rustled boughs, attention seized and fatefully decided. Instantly Ishtaac turned away from staring stunned to face the angered crowd now mobbing to suppress him.

A relatively small but stealthy band of soldiers, dressed equal to their riding counterparts in coverings of bright, reflective discs affixed to heavy quilted tunics, had suddenly appeared to revelation from sight's secrecy behind the shack. Upon each head they wore a curvaceous leather helm interspersed with a studded fabrication which shone and gleamed as captured for to mirror harsh late morning's light. Scarred hands well used to battle carried spears, tipped again with this most versatile of substances and long knives too about their waists seemed fit to stave off any close called challenge…it was the drawing of such weaponry that had betrayed the deceit of inattentiveness.

Menacing, dangerous shrieks of savage threat, jostled to the fore and a sharp, keen stabbing realisation was known pressed as coarsely dry against his throat. The tensest calm ensued whereupon Ishtaac's jaded necklace was harshly snatched and then removed. The aged couple offered verbal intervention fearfully, on his behalf, although both futile and to great expense those efforts were to prove. In one single, arrogant thrusting of malevolence the husband's life ordeal thus ended and her's increased beyond all dreadful measure. Aloft the timid fisherman was held and buoyed so easily along the battered shaft, to retch subjected to the mocking jests of final writhing moments, prevented from the dignity of falling by a slayer's ruthless hand. Hung twisted, tortured in his agony, caught with eyes imploring behind the frailest arms outstretched and groping weakly, the old fisherman sought for one last time, embracement of his loved one being held at bay, unjust beyond, to taunt his dying reach. Crying then the tears of impotence he passed on limp through clemency's denial.

Ishtaac felt the pain of steel himself that day and for the first, compelled to standing idle by whilst helplessly the widow fought in vain against a vile intrusion from the odious dead at heart. Struggling on clawed nail and teeth distressed for biting, eyes ablaze with thwarted fury she screamed demands upon her gods for retribution, but remorseless was she dragged from sight inside to shield obscenities from any audience view, desiring rather but themselves to be their sole accusing witness. The hollow shrieks of her protesting scarred as flailed on Ishtaac's soul relentless, unheard by all excepting he…and never would those wounds inflicted on that bright, ignoring day ever truly heal.

Prolonged and brutal did the time elapse until, lamentably the muffled hoarseness of foul drama would subside towards subdued and ponderous sobbing shame before the fretful silence of one fatal, everlasting crime, whence calm restored itself once more. Only the gulls above returned their plaintive cries of pity to assuage….as the surf crashed on regardless.

Awaiting doom at the brandished end of spear point, Ishtaac heeded the riders approach with the resolved air of deep foreboding choked within him. He watched them turn inland and speed up from the water's edge to greet their comrades now emerging. Standards unfurled they came, sharply radiant wrestling with the breeze, to a clumsy halt enclosing.

Monstrous, wild-eyed beasts agape with flared and snorting nostrils bore disturbed unease to pressing close upon him, champing out insane an orchestrated torment to the tune of callous, inner demons. Contesting the riders authority they reared up to kick and jerked unsteadily whence sought to charge him to the floor and all around the passage of an undeciphered, animated converse hurtled back and forth in argument between the horsemen and the inhumanity that soiled the ground beside him.

Prodded continuously in the search of some compliance, Ishtaac was at loss to offer naught but gestures in return. And moreso, roughly was he handled for his failings, with coarse derision thus provoked delighting to their high amusement in a ridicule now brought to bear on unfamiliar lineage.

Ishtaac forced his laugh appeasingly, for there was little other hope of preservation, taut then without humour he suffered fearfully their jeering him, expectant of the worst, whence from his waist the bag was cut and with it went the precious key, his blade and trusted guiding stone. All physicality of his worth was plundered but for the band about his forehead, which likewise, as regards the clothes upon his back, they thought unworthy of their seizing. Ishtaac's life hung wan afoot the most delicately woven thread of single strand decision and knowing this he chose his option wisely, so in spite of sternest reservations let them go, spurning indications of reluctance but avowed unto himself, one day, a recompensed return.

In the longest moments that would follow without a single utterance, Ishtaac eyed the undisputed leader of the riders, closely noting details so that when the time demanded, recognition he would know, by feel alone in deathly, quiet corners, if such cunning was required.

The rider withdrew Ishtaac's blade studying its ornate character with an accustomed eye to arms. The likes of this peculiarity never had he seen before, so was therefore curious to conduct a trial of sharpness. Taking a thong of robust leather from about his saddle he sliced it through with satisfying ease. His companions remarked approval and in return he nodded his agreement before then tucking it away inside his belt for due consideration at a later date. Proceeding then he leant attention to the remaining contents of the pouch and removed the key for close examination. An unguarded display of terse objection from their captive betrayed a valuation to the rider's interest whilst immediately correction came administered as driven deep in sharp response preventing any further thoughts of outburst. However, the action carried too, an unpredicted worth in that the rider's nomination was let slip, to burn forever branded on the inner wall of Ishtaac's mind…and Shen Song was that sound declared sufficient to locate him by.

The horsemen eyed their vagabond anew, severely spent of any previous naive condescension, but instead with experienced caution and suspicion they would keep him in restraint. The rider continued to examine the item, reasoning its purpose with a puzzled expression fraught upon his brow constantly referring to Ishtaac's reaction at so visible a trespass, although despite resentment gnawing at the mental bonds of his endurance he gave no further indication of a hostile nature or affinity towards his longing.

Bidding Ishtaac to approach the foam, flanked beast its rider looked him over with advantaged posturing and then clearly gave appeals demanding explanation, which foolishly or otherwise Ishtaac opted to ignore lending only to annoyance, preferring moreso shrugging innocence and a feigned attempt intent upon dismissive revelation. Shen Song, having greater concerns at that particular time, soon decline the tiresome chore, but deciding that the object held as yet an undefined, potential worth, chose to keep it also, for his later contemplation, and issued forth an order, casting down the leather newly cut, which would prompt adjacent soldiers to complete as trussed their capture. He was marched then forcefully away across the beach without a single backward glancing to the little home and every sad reminding of misfortune his acquaintance had condemned with ill upon it.

Forward to join the similarly bound company of wretched and beleaguered, jogging wearily along the tide mark's course of shingle stones and jetsam. Where outriders were the guardians of order among their human herd and forced a pace beyond, for some, survival's speed, urging ever onward with their animals to crush behind the burning sting of whip struck hide as dismal to encourage. Shrill oaths arose above the suffered mourn of anguish, but hanging over all a nauseating stench that gagged to equal any rank and festered sore.

The sand grasped leaden, dragging tiredly on sore and pounding feet. Ishtaac knew now at least, the reason for the absent generation, they, like he, were here or gone before. Rounded up, collected to perform no doubt, some task where voluntary willingness showed rare. This land then, was maybe not so strange or different after all he thought, picturing its ruler of ensnaring who would order wisely from afar…and thereupon inquiry saw truly once again the familiar face of hopelessness bemused beneath its ever-present haunting of despair. Perhaps all places where people dwelt were on foundations made the same. Considering this delayed sufficiently to find himself reminded of intolerance's harshest, smarting bite sensation wealed across his back provoking thus the curse of knowing more than ever the wrong side of imperial favour.

They travelled north that day exhausting afternoon to fading light, when thankfully they turned due west and onto firmer footing. Following a river's run they passed inland through idle, barren fallowness, where farmsteads stood long empty in decay. Through the coarse grass cut that slashed bare flesh to weeping red and over rolling lowlands where nothing stirred but they. Also to the night the company maintained their jarring, trudge of dire repetition until at last were put to resting, sheltered in a dale.

Ishtaac sat upon the ground, moistened in the chilling air to while away the numbness of his being, forsaken utterly and cast adrift upon his woe…though soon was roused again on noticing, despite his dulled awareness, a movement and a murmuring, its ripple surged through disarray. There appeared at length a bowl and settling within, a meager serving of the now familiar swamp of husky grain, to which his stomach earlier that day, was thought become accustomed. The young, dishevelled woman who handed him the food smiled pleasantly concealing well her conflict then proceeded staring with, primarily, a disconcerting interest bent towards his features, prompting but the gentlest meet of tender exploration against his neat-trimmed, grizzled beard. Her pretty rounded face though grime ingrained, held bright the fragile, freshened breeze of youthfulness to envious gods perfection and graced to gaze upon the world through vivid eyes that shone entrancing, as the morning star. Unsullied was her vision framed by the tousled fall of long, dark, unkempt hair to the point of overborne endearment…and resentful more than ever previous was here Ishtaac made on seeing such poor-circumstance.

Nervously she spoke at first, whence halting over unknown matters seeking not replies or falsehood's reassurance but rather more looked simply for to comfort him instead with charm and quiet, dulcet tone. Ishtaac tiredly though, ignored her attempts to associate herself with him and simply ate in place of her acceptance, indulging as forlorn a misspent, selfish moment's squander never to forget.

When he had finished, she politely received again the bowl and passed it back along to waiting, outstretched hands choosing to assume a closeness there beside him huddled daring almost to the touch.

Shivering, the young woman timidly sought the further pleasure that his warmth could offer whilst the night swept cold its brush on drying perspiration. Ishtaac allowed her nearness now that part of him in some small measure was content, and snuggled down compliant, for both their mutual needs. And forged, entwined as one, serene in contrast to the tumbled sky above they found necessity became the natural pleasure of caressing. Where despite the screams of failed escape that marked the clouded, starless passage, they lay exempt, untouched by harm, distracted free in blissful isolation, and knew upon that night from hopeless situation that a bonded love was formed, where hearts exchanged embrace and so remain forever bound in memories by the ponderous whims of fate.

Morning light rose pale its revelation over the deceased diminishing of their number, spurring on, severe with truths and nothing more than water to sustain them, the recommencing of that trudging march of doom. On toward the distant mountains, on relentless through the days, and as they fell, and many did, the riders would return to swell their ranks, again. Reaping from the crops of unprotected village caches hidden insecure beyond their sight within the woods, or seizing from the placid, nestled places where innocence slept idly unsuspecting still, behind the secret look of spur and rising hill.

Thus their journey continued brutal in its manner, beholders to adversity, always together, side by side, tired and hungry enduring hostile plight in bitter harmony, Ishtaac and the lady whom he came to know as Shant-lei. A corruption developed from his failing efforts at mastering her name and a similarity found existent among the neglected words of long forgotten usage, meaning appropriately enough, or so he thought, sweet fragrancy on evening breeze. Such entitling amused her and upon each utterance would induce a needed smile which leant its promise to the welcome of attachment, and offered eagerly a tender recognition to reflect as dearly prominent within the focus of bewitching, hazel eyes.

The road, improving recently along the verge became as cobbled underfoot, and soon united with another equally so rendered. At the time of their arrival at this juncture, came as they themselves, more driven pale and weary victims trailed upon its length. Three score docile, haggard forms hung pitiful on staggered limbs, driven ceaselessly ahead the cruel will of ruthless masters, with the dead eyed prospect of to live another day in misery as the only hope before them. It was for each alas, a sadly welcome sight for as their number grew, then so the pace resisted in accordance to constrictions now imposed by the very strangling nature of their route. Ishtaac however, whence trampling here, as deemed upon the last and nearing enlightenment's conclusion found again his thoughts came pressed to dwell upon possessions borne aloft beyond retrieval's reach.

Shant-lei indicated often to the mountains with evident unease, sensing also the foreboding of a purposed end was looming nigh upon them. An impending anxiousness that echoed grim within her when they lay in unison that night.

The following morning saw an unexpected smartening of appearance among the soldiers' ranks as if in preparation for some unforeseen procession or parade. Personal grooming, weapon polishing and bindings also re-examined made for a later start than usual…but despite intrigue's commotion and bewilderment enough to stir distraction, the dreaded thought of imminent separation draped its spectral shadow for to settle firmly over Ishtaac…though now not solely with a distancing from blade and key. The notion sprung acutely to alarm, and forth, the feeling that the time to move was close at hand, although as yet, with guile or otherwise, his mind forewarned of little else but wasteful death awaiting at the end of freshly sharpened spears…so patience must he knew, persist among the present time at least, but also must he keep his fealty to the words and wisdom of the Quauchen. This latter of determinations, however, was reminded many times without as now, his utterly convincing.

Throughout the entire, desperate affair thus far Ishtaac, compelled somewhat reluctantly until this moment by the most fatalistic of intentions, had managed to work his way gradually to a frontal position accompanied by, as always, Shant-lei, and so, when setting out that early mist hung morn' was claiming an arrival to within a reckless striking distance behind the leading horses should any opportunity arise. The process had been executed over time with caution, passing undetected by their overseers who looked only for escape, and occurring largely unchallenged by their fellow prisoners…actively encouraged even by some others. The majority not wishing themselves eagerly to fall upon their fates with undue haste.

Raggedly the captive reinforcements commenced the sluggish day ascending along a steepening incline where on the left was seen the landscape rising sharply to an overhanging slate wet, grey. Shattered sheer, fragmented faces pressed a closeness nigh on overbearing with its crush, and to the right they oversaw the barren rocky, scree-sloped slip, fall harshly to a valley floor obscured snug by stunted, gnarled and crooked tree tops. Across the widening gulf the mountainous terrain thrust jagged, soaked in hues of purple tingeing overlay to cramp a crowded sky, and overhead the black washed storm clouds whispered misty fringed, an end to yearning's ache….and then the rain came down to weigh and cow them further.

Succumbing to an instant of despairing realisation where loitered hope exceeded all allotted time, Ishtaac raised his eyes and saw the outer city walls of nearing destination, reaching high, impenetrable with adverse threat of dour incarceration offered only from its stony frown, standing resolute and sentinel for marking sound endeavour's journey to untimely, thwarted endings. The soldiers hence, presumption made, would get their reassignments for to harvest lands anew and thus the key would then be gone forever, held at best, as curio somewhere lost in this accursed, strangers' realm or worse, perhaps an inspiration unto future wars with unrest cast as far afield as even to his homeland.

Heart and shoulders sank as Ishtaac there became upon reflection, visibly distraught, Shant-lei whispered words of strength and comfort to enable further passage to the last but all was seen confounded now alas, so very, very late. They had arrived, and he now met conflicting guilt's rebuke for entertaining overlong the hesitation in his craven hand. A contentment personal and hitherto unknown was he gifted in Shant-lei's companionship…an ease to mend his troubled soul, and through great hardship he had found himself a fortune, in this his present failure, to have experienced fleeting gladness truly for the first…but what indeed, would the Quauchen order think of this so costly and diverting an indulgence amid such vital undertakings? He could only surmise their judgement as ill-favoured and thus could temper it, with nothing else but useless sacrifice and shame.

Surging forward with nothing more than rashness for determination's sake in haste to rectify his sins upon one final try at cleansing stains and salvage that so easily lost, Ishtaac hurled diminished chance upon the fickleness of gods. Shant-lei tried in vain to prevent what seemed a certain death. Stumbling helpless with neither balance or a personal care she lunged her all towards his unforeseen impulsiveness…though much too short the effort proved to gain his arm and stricken, would her fall reveal itself denied as empty handed.

Ishtaac, unaware of his cherished's plight behind came headlong, arms outstretched and diving blindly at both beast and rider with poor wisdom from the rear. Ignorant, the horseman showed himself to be, his mount however was not so easily assailed and in a wild-eyed moment of alertness caught the woeful sudden movement, panicked, then struck out in trained defence on smart and powerful hooves. Neither he nor Shen Song saw or felt the next but roused instead to find themselves upon the hardness of the unforgiving floor. Shant-lei's distress called lamely from across the void of his adherence whilst the world spun on relentless from his grasp, just as dismally, through blurred and effervescent senses Ishtaac stirred and saw his opportunity elude him.

Sensations buoyed to floating airlessly upon protective cushions far removed from all severity about to wake him with the stinging jolt of deep grazed blood loss, burning from the wound about his forehead. Muffled then he heard again her crying out for quick response before the soldiers intervened, crawled and gained one knee as menacing, the mirthless grin crammed close in spiralled vision, followed swiftly by disdainful tones of malice which of recent he had more than grown accustomed to.

Thrown back into rank, Ishtaac buffeted heavily from Shant-lei whose firmness urged him staggering forward with encouragement enough to struggle on throughout the swoon of footing's unsure labour.

Ahead the city gates approached, ominous and final. Once inside immediate fate was surely sealed, suffice to last maybe his dulled and docile understanding of the concept, evermore. Ishtaac sighed regretful and forlorn, an aching head no recompense to justify for consequential losses, as watching vaguely and subdued, displeasure's ill-defining saw the leading riders soon dismount to bring both travel and their discord to an ordered, swaying silence.

Beneath the shadow of the imposition they lined in preparation of admittance. Ishtaac swayed his faltering alongside Shant-lei who leant supportively against him when together they would shuffle meekly on in turn towards a long, decrepit table, at which a disgruntled man in once fine silks sat weary with despondence to receive them.

Ishtaac watched the portly man lamentably unroll a stiffened, cloth like substance, wheezing through his muttered utterances whilst wrestling with the ungainly document in hand. On the roll he saw the alien scratches previously recorded there and looked on curious as yet more were added with the aid of a thinly pointed strip of wood, stained as were the author's fingers with the blackened, oily liquid drawn from slender china flask positioned near to hand.

The administrator paused, looked up and drummed impatiently the plumpest fingers, prompting for the waiting soldier to react some way to end stagnated silence. Shen Song duly announced his surly presence with importance unabashed but little impression was there made, despite an obvious acquaintance. After a brief, fatigued exchange where tiredness suggested of formalities, the administrator nodded permissively to an understudy standing beyond the gate and proclamations then were issued loudly, whereby in response, after the echoes had long since died away, several rushed, apologetic looking guardsmen appeared hurriedly from within, despoiled and battle worn, bearing wounds and amputations fresh and poorly tended.

These were the begrudging spare, the corrupted few of many from a front-line fortress under siege. Each had come to collect their allocations defined as written by the clerk and led their charges on to entering the stronghold, forthwith to separate destinations and whatever use, the defending of nigh fallen cities need…and all the while Ishtaac leered with loathing undisguised upon the bag tied firmly to his captor's belt wondering of his chances once again, feeling bitterly torn between the relief that Shant-lei was with him still, and that unmistakable empty tasting of defeat's sensation knowing that the key, his blade and hopes for she and they were about to drift without his further protest, off along the ebbing tide of failure, much too easily away.

Through the mazement of deserted, empty streets, their march tramped flanked on either side. Doorways, walls, in part and whole removed and taken for the cause gave an eerie, haunted feeling to the hollow wind that whined its way unhindered. Buildings, tall with layered, sweeping rooves showed rude their pillared standings, exposed in cold and skeletal appearance, stripped of comfort, bare of fixings, sombrely expectant of an aftermath's destruction in the wake of bloodshed's confrontation. A place of apparitions, a testament to absence where the merriment of long gone children echoed yet, discarded in the remnants of their play. Broken toys of wood and ragged dolls of once so dearly gathered straw marked trails of hastiest retreat, flung or cleared as spent aside to jumbled corners, lifeless and unloved, henceforth to lie forgotten and to wither in decay .

Ishtaac was the first of their small group to hear the murmured battle rumblings troubling towards them and tensed as vivid, grim reality riddled with its looming peril, crept on every footfall ever nearer.

From a side street, a wooden cart trundled across their path on circular spoked configurations, bearing the bodies of more fallen to some morgue's misguided haven, propelled by a solitary comrade harnessing the entire barrow's weight alone and almost with an ease. Ishtaac wondered at the strength and ingenuity required to surpass such feats and considered strange, Shant-lei's apparent disregarding to events but would even moreso whence the now familiar clash of steel grew noisome to be overwhelming with its din and mournful in its forecast.

Sooner than enough they were passing by the glare of strictest looking guards, projections of horrific sights whose presence there beside the narrow, single entrance way prevented all attempts to flee with promised death reflected absolute in dread, remorseless eyes alert to any sign of cowardice. Into the wide enclosure they were marched and once inside predictably, were trapped.

The compound was ringed to complete containment before them by an high, compressed earth wall, thickly based and almost sheer. Impenetrable at the moment but judging by the fevered activity that fought tenaciously along the battlements, its challenged strength was ailing. Adjacent to their entrance it was also overlooked by the scarred and eyeless plain facade of a civic building's walling, adorned with the shabby hangings of its ripped and char blacked, ravaged ensigns which ran the breadth entirely of the yard from the perimeter wall close by, dissecting across to its distant, arced demise.

An outcropped, semi-circle of detention defended by those condemned it seemed in equal measure as were they, weakened only at its central reach by mighty, steel braced, wooden gates, barring heavily against the tumultuous rampage of the outer lands beyond. Their only realistic means of escape would be either through that guarded portal or over the wall as yet, unbreached. Which, despite its close hand dominance was proving, in reality but a frail line of resistance and all indeed that separated they and their captors from the warring tribesmen's grasping…and alternatives, perhaps no worse than those already suffered, though inflicted by their own.

Plaster and fallen roof tiles littered the floor, thus they crunched a trail across the pavings to their halting near the centre of the square. Everywhere within his prison's yard scenes of distraught or dazed confusion unfolded with lucidity amid the mayhem, the clearer for observing. Soldiers and civilians alike rushed from place to place barricading and resisting the onslaught as and where were needed. Arms carriers, water bearers and physicians aided to unfulfilling their ability together in the striving. Stones, clay bricks, shattered wood, even the slumping bodies of their kin were called to act upon defensive service. The main gates looked to be the concentration of the attack without but along the ramparts and the hastily cobbled gantries figures also charged to and fro slashing desperate to dispel or hurled instead defiant anything at hand toward the engulfing human tidal surge crashed wild and stubbornly against it. Archers too, with discipline, worked frantically adhering to the task sending their impaling storm continually outward as a rain to fall from darkened clouds so deadly tipped upon assaulting waves below.

How long the stand would endure before somebody finally came to terms with the inevitable succumbing of the city was difficult to determine, but Ishtaac saw clearly that the desire to capture far outweighed the ability to defend, and having to drag a far flung peasantry in under duress to support the effort promised little in the way of substantial reinforcements for the future. He felt it to be simply a matter of time, and brief at that.

A fretful, red-faced, fat man with sleepy eyes bound inside a tightly fitting uniform, whose stressed appearance owed as much to personal indulgence as to the hardships encountered thus far in the conflict, blustered orders at any who would listen, and found suddenly the trespass of a foreign ignorance objectionably upon him. The bulky individual's arms flapped livid, bowing at his sides to demonstrating puffed frustration, before conceding utterly, submission, whereupon he thrust a nearby yolk and buckets miserably at Ishtaac and then subsequently threw repugnance in the direction of a rubble pile.

Reluctantly, but without voicing his contention, Ishtaac shuffled slowly off about his newly given task.

Ishtaac, the learned, he thought to himself derelict and dejected along his lowly amble, from atop the hierarchical tree to the indignity of incarcerated rock carrier, wearing the borrowed harness of such station on his back for everyone to see, and make complete the picture of his wretchedness. He smiled wryly, considered pride redundant for a moment, then crouched to gather stones. From his huddled position near to the ground he saw Shant-lei being handed a large bundle of linen and given the undertaking, he assumed, of tending to the wounded. She could be good at that, he decided, with an obvious benefit passing over to the assailants also, when eventually they won through. A fortuitous obligation that may just have saved her life. The idea lifted him a little and fuelled his labour from that point on with only slightly less concern.

With relatively more freedom than he was used to since his capture on the beach, Ishtaac found himself able to roam unchallenged to the boundaries of the courtyard, so long as his buckets were full and he maintained a sense of purpose and direction to his dawdled stride.

Whilst toiling away the waning afternoon in this unenthusiastic manner, he happened across the foot of one of the numerous rickety, makeshift ladders propped against the wall, and after furtive glances all around scaled to gazing out upon the landscape and his first full preview of the enemy horde without.

A steep-sided valley littered with the dead or dying and the fractured debris of numerous lashed together frameworks, coloured, on the margins, the bared fragmented rock but down the central swathe of tumbling grassland where the roadway wound its jagged, eased descent as best it could, a listless human carpet clogged, the fervour of approach. It was clear to Ishtaac that these invaders held determination beyond the realms of compromise, for evidence there was in great abundance to show their arrogant disregarding of the casualties inflicted on them, lying wasted there, even to the extent of its hampering their own progress.

As far along the wall as the structuring allowed he saw the swarming lines of attack recklessly advancing on a city in its death throes. He cast his sight to view the saddening despondent, devastation behind him and thought once more of his escaping. Shant-lei was someway off among the dying. Her gait was unmistakable and a comfort also to behold but all too soon her beauty was obscured, engulfed by staggered reinforcements hobbling in to feed the fray, brought from other quarters deemed less needy or from causes finally abandoned by the way.

The high pitched, sucking noise of arrow's flight, charred overhead startling him to seek protective cover, but sighted high with trailing plumes of blackened vapour smoking in their wakes their deliberate trajectory was to land them well within the compound and to stretch the scant resources even further, but as none could be afforded to attend the less immediate destruction that they caused, they were merely left to burn. In retaliation, the rocks of his supplying along with those of many others, were heaved or thrown by hand or slingshot, depending on the size, and sent forth crashing down among the rabid cloy without their need for aiming.

The barbaric savagery of close quarter combat priced a life as cheap and so was carefree with its spending, with inroads made then shored again and few remaining able to account the cost.

Throughout the late afternoon the ferociousness of battle soiled complete the wounded day, but despite the fragility of their standing the city held, and with the onset of the night the turmoil gradually receded to the goading hails of floundering frustration and the subduing prospect of their plans to reconsider, leaving only those to stain the peace with bloodied cries of lonesome suffering since discarded to the illustrious fate of noble battle's lulling aftermath. Ishtaac found himself then put to different usage, continuing nevertheless under only temporal watch, repairing the battlements with anything moveable not better suited to the likely task of killing.

Options, as Ishtaac saw them, ran in two directions only, to remain and face, if not a certain death then a lengthening detention, or place all trust in faith and Quauchen foresight and risk his head outside…it was a decision easy with solution.

Edging cautiously he slipped away, when chance permitted through the choking haze of dank wood smoke that lay as trapped as those besieged inside the walls, with intentions of to meet again with Shant-lei and escape the shackles of the square. Eventually he found her near the debris of a long, low building barely housing the overworked resources of a sorely inadequate well. Bloodied and weary, she applied her care unreservedly offering comfort as she tended. Ishtaac marvelled at her willingness to lean toward forgiveness and smiled a heartache's revelation.

Touching her gently on the shoulder, she turned to see concern upon his brow and buried deep her face, to hiding within embrace instinctive, momentarily excusing herself the horrors that abounded. He held her tightly and protective, whispering gently of her name, soothing fears and steadying her whilst wrenched to feel the tender shivering of her precious tears as openly she wept upon his tattered robe, returning freely of himself and giving wholly his compassion.

When at last she settled, Ishtaac indicated his ideas for their release as best as he was able...or indeed had hasty forged, but reluctance to leave her fellow countrymen, regardless of morality or of the reasons that had brought her and them alike to this forsaken place, showed through in the gentlest of rejections when was severed lightly the sweet sensation of her contact. Conveying in so doing that she felt it likely most had arrived here under similar circumstances as had they, as indeed had all her family gone before her, and as such could never simply choose to abandon them...not now. For there, by chance or doomed ill-fortune was her brother found and put to lay within her lap, a harrowed scene from which dependency and undeniable likeness struck to smiting all remaining hope into a myriad shards of damning failure and regret. To Ishtaac unfortunately the way ahead was clear and thus was caused profusely so to weep when then she urged instead for him to stay, tending by her side, if only for a short while longer, offering pitiful her makeshift bandages, imploring him with tear-filled eyes to aid. He looked upon her understandingly with an honour previously ungranted, though sadly doubted of her kindred such allegiance, as now the pain of parting welled torrential to consuming totally within him. Smiling through the bitterest tears, he kissed her forehead and thought of things that might have been. Then empty and beyond the reach of futile comfort arising to his feet, resolved retrieval of possessions wherever they might be. Slowly thus he it let fall, that soft and clinging gentleness of privilege he had come to know so dearly, and gazing then one final time upon her unstained natural wealth forced to tear himself away with broken heart on rueful promise to return.

With practised quiet stealth to clasp distracted, fragments of a once thought hardened heart he stole across the yard, hastening ever closer to the guards still holding fast departure's single exit between the outer wall and lofty civic building. Without a weapon or diversion that route would he sensed, prove far too hazardous to justify attempt but needed still to satisfy himself that the opportunity was unavailing for along that path he thought to reach his goal directly…and thus it proved to be. His actions merely caught the sentry's interest turning him to run suspiciously instead unveiled, towards the nearest ladder standing propped against the bulwark…and as expense for such mistaking heard the cries of provocation growing louder in his ears and knew attention he had drawn, from each of those around him.

Scaling the rungs easily, now devoid of heavy burden, Ishtaac raced along the gangway, silhouetted lean with eager purpose against the cold night sky, agile and demanding sport though for exhausted bowmen was his target to be rendered. Shant-lei watched his daring escapade transpire, tense and hopeful from across the court, with emotions raw and rent apart upon the tear-soaked remnants of her rags. Returning only about her crucial business whence finally Ishtaac dropped away unscathed from sight, forever from her life, outside of harmful bow shot and the hostile city boundary, safe, beyond the recall of her love.

Ishtaac had chosen his route without much time for forethought at the last but still it served him well enough. He had run along the narrow ledge to where the wall incorporated cleverly the mountain's natural defences, from whence he'd leapt carefree to chance his fall upon the steep rock face below, sliding free from capture into an unknown, darkened wilderness of open draughts outside. Down the slippery lichen-covered surface, he sped without the means of slowing his descent until coming to an abrupt and painful halt, hard against an unforgiving outcrop. Freedom, though saddened through its earning, was once again just like his solitude, returned, but his homeland more than ever seemed so distantly unreachable and without the key was known that always would it be so...for now however, thoughts on that must wait.

Rubbing pointlessly the smarting in his shoulder, Ishtaac made his aching way quietly among the ferns to meet the valley floor, following the stench of man and beast that dwelt much time together closely side by side. Hurriedly from there he stole along the grassy bank of a shallow, splashing brook which layered silence on his progress and carried him unchecked to within the sight of wind rushed, glaring campfires, sparking hereabouts between the temporary, fabric-covered dwellings providing for their host's protection from cold, wet nights abroad. Lookouts were visible on the outskirts of the clearing, their earthy dress and lack of flagrant colouring portrayed a force concerned far less with noble, honoured, ritual slaughter and more at ease with guile and cunning murder. He listened from his vantage point to casual conversation and considered now... approach.

In truth, little did he have to offer other than suspicion although had much to ask for in its place, and what was more, without his wishing to reveal it. He needed to get back behind the walls to secure Shant-lei's well-being and regain his stolen losses, but knew that that would take an army to achieve, so this must surely do....though not content was he to be a prisoner this time.

Unarmed, dependant entirely on the utterance of a Quauchen priest, made it seemed, so very long ago, with the prediction that his destiny was scribed and seen as finalised elsewhere, he raised his arms slowly above his head with hands wide open in a gesture of his honesty and emerged to full exposure from the bushes proceeding nervously upon the draw of smiling, crescent blades, hopeful of their understanding or at least sustaining intrigue. Ishtaac carried himself towards the guards with the mixed air of vulnerability and worthlessness that had served him often in the past, who in turn responded with conflicting reservations based on humour and bewilderment, but were nonetheless quite thorough in their searching him. Their pliant figure of amusement was then escorted close at either hand, through the encampment, assisted by the occasional coax of prodding steel on to where a troubled figure sat for warmth beside the growling firelight discussing matters with his comrades midst the finals of a casual bone strewn meal.

The aged, greying warrior looked up with eyes ablaze, surprised and clearly annoyed at the interruption then stood defensively to greet them, casting braided hair tied off with leather thong on doing so, to drop from interference, long behind his back. His hungered, sallow, leanness and hollowed, sunken eyes sat well upon an angry disposition, expressed with force whence on demanding swift, curt answers from his men whom they respectively, addressed as Tsai Chi Min or sounds to that effect.

Ishtaac became increasingly concerned, reassessing gravely his decision to have disclosed himself so readily and appeared noticeably distraught, an obvious discomfort which was met with scoffing and derision from among those present in his company. One in particular projected his dominion over Ishtaac by taking him so roughly that his robe was almost put to forfeit whilst he mocked for entertainment with the greased intrusive probing of his ravaged, part chewed animal remains. The old soldier looked on unmoved, stroked his delicate, wispy beard and eyed him with a dubious scepticism. He considered circumstance and motive then returned his mind to profit and, on giving out a signal, prompted Ishtaac's physical forcing to a seated position overly close to the crackled burn of campsite flames. Limping a wide encircling path behind his captive's back he further pondered on this sudden bold appearance before eventually coming to rest cross legged, opposing through the dancing glare. Moments later a soldier returned from the darkness beyond illumination accompanied by another. This latter scrawny mis-shape of well spent, undernourished manhood sat unbidden and without request alongside the evident authority. His stare contrasted to the weakness of his presence and held intently, delving ceaseless into Ishtaac's manner for the slightest revelation that might betray a hidden, inner purpose. With steepled fingers gently tapping on thin, dry pursing lips he exuded an intentional display of wisdom, to which Ishtaac responded pleasantly with a smile, nodding also to concede a due respect. The gnarled old man turned favourably toward his captain and emptied several small white objects from a pouch into the palm of his twisted, claw like hand and together they regarded close the contents, which from their faces of approval appeared to endorse some preconceived, conclusive outcome. One of the younger tribesmen however, reacted with unconcealed disgust through an apparent disbelieving of events, slapping his flanks in a show of unbridled exasperation only to find himself immediately disciplined with a severe tirade of bitter, verbal lashed reproach. It was clear that wounded pride struggled in one fleeting moment of abandon to defy its master, paused, then stormed, with seething on a crushed and staggered rage away into the night, leaving leaden as a wake, the pensive silence of his absence. The seer muttered some unconcerned aside, stated with the nonchalantly dismissive flick of his thin and bony hand which duly caused their captain then to laugh aloud, humourless and haughty to the breaking down of mounting tension. Tsai Chi Min then called upon another of his men and released him on an errand, returning himself to watch the ever changing thoughtful inspiration of the flames.

What they had foreseen was only to be guessed at, but their reaction had offered Ishtaac a little hopeful inclination to his near future, and for the first time now his vision strayed to his surroundings. Carts heavily laden with the clutter of a wide array of flasks and arrows by the bundle tipped in various fashion, the likes of which were aimed in his direction not so long ago, lay nearby to hand. Spears, bows and other curious weapons made of steel, stood in clustered leaning ready for to use within a moment's notice. This, to his perception, was an army on the move, mobile, well disciplined and led, fearfully courageous but not overly used to the spoils of conquest and indulgence, thus also he deduced, they had a purpose higher than this precious gain alone. They trod and beat new ground beneath their feet from homelands far away but managed still to keep their spirit and a rigid strength regardless, sufficient to reclaim territories long thought perhaps, initially as stolen…and with their animals for warmth and comfort he would see them lay before that night was done, to ease the cause of heartfelt retribution.

Ishtaac found himself addressed by Tsai Chi Min who bade him near with a friendlier or at least less hostile tone. Taking a smouldering branch from the fire he watched the dying flame with fascination for a while before decided, scraping clear an area of soil around his boot and there proceeded to inscribe quite obviously, a bird's eye viewing of the city up above, within its outer wall, to test the depth and fortitude of Ishtaac's will and understanding, marking areas where he supposed possible sites of fracture or strategic vantage lay along its length. Then under the observation and approval of the seated oracle handed Ishtaac the wood to impart his knowledge onto the depiction. Ishtaac indicated his point of exit, prompting both to smile the knowing smiles of those who understood the necessity and nature of escape but also there implied a weakness in the northern gateway, adding too, the number of defenders and the ebbing of morale. Appearing satisfied with this submission for the moment, subsequent speech passed earnestly between themselves until the drawing of conclusions. Ishtaac spoke also of Shant-lei declaring his fondness for her in the hope of courting sympathetic favour. Tsai Chi Min conceded little or nothing on that particular issue though, merely brushing his request aside as the soldier previously dispatched came stepping quietly to the fore returned, in order to convey his gleaned report in whispered tone. On seeing him the oracle rose to his feet and bade the visitor do likewise, loitered anxiously as the message was delivered, then followed Tsai Chi Min's impatient lead whilst continually ushering Ishtaac's journey on throughout the vast encampment.

Skirting nervously around the innumerable scattered pyres that lit to trace the contours of the ragged river valley, Ishtaac saw the soldiers lounging with their animals awaiting with indifference, the prospect of another dawn, whence heading on to where a trusted battle hardened guard of swarthy men stood ringed defending of a tent, its fabrication singled out remotely for importance.

Despite familiarity and rank the captain met the challenge of approach with care and searched his memory for selected words to verify his standing and was soon permitted sole, his access on demand. Ishtaac remained outside with the soothsayer under threatening suspicion until a short while later the ageing warrior reappeared from behind the folds of pelts and hastened them within.

Therein a lonely figure sat, lost to contemplation, head bowed almost nose to touch upon crossed legs, beneath a woeful, weary mantle exuding private thoughts. The ominous gaze turned up to silent greeting, showing grim the price of previous conviction upon much scarred and mended features. A repellent guise bearing tales of countless, virile conflicts that burned a stare to branding Ishtaac's soul…uncompromising was the eye that held him.

The oracle bowed respectful low, submissively avoiding fearful, his commander. The captain on the other hand stood sterile to attention focussed straight ahead and proclaimed due name and titles, Warlord Shakmil Khan, courageous and beloved leader of subjected many, emancipator from the thraldom, monarch of the northern reaches, illustrious and without a living equal but accursed proudly, on the acrid tongues of spurious emperors.

Ishtaac understood the predetermination but heard clear only the inflection raised upon the name of Shakmil Khan itself, noting also there a nervousness betrayed by Tsai Chi Min when beckoned now with trembled hand.

Shakmil Khan arose smoothly with a balance stolen from the feline to examine Ishtaac closely, sensing strange his clothing but, more importantly for to search his eyes for honest answers. Ishtaac swayed under scrutiny not felt since Rashkulcan maintaining an expected silence and stared ahead appreciative of the strength and loyalty that provided for such power. Shakmil Khan encircled slowly, ponderously measuring the intruding uninvited, then asked at length, with cautious interest, awkward questions of his captain who, by way of illustration was thus provided through the seer with an effigy an age possessed in secret, small and dark, delicately carved from ancient amber resin. Placing the piece reverently to its resting in the palm of his sovereign's outstretched filthy hand, the soldier surrendered then to shake beneath the intensity of his master's full attention.

Ishtaac dared himself a stolen look and saw a robed depiction little more than the length of his middle finger expertly fashioned with a cunning detail reflecting warmly of the dampened fire's glow. The commander held the tiny figure up to pierce visually its opaque lustre and sought dubious, for comparison between the image and the guest. Rightly he was unconvinced and so returned to encircle thoughtfully, the fire, nodding as he did so to the sways of an internal disputation clouding further still his indecision. Suddenly arrived at snarled contempt he threw the article to the ground with fitting malice.

Tsai Chi Min gasped lacking Shakmil Khan's intention, and looked imploringly at the old soothsayer for assistance, who when at last responded, uttered softly and with reason to their chieftain in a patient, almost perilous to condescending manner. Without a motion to detect, he produced a pouch containing the small, white bones as fragments of corroboration from the very air itself it seemed, and spilled the contents for their falling lightly to the dampness of the earthen floor. The three and Ishtaac at his distance, examined the apparent randomness to carefully gauge their fortune's meaning yet, despite the convictions of his oracle and captain, Shakmil Khan refused to believe there any claims of worthwhile finding. Ishtaac watched and wondered whether he could, or indeed should offer meaningful suggestions being warily unsure of his reception. The old man aloofly replaced the pieces in the bag and poured them out once more spitting defiantly his portrayal of the second outcome as some undeniable, ancestral confirmation.

Shakmil Khan was a warrior, he trusted in the strength of an archer's aim and in the edge of tempered steel, the swiftness of his horses and the acquired strategy of warfare. He was not able to concede completely to the dreams and prophecies of mere advisors, unlike certain predecessors he despised, but then their achievements measured nigh inconsequential when placed to flanking near his own. He was Shakmil Khan, he relied upon his own judgement and the gods must interpret that in whatever way they would or could, simply drawing their contentment from result.

Ishtaac spoke haltingly the few words that Shant-lei had taught him, he was not even certain whether or not it was the same frustrating language, but began anyway by offering his service and acknowledging the warlord's worthy status with all the proper due respect and high regard. The humble manner of approach, if not the words appeared to agree with Shakmil Khan. Ishtaac nonetheless, saw his non-conviction clearly though and envisaged credibility seeping helplessly away with each embarrassing emission made for marking painfully the creeping passage of that difficult and anxious time. He decided then to make so bold and redraw the outline of the city wall, daring to disfigure the soundness of the ground upon which the regal chamber stood, signifying where he thought successful inroads could be made.

Taking a glowing branch from the fire, he laid it across where his depiction of the northern gateway stood, knelt and blew gently giving birth to tantalising flame then poured to good effect the oozing drip of wicked lamp light's oil to fuel. Ishtaac was proposing to subdue where arrows and the sword alone had previously failed, to achieve an entrance through their burning down the wooden structure and thus gain a rightful passage. At this point Ishtaac found his host become agreeable but conversely to the situation saw also, there develop subtle confrontation from the oracle whose whined objections were becoming, to Ishtaac's ears, invested more upon the emotional content of satisfying deity than obtaining vital military objectives by any other merit. He was however, only meekly supported in this precarious standing by some indirect and nervous utterances from Tsai Chi Min's reluctance.

Prophets suggested their ideas based on fanciful delusions or at best, unreliable sources and often they would contrast to a soldier's better judgement, were the thoughts that Ishtaac rightly had determined.

As far as Shakmil Khan was concerned they were an unrewarding liability. His opinion was the only one that held a value, despite the warning reservations of the older, inherited generation inflicted on his progress and design, so had gradually reduced their number and importance within his ranks accordingly and was therefore ready to dismiss them both, to favour Ishtaac's counsel as his own instead.

With a surprising, severed, drawn out gasp, the seer suddenly noticed the tiny amber figure that Shakmil Khan had thrown aside, ablaze and drinking thirstily from prostrate leaning, at the edges of a flaming pool. He continued looking on in humbled admiration and with wonderment relenting, aglow upon his face as if a sign was sent for ratifying Ishtaac's plan then turned to his commander who also watched events unfold but with instead, suspicion, tingeing interest. Ishtaac for his part though was becoming more unsettled at the numerous, all dreadful, implications entering his mind and grimaced with alarm as his supposed counterpart burned so eagerly whilst yet remaining seemingly untouched, wrapped for life eternal in the searing lick of an unkind, baking fate. He felt the air suck quickly from the shelter and looked for answers from above...but came his gaze returning downward as the little likeness flared one last, dramatically before their eyes, blackened sinister as the garment that he wore, then fell from sight beneath the char of ashes and submittance, towards an unknown destiny that struck him deeply to the core.

Thrusting the smouldering branch forcibly upon Ishtaac, Shakmil Khan far too graphically displayed his worrying intentions...that he should carry out his own proposal personally. Ishtaac flushed at the prospect, this was nothing like the outcome he foresaw when first he had an inclination to acquaint himself with the usefulness of nomads. He had envisaged with, it seemed a naive preference, himself re-entering the city in the wake of a triumphant army, or on its flank at worst before then moving on to claiming his belongings from about the courageously defiant, but nevertheless quite dead, Shen Song.

To his reckoning, it was to have been simply a matter of locating the thief, and with each hand pressed in desperation to repel the onslaught of their next forthcoming effort, he knew that he would not have to look much further than the enclosure high above. Unless the man took to flight, but then that was one consideration Ishtaac was confident of having measured more realistically. The soldier was more likely to die fighting or even suffer unconditional surrender than flee in cowardly fashion. At least, things fitted neatly into his reasoning that way...he had seen it in his eyes, or so readily, he'd convinced himself. The reason probably why the vermin had been assigned the entrusted task of rounding up assistance in the first place and had continued to prove, no doubt their twisted faith in him correct, upon each of his returns. The vile secretion really had that much evidence of postured, foolish pride about him…but here he was being allotted a task of his own…and appearing equally, if not even more ridiculous.

In the guise of feeble-minded scapegoat he would risk his neck to go achieving access to the city for those whom earlier had sought to kill him. He wondered whether they were all secretly laughing at him, wagering upon his life's expectancy or some other macabre form of campaign's levity and thought, if not himself involved whether he would laugh the same. Whatever the reason for this allocation he was, through some bizarre obscurity being regarded by Tsai Chi Min and the dubiously wise old man with his bag of superstitious rat bones, as some sort of divine deliverer, whose expectancies unfortunately were all too inescapably predictable and clear. What he needed now was to find a way to apply that adulation to a better end, and fast. Ishtaac sighed, somehow he had found himself chancing everything for strangers and their unclear causes or worse and less rewarding, the aims of unknown gods, but then he did suppose himself to be alive, for the present if nothing else and was as yet, unbound….It was a truth then, he surmised forlornly, things that could only get better could also, often get worse and usually did…for him anyway.

There was too much to go wrong, terribly wrong, beyond too much in fact. He looked sympathetically at the little, mournful pile covering dismally, his likeness. They needed to plan carefully, he needed to plan carefully. Perform some trials, discover the abilities, but more importantly the weaknesses of those around him and do so rather smartly.

Taking up the stick as a symbol of his dutiful undertaking, Ishtaac frowned with a ponderous apathy hung heavily about his manner. Shakmil Khan smirked a heartless smile, the best that he could manage to encourage, being unused to coercion of any tempered sort. The old seer and the captain exchanged glances and even dared to speak congratulations that implied they knew or had imagined, one way or another to have been right minded all along. Ishtaac bent to carefully search the remains, probing with his stick whilst suspecting a vague and horribly disfigured creature to emerge as ill-befitting omen, and tried not to show revealed surprise quite so obviously on finding the figurine there perfectly intact, but had caught their attentions nonetheless as they in turn observed his secreting of the item quietly away with delicate attachment. Tsai Chi Min came and placed consolation's weighty arm upon his shoulder, passing courteous conversation with his chieftain as he did so suggesting all was well, before his leading Ishtaac solemnly away for doom and preparation.

Ishtaac accepted the hospitality offered such as it was, eating and drinking politely that which he could stomach of their fare whilst not wishing to cause offence. Others watched him curiously, half seen bathed among the shadows that swept and swayed around the campfire. Tsai Chi Min sent out his messengers to return selected personnel regarded sufficiently expendable for the task and to formulate, if not the best then some coherently effective plan within the briefest time available. Thus, eventually, the vulgar lumbered forth from night's enshrouding, their smell allaying all surprise, suffice to dash the hope of incorporating any stealth to future projects. Tsai Chi Min held counsel freely as each were urged to put forth such proposals deemed of even slightest relevance, a sight and experience Ishtaac was quite unused to, but from it, through uncouth physical relieving, farted animation and the crude inscribing of the ground he saw ideas rendered take a tangible and somewhat helpful shape. The heavy losses of the unexpectedly resilient city had indeed challenged these simple, low browed, front line soldiers to accepting other methods of approach, in fact any other method of approach appeared preferable to those most recently experienced...and so of those that could or feigned attention, they listened to their comrades' converse well.

The assault would have to be made before the dawn while still beneath that very darkened sky, this he learned, was their impatient way. From various directions each would come, ensuring the avoidance of simple target clusters until, unfortunately, well within a bowshot of the wall, thus with hope enabling some at least to achieve the gate whilst bearing with them, on their backs, tightly packaged bundles of combustible materials consisting oil-soaked fabrics and the lightest kindling brushwood for to spur commencement of the burning. Behind would arrive the heavier bones of the fire as speed of passage might allow, along with oil in flask and barrelled timber which would then be added to the pyre and ignited when sufficient quantity was amassed to sustain an adequate inferno.

Ishtaac demonstrated with the use of gathered firestones the speed at which he could summon up the demon's lick, thereby relieving the need to transport conspicuous flames aloft upon the hillside, a skill that was received with the general high acclaim of the very easy to impress. The arrows Ishtaac had seen smouldering through the sky the previous day were proving unsuitable in testing to fulfil this vital need due both to the moisture content of the early morning air dampening the embers whilst in flight, which caused their almost certain dousing, and the lack of uphill accuracy achieved in poor light. The latter having provoked in Ishtaac a serious disturbance, knowing over eagerness and disregard would have them standing in the way when Shakmil Khan with all his depth of carefree wisdom decided that the time was right and theirs adjudged of little further consequence.

The languid, tired airing of despondency that had drifted lazily among the slumbering camp was now dispelled by the vibrant buzz of expectation's poised activity. Rumours that their long awaited talisman was finally among them lifted even the most guarded spirits to honing blade and spearpoint, as warriors prepared their weapons with a renewed and driven purpose, feeling that the dawning day would bring the siege to bloody climax and the city tumbling freely to their hands. Ishtaac rather thought it was more down to man's inherent lust for entertainment that brought a sparkle to their eye and full attendance to the field that night.

Ishtaac's accompaniment were assembled and re-informed of plan and duty, lest any had forgotten, whilst over emphasising the anticipation of a glorious success. Many would not return, perhaps none would ever see a different day to this, Ishtaac was keenly aware of that but it was the 'at all costs' part reinforced he found a little over laboured.

Another striking force comprised of worthy archers, or so he was encouraged, would be deployed as near as possible in the event that those defending should unbolt the portals and attempt to clear the gateway before the blaze took hold, deeming them sufficient in number to hold the breach until the greater horde to follow could secure it. Compromised archers was probably nearer the mark Ishtaac would suppose when caused to view the motley ape-like gallery on offer. The tactics were simple, swift and clearly suited to the heavy handed full frontal, confrontational assault that Shakmil Khan agreed with. The concept of a victory either gained by death or outcome having become a well-established tradition in his ranks.

Ishtaac stood unconvinced staring at his fate with an anxiousness and sickly feeling knotting in his stomach. He saw the grim determination that formed around him, the piteous faces of eager men willing to make their mark or leave their stains in battle. He had seen it many times before, but was never so involved.

Heavy packs of saturated rags and hasty manufacture were being hoisted awkwardly onto the backs of the selected dregs. Ishtaac also bore his burden, and in each hand was thrust two loosened faggots of new cut branches wet and woefully uninspiring, more as an optimistic gesture of assistance than of any actual worth.

Frowning heavily he rued his lot and glanced about morosely. Overall opinion was holding sway that brushwood and backpacks were no way for a real warrior to enter the realms of final courage, for many of the soldiers were complaining of being denied their protective shields or any other means by which to defend themselves. Bearing pots instead to beat the foe was making heard its restless insult and looked as though, for one elusive moment, things might, upon a stroke of luck, turn sour. These misgivings were assuaged however, when Shakmil Khan himself made timely his appearance to oversee proceedings, stunning each to the silence of exaggerated personal value. Ishtaac noted the pride and bravery their leader seemed to impose upon their hearts by his mere presence alone, and despite himself also began to feel strangely a part of this alien escapade, swept along on a tidal resolve of misplaced loyalty and over estimation. These he assumed then would be the last faces he might ever see and they likewise were to look on him, portent's acclaimed deliverer, with an uncertain, yet familiar association…but they had their cause he reminded, and he had his…and although both might be claimed delusional they nevertheless remained, very, very different.

All too soon the preparations were professed complete and Ishtaac found himself awaiting on that dreaded signal to be underway. Together they stood afoot the hill, momentarily in the darkness out of sight of bowmen on the wall above, cresting black, the man-made edge of night, dominant and brooding high against a troubled sky.

The twisting wind of cobbled roadway that meandered from the top recoiled as silver to the gates before them…but they could ill afford that leisurely ascent of child and trader's cart. Theirs would be a quick and perilous climb using fallen comrades along with any barren cover they might find, ultimately forcing a convergence into channels at the last whence up against the deadly teeth of pending storm known lurking near the gates, to present themselves as ripe and bloated targets for the archers who remained inside of use and able sight.

Ishtaac was not prepared for the discourteous shove that propelled him forward, and it took him several ungainly, staggered, tripping steps to master control of his wayward bulk. By which time he was already overtaken on either hand by the thrill of new-found fellows. Perhaps they thought to reach the summit promptly and be rid their loads, to be away before alarm was raised. Maybe they lustily sought the celebrated death that only battle could provide them. He shook his head miserably and tried to keep up, to lose himself among the wave and not become the target victim, lonely straggler. Fortunately the irregular shapes they had assumed did provide some illusion in the darkness. He watched as those around him blended into the mounded landscape in a cumbersome, unwieldy way as large and overladen bushes might advance impeded by a strong and swaying gale. From above, he hoped the effect might hold deception more complete…but in that faith alas, he harboured serious doubts.

Half way to their goal and already the steepness was taking its toll, Ishtaac's legs buckled unsteadily through exertion upon the unseen, stony interference strewn concealed below the sward. Many times he fell, but on each was found reluctantly assisted to his feet by those who followed on behind. When he rested temporarily, as ever frequently he was having to, he could make out the stifled agitation grow from watchmen peering at the unconfirmed activity below. Grouped together in small bunches they pointing out uncertainly. He saw it several times before eventually, the long expected calls rang out of apprehensions finally realised.

Delay had however, unwittingly allowed some of the most vigorous advancement to arrive almost within reach of the gates before the initial avalanche of arrows descended fatally to cover them. Ishtaac saw their numbers cut to heavy losses and was stunned by the sheer weight of onslaught, sufficient to invoke a sickly feeling that all was surely lost. At that despairing moment, there upon that bleakest incline so early into their inept attempt or more precisely another of his blundered failings, he sensed the need to drop. Cravenly in that foresighted instant he fell to ground and buried his head for pressing firm against the trampled turf biding there until the barbed and whistling wind had ceased its bloody shower.

Lifting his head slowly after many lifetime's had expired, Ishtaac dared to view the outcome of that first assault and saw increased the bodies cluttering up the mountainside amassed from previous days, this night also it appeared, was to be no great exception and looked a total rout. Pierced and motionless the slaughter lay everywhere and absolute, as again he rued decisions made with the highest costs entailed. But when his hopelessness had nigh consumed to almost overwhelm him with its settled crush he noticed rising tiredly as the infirm often do from torpid slumber, one by one the quill struck backpacks taking to their feet once more as deathly, stalking phantoms, spectral visions from beyond the mortal world of men. A strange, uneasy stiffness in their gait projected nevertheless, the unforeseen good fortune that had prevented the missiles from a harmful penetration through compacted wads' protection. A relieved, dared murmuring cheer sounded out along the lines for greeting Ishtaac's unexpected smiling, as all but few would set themselves erect once more and doggedly proceed towards their goal.

Time and again the air rasped hoarse its whisper to the strum of steel tipped fletching. Time and again the packs provided ample cover on the whole. Some even began to trust in the divinity of their charge, regarding themselves impervious to the lowly bow strung aims of men...and some paid highly for such frivolous beliefs. Often Ishtaac would be forced to use the protection of the fallen dead or dying to continue his approach, and sure enough, over the shuffling confusion of the foreground, he began to see the first successful parties unloading hurriedly their contents, rendering themselves then unprotected and vulnerable to the archers' sport above. Some held tight against the wall as flat as they were able and lived a little longer, but those who fled retreat were also callously denied escape and fell with frequency among them only for their mournful cries of uncompleted slaying to upset its promise down throughout the valley. Then came the unforgettable rain of fire as scorching arrowheads would singe the air and strike with thudding cinders and a sparking eager to ignite them. Many flared and ran without control, gripped by panic, driven to the brink of human torch lit madness, fleeing in the struggle to shed the flaming packs that ceaseless followed them wherever they would flail. Some would roll and thrash as helpless on the ground in a vain attempt to douse the fire spewing forth to their engulfing from the shattered pots once held....It was a perverse and sickly game the archers played, as too their taunts of mocking challenge rang deplorable and crisp, ashamedly above the drawn out, wails of suffering beyond the consolation.

Onward unrestrained by futile caution, Ishtaac dashed the remainder of the way, upward through the endless raging deathly rods of terror on legs that cared no longer for the labour. He neither saw nor thought much more of that which stood or fell around him, of things that might or may not be, of chances slim and fickle, only of to gain a desperate foothold on the summit and seek elusive sanctuary there, away from that accursed openness and immediate dilemma.

The gates hung tall with threatening imposition, to gravely scorn upon the toppled jars of oil, some still with content, sacks unshed and fronds of carried kindling, scattered, cast amid and on the knots of twisted, overlaying bodies....and aided thankful through confusion and commotion, Ishtaac found fortuitous his haven from hostility beneath its own restrictions, there to gain the briefest respite from an untimely, tortured end.

Tucking himself tightly into one hinged corner of impeding he could escape for moments from the mayhem and make his timed excursions, darting out among the deadly issue of those awaiting him above. Each chanced attempt collected more expensive fuel though only by the handful or the individual flask, yet somehow, despite concerted efforts to prevent, Ishtaac managed to pile the minimum he thought as necessary for the task and worthy of igniting, then primed his labour with the phials of luminary liquid.

Huddled fearful on the brink he searched himself to no avail and realised on dashed acceptance, the unbearable cornering of truth, distasteful with its mirth. It was no use, he declared aloud and to the gods with bitter accusation, the firestones had gone, and with them that essential linkage in the chain towards success, he understood as forged now on the anvil of his doom. Standing on the threshold of endurance, he had found his efforts thwarted by the mountain's stern resolve, protective of its residential hosts, and he himself abandoned on the humoured whims of deity. After every sacrifice was made and more besides, always he would ultimately fail. He would fail them all, Shant-lei, the High Order, his land...a list continued where none had blessing for exemption, even the wandering nomads it appeared, were at the mercy of infection from his own perpetual cursing.

Ishtaac laughed to scoff at faith and ruined men, of hopes and dreams and bitter, foolish life about to end. The fallen lay in testament, and ever would they do so to accuse him of his treason, cast about as spent and cruelly robbed, their foolishness to trust or chance in him, their path to final glory.

Upon this, his reckoning moment, all consumed by anguished self-reproach, he knew astonishment as seen through the sight of one defeated whence espying there before him another of the tribesmen, the last to make the climb. Cresting the roadway's ridge he came, prevailing dutiful with precious load, driven upon the dire, expectant winds of foretold victory. Ishtaac watched poignant over the futility of such determined conquest, for regardless of the many arrows bedded firm within him, still he laboured on with desperate hope to glint from woeful eyes, whilst yet many wooden shafts still broke abundantly across the pavings at his halting, shuffled feet, splintering away on clattered flight to unimportant ends. Ishtaac smiled helplessly conveying the hollow emptiness of gratitude that saddened him to sickness as the warrior received his fate with a passing smirk of recognition and so dropped unto his knees, discharged in full of honoured obligation.

A bolt of dirty, smoking filth shot blackened forth, remorseless to the soldier from aloft, gods sent to needless mock, igniting pride with flaming passion, devouring ravenous all manner of combustibles, hair and flesh and clothes alike…nothing missed their new-born's eager tasting. Nonetheless, thus bathed amid the glare of any hope eternal there burned to fuel ideas wrought of desperation, apparent whence the nomad cast his embers forward for to crawl the last of fabled missions. Reaching out in vain, he came up wanting of his target though, a fitting jest perhaps, his goal a mere fingertip beyond the stretching touch of dreamers.

Assailants gathered to observe his striving from on privileged high with gleeful relish and relentlessly they took to pounding merciless for humour's sake, his wretchedness to death.

Drawn unknowing to exposure, in the isolation of concern, Ishtaac felt the sudden, stricken weight of accuracy plunge deep in penetration of his shoulder, with a force enough to spin him round in protest and to cause his stumbling out to beckon sure demise. The stinging tail of death was hovering mere yards above and poised, and yet unscathed, he noticed from the remotest recess of his darkened mind a slow and vengeful creep, the thirsting of insatiability, potential in unmastered flame. Having consumed thoroughly of the victim that had brought it life, the blaze sought now to further its existence. Along an outstretched sleeve it flowed, hugging low in profile as the wary, skulking on the fumes to leap in silent grace, the sparking gap abridged from hand to unlit, cold and costly pyre. A flashed success of warm, blue luminescence washed up gently without trace of fuss or hindrance, smoothly to embrace the fuel and thence the timber sourced resistance.

From behind the hitherto steadfastness, cries soared high in pitch above an end's consuming roar marking now, for one, a glorious achievement but sounding out the ruin also, for another, as heat suffice to boil the watcher's blood, singed and soiled offensively the air where those still living, sane enough to fear, took flight before the purest rage thus heralding the fractured moments of defence.

Overlooking the very boundary of despair itself, an act of utter hopelessness brought the gates reopened in attempt to cleanse the burning from their doorstep, the ultimate of options taken before the maddened horde without could overwhelm the breach. But further down the valley, hearing only victory calling unto them unhinged, the wild, nomadic throng screamed clear their hails of insult and came advanced as swarms across the mountain's incline, unprepared to let it slip, their claiming recompense for untold wrongs on thoughts of welcome conflict.

Thunderous the ire of battle growled its barest teeth at onset. Drummers beat intoxication from their march of non return and horns blared loud the summoned urges for exacting deeds of courage to extend the reach of heroes. Grappled chaos, rampant in the melee reigned unchecked exposed by morning's early waking drizzle as the imminence of dreaded downfall threw defendants to their lots courageously on folly in attempt to seal the inroad, but came rushed, the tidal onslaught, smashed repeated, undenied.

Ferociously barbaric the fighting clashed and screamed along the standing bulwark's length, yet saw its concentration firmed against those climbing scaffolds hoisted up to lodging fast, and ceaseless also, rose their clamber. Steel on steel struck fiercely hence, submitting severance to the bone without delay or slight regard, where limbs and flesh were torn asunder by the bladed hand, released its burden of a single care, rancorous and deadly numbed to feeling. Desperate was to be the ending of the struggle whilst morning bled away the surging choke of warriors throttled life's submission, from the now bared throat of ailing, newly vanquished. Thrusting heedlessly upon the shameless pleading for survival there issued forth the tendered fates that drove insane beyond keen measure, snapping cleanly to unbalance and hurl forever furtive forms to gibber out dependently their days.

When at the noon's grey zenith the siege was witnessed given up conclusively to carnage, and in entirety its relished triumphing to languish still, a cockerel crowed alone for desolation's sake and marking. On rushed the crescent scalpel tide to scythe away the sore they deemed resistance culling mercilessly onward to the remnant cowered folk within. Unstoppable, for spreading where they would unbound, despatching everything from right's deserved path before them.

Amid the smoke and ruined ashes of forgotten loyalties, once humbled people turned their bloodlust there against the old, established order. Those brought through duress and put to cruel service, seized their timely moment for to reek revenge on previous masters standing, caught confronted or who sought a freedom rather in concealment under newly changed allegiance, dealing swiftly out their hatred to replenish then the fallen lines of Shakmil Khan anew, whose conquering horsemen charged on rampant, released for savage overwhelming, on throughout the streets to overrunning every open plain and corner with their infestation, purging all inherent life as found on sight and view.

Ishtaac staggered in the vanguard's wake bowed beneath the dragging weight of realised pain and began his quest for love forlorn and one despoiling individual, in particular. He walked among the stricken, fighting hard against the plaintive pleas for help from most long past assistance, calling frequently to Shant-lei…but alas, denied despite desire cast words to no avail.

The gathering storm encroached upon his heel and swift, encompassed from behind to cause his flounder, its dragging cloy compelling to the contrary of his will. Pressed, cajoled then tossed along the current of invasion, Ishtaac swirled propelled reluctant by another's motive on toward the heartland of a barren city's corpse.

Stubborn opposition, cornered and entrapped, clung fiercely behind the crumbling walls among the long since raped and plundered gardens of once wealthy citizens now gone. Buildings one by one were overcome with bloodied ease, floor by floor and room by room they cleansed away the memories. Monumental obstacles that housed the tastes of rich abandon now yielded up old dead for favouring returns of mere salvaged dereliction from the passing of most recently acquired guests.

Ishtaac fought successful to be free of the tangled, boiling mayhem and from promises of accident therein among such self-defying ruthlessness. Crouched then, huddled in an open doorway, the ground he tentatively held proved sound enough to frame escaping lea from the crushing swell that hurtled past. Long cowered there as fallen among the echoed din and turmoil would he hide until the human torrent gradually reduced itself to the bewildered wandering trickle of those straggling sheep confused and yet obliged to follow on.

Quelling the tremble in his heart, Ishtaac knew that somewhere in the madness, if chance had not again eluded, his belongings might be waiting, yielding to collect, but also that he must locate them before the placid, reassured aftermath took hold where ransacked claiming of another's trinkets would surely then begin in systematic earnest. Shant-lei was gone and there was nothing else remaining but to place reluctant trust in fortune and continue through a city hazed beneath its blanket fumes of gagging black, thickened by the misting rain. His eyes streamed and burned for staring into every gloomy, smouldered dwelling. His mind further blanked to anguish on examining each damned, dismembered cold or steaming body that he stooped to rifle in the hope of finding that or those he thought increasingly as lost.

And so it was whilst moving stealthily along the maze of debris crowded streets and alleyways about his grisly business, reminiscent of the scavengers he once despised, Ishtaac came upon a hampered knot of forces, cautiously observing the deeply lodged remains of a once imposing proud and numbered army. Isolated, severed clinical from both route and aspiration towards escaping, if indeed that was of late to have been their dismally intended purpose, they stood in open contest. For grim determined and united they would dare to face with dignity their victors, asking not for clemency but clean decisiveness instead, foiling easily upon the end of bloodied spear point's length the spiritless opposing hemmed disgracefully on offer. Obstinate and resolute unto the very last they tightly packed that courtyard's centre back to straightened back.

Access from three corners along each a narrow street, allowed but few to enter for the final conquest and those who had were noted to have paid a dear, unworthy price. The numerous others who had found themselves on hand thus gathered simply for to watch instead through preservation's intervention sensing the initial, fevered sting of thrilled invasion somewhat dampened by the splintering of now fragmented forces with its trampling fervour waned. An uneasy, simmering stand off was occurring. A matter of time, that was to be the certainty before their end but with the city gained and profit's plundering in store neither wished to throw their lives so pointlessly away upon a needless after battle skirmish.

Shakmil Khan could be seen atop his horse, surveying the scene ahead, toying ponderously with a sharp edged, rooted foe…but beside him, Tsai Chi Min incessantly would shift, as nervous in the saddle. Ishtaac pushed his way to the fore between the horses and looked upon those valiant few who gave such hindrance to the progress of by far superior numbers. Laboured, weary gasping breaths he saw essential but as stolen, ashamedly revealing weakness unbecoming, for to him they had resigned themselves to flinching not before a brutal destiny, and therefore stood among the dour elite of all damned men…but there also, unexpectedly, amid consolidated faces he espied the only one he sought with ill-intent.

Ishtaac counted henceforth Shen Song's life as short and was glad to have come in time to watch him pay, but strong though was the will that bound the enemy together still and never is more dangerous than when nothing can be lost. They were a stone in Shakmil Khan's advancing shoe, Ishtaac knew it well and so he waited, unwavered in attention, firmly fixed.

A sneering flash of recognition scorned its pierce through the cornered soldier's eyes whence his glance returned by chance to settle grim upon conceited accusation, with contempt and stifled rage. The lowest of the surrounding trespassed low had come again, the one from lands afar to gloat and then to pick his carcass clean.

Removing Ishtaac's bag from dangling limply at his belt, the soldier proceeded then to hold its provocation loftily at arm's scarred taunting length, for all to see, and he in turn, to take his coarse enjoyment from the goaded pleasure of a much despised opponent. If there was but one breath and one alone among that baying crowd he might receive the last of, it would be inhaled, reclaimed from stolen acquisition by the most foreign of intruder's lungs.

Shen Song called him forth, jeering and confident of at least one satisfying kill. Shakmil Khan looked down upon the object of the soldier's threat and waited for his puppet to respond with avid interest. The ragged sham of a deliverer would doubtlessly be culled before them, here and now, a fitting end to one so laughingly esteemed as brave. An honoured duel to publicly remove all further sway of falsehood and any need for unjust recompense he mused, but tidy finish also to another good Jin victory. Shakmil Khan considered options for the briefest moment, spat needlessly as one decided, and then shoved Ishtaac forward for a second time and last, that day.

The sudden jolt upon his shoulder sent him wincing, lurching from the safety of the crowd to know the hollow, void of pity, gaping thirstily between them. All eyes fell instantly with weighted expectation upon his due demise. The soldier smiled a welcome grin and boldly flashed his life-stained sword, wet with others spent in mist it ran, unsightly and conclusive amid the cold noon's mounting stillness.

Ishtaac held his arms aloft, weaponless, and limped a halting stagger. There could be no eternal dignity recalled from this particular act, his intention would enforce. This was the inciting of a coward and not that of a real warrior he furthermore implored with frantic gesture and scant words. A condemnation which indeed gave cause for Song to contemplate the lasting judgement of the crowd upon his head, on Ishtaac's vulnerability and the lack of honour in the fight. The longevity in the memory of so disreputable a final deed would rightly haunt the patriarchal concord to exclusion was his fear, and therefore threw him back returned in full the blade long since admired, marvelling as it spun and sliced the air in perfect balance to the fleeting glimpse of Ishtaac's outstretched, speeding hand.

A keen reunion of old acquaintance met deftly in the cleansing of an eye's perception, it was thus that Ishtaac felt complete, if not content to face his shadowed future…and though fears dissolved, he tempered yet impassioned longing bent to kill his foe, assisting guilefully instead a favoured outcome by the feigned, stressed cunning of an overtaxing toll of previous injuries incurred whilst adding fumbled clumsiness he thought might also prove deceiving.

Shen Song, satisfied requirements were fairly met, snatched his moment and charged unwary with a terrifying din raged upon his hapless victim. Fearless malice, angrily he vented in one final, proud display of empty, heartless courage.

Wielding skilfully his sword with combat's seething frenzy, both violent and accomplished swift above a bared and blood-gashed head, he came to slashing strikeless clean across the vanish of his aim. Penetrating thin, the air with unaccustomed ease his blade had spawned surprise, propelling twisted through off balance almost to the detriment of tumbling. Ishtaac nicked an ear on ghostly passing and rounded ready to repel attack once more. Shen Song tried to compose and muster from the shock, whilst putting swordless hand to staunch the soak of attribution's burning wound, confused with startled disbelief.

The crowd roared appreciation of the spectacle presented, somewhere in the background tapestry of concentration, and stoutly urged their wayward, comic champion onward for to fill a matinee performance with the highest entertainment.

Incensed beyond the realms of wit's retrieval by his fury, Shen Song, sparing caution, pounced again swinging wildly at the spectral blur of shadows teasing to aversion on the hazy fringe of sight, turning thus repeatedly to face it. Time and again however, Ishtaac eluded each attempt to bring his life to closure always there reminding of his menace out of reach, until the flourished sword point crashed its last to jam then snapped, securely lodged between the paves about his very feet. Upon this instance of good fortune long awaited, the unseen sting of Ishtaac closed with final purpose, that to cut his opposition deep with disadvantage to bone, and thus the blackness followed quick with lethal savagery whence stabbed deliberation cut incisive through a lapsed unguarded eye…further crippled nevermore to clear.

Spiralling through a reel of acrid senses Shen Song was forced now to return in feeble swipes with incredulous and near blind abandon until defenceless plunged, humbled in the death throes of his turmoil so to falter lowly felled, receded at the knees for helplessly succumbing to yet even more, abhorrent lunges, as the scorpion punctures likewise without pity, stunning prey's endurance to surpass the stillness of submission.

The captain of the riders lay buckled spent and fatally defeated, whilst about his devastation the bedraggled stranger stepped as gracefully unscathed with spriteful fluid malice. A soul returned unto the darkened fold of joyous, learned detestation not forgotten, long denied, it watched content once more whence sacred blood poured forth from absolute inflictions. Deception's tribute to appearance, thus he stood beheld in quiet awe, and never would those memories gathered there soon lapse, nor judge again with hastened scorn on looks like his alone.

Ishtaac collected his belongings intact, and secured them tightly at his waist, placing reverently the necklace of high office around himself once more, though loathsome would it bear imagination's stench and tarnish so imposed by thieving hands. And task completed he emboldened, would defy them each, their contestation of his privilege to freedom fought for and deserved.

Shakmil Khan however, was quick to assume the triumphant mantle there proposed and welcomed Ishtaac freely back into his order bearing witness also to the demoralising nature such defeat imposed. A tried and tested champion vanquished with apparent ease by a lowly beggar vagrant whose death, like they, had been deceived.

With little else to fight for those remaining chose their end in brevity and forced themselves upon their upthrust, keenly waiting spears…a finality which fell to ease their suffering but tainted nonetheless a fallen city with their passing.

The victory was utter, his lust for now fulfilled, the moment like his stronghold...seized, a warrior's battle won. Shakmil Khan thus presumed ancestral favour with attainment's pleasure once again, and bearing arrogance aloft in torn and severed, eyeless heads he cried aloud his proclamations through the streets for all who followed to pay heed and know...and so his multitude would grow.

Ishtaac searched unhindered every quarter, for any tell or trace of Shant-lei. Long daylight hours of eerie calm thawed slowly to the imbibed debauchery of a celebrated evening and beyond, from which his quest would thenceforth carry lamely crept unto the widest points throughout the changing seasons...but nothing of her fortune came he ever to discover. And so it was upon one bitter, autumn afternoon, forevermore a special time of scented breeze regretful to imagination's sensing, Ishtaac resolved to leave behind that land with cherished recall to despair, to contemplate alone, the disposition of mourn's yearning peacefully, and seek instead elusive refuge from his scarred and wounded soul. Though always grief struck he remained to dwell upon the pensive sadness born of but a single moment's compromised reluctance, never to amend.

Chapter 3
Trade Winds Blow

Sometimes with the caravans endured along their diverse trade routes, more often though, alone, Ishtaac saw himself condemned to roam through troubled lands and shy away recurring from the dogged clutches of unwanted interest. Frequent was his hunger and ever fearful of encroachment, from those dreadful left behind, driven thus it was he chanced accommodation whence available, away and safe from any other but more crucially from brutal mountain bandits' short acquaintance who would rob and coldly slay uncaring of the roadside traveller, to seek in preference more concealed and lasting refuge when and where he could.

In this wary way, the ravaged and forsaken figure trod his westward march meandering through hostile scenery from town to lonely town along the ancient, stony highways. Settling on occasions to pass the seasons by in each and every haven as and when disclosed, to elude disquiet's stalking and so soothe the furtiveness of burdened mind's fixation.

Mountain shepherd boys he heard as, at times their dusty hillside lairs played host to calm, melodic, music drawn on reed constructed pipes, haunting him unseen from beguiling shades of starving cave mouths' gape. Languages and tales in wealth rewarded also much attentive listening and compelled his feet to places far away and distant from his plight…curious places unassayed, proposing welcome respite for dissolving threat's pursuit.

In time, he found as wayward on the trek, a mule to tempt his transport, strayed and living of the simple life escaped and masterless in labour-free emancipation. Content with ideal, carefree wildness, he was come upon with ease, though riding proved ordeal's reluctance, weighing heavy on both parts.

Into the west along the ceaseless path they plodded for to share companion's fate together, and with every jarring step that Ishtaac could endure, he found his anxiousness diminished and too, he sensed the shadow clouding urgently his mind dispelled to mere fretful vapour beneath the glaring scorch of ever-present sun.

Through bustling, crowded cities wading in the torrents of the street bound, harried faces and over the remotest mountain passes, where the villages that were, died coldly parched, grim lonely and deserted. Down into the high ground's fertile pastures and beyond for passing wary through the busy, cultivated valleys, always was he drawn towards the allure of sparkling, suncrest sea, and its beauty's unquenched prohibition that would fill him with remembered dread at thoughts of thirsted crossing.

Guided solely by the word of unknown, passing travellers he meandered under slowly circled skies until at last he came across a daunting sight with compromise to ponder.

Unwelcome was temptation's aura shimmering as far as glistened eyes could see, sprung forth abruptly from a ridge of hard-baked, desert soil providing dubious invite to expectant gain's existence far along its crescent shoreline edges, urging also of decisions from dilemma, here upon the asking.

A gentle trickle of goods and traders had swelled itself towards a thriving population, through doubtless, an unwillingness to risk again the tread of desolation's arid lands from whence they'd prior come…and so they stayed to deal anew with destinations oversea.

Vessels large and small differing greatly in design and purpose, nestled in the gentle sweeping arc with intentions to embrace both seabound and the residential traffic equally, with either outstretched hand…conjuring an imagery perplexed to frame the landscapes of their varied origins among the forethoughts of the mind. All things then, were reached and catered for upon this thin but rich expanse.

Cargoes made their way excited to and fro form hand to ship and boat and back again defying the bewildered stand off's gaze as fervent boiled the chaos of activity that swarmed disruptive to the ordered neatness of both storehouse and the mooring craft alike. A coastal vein of commerce here exchanged its wares to be again removed as tidal currency dependant on wave's banking ebb and flow eternal, leaving in untidy wakes, congealed conglomerates that vital showed, residual hues of profit.

Places of religion built as praise and testament to one's personal acquisitions stood proud above the flattened dusty rooftops of the commoner's abode, rippling translucent crystal in the afternoon's soaked heat haze dewly clinging with consistence all about. Centres of high learning solidly robust, boasted out their inner strength of knowledge whilst too, proclaiming loud the prowess of a stabilised metropolis…but with it, more profane and daily earthbound needs came also well provided for, with pleasure and in number. The whore houses, taverns and the squalid smoking dens where deals were struck behind the backs of gods…and here, inevitably skulked the lowest, scourged excretions of the low who would, allowed the chance and undenying, steal from deities themselves. Dwelling largely on the outskirts of the desert city-port, an evasive flight to refuge in the wilderness whence noticed, being often, their only route's solution to dishonesty's survival.

Ishtaac displaced his bagged possessions reassuringly about him regarding the weight and presence with a gratifying comfort. He had very little worthy of a retail value to expend, his necklace and such he thought too precious for the trading, only the mule that bore him remained therefore, to bargain with. Although not young, strong and fit enough to work, dehydrated perhaps, and more than under nourished, but still….each thing had its worth. Ishtaac decided wisely then to take his bearings of the market before agreeing with himself that any possible transaction could take place. He was able, after all, to continue as he had, if propositions proved themselves as wanting.

It was not to be long, however, after a quick yet thorough assessment of accepted currencies and economic rates, before Ishtaac was easing down from soreness to whisper gratified farewells.

Considering the deal as beneficial and himself now affluent enough to afford some lodgings and a frugal meal at last, with hopefully a skin of wine to aid consumption, he stored the coinage in his pouch and sought reclined position, snug amid the cooling shade of an olden, gnarled, dry olive tree to watch with caution, his surroundings be.

Soon reposed, Ishtaac would assume himself sufficiently with acumen and standing then, to work free passage, to any, if not all the strange new lands enticingly within his grasp, but sat for now there merely glad to listen basking in the warmth of civilised companionship once more….Maybe he would stay a while instead and make some usage of the learning in those grandiose palaces where only lore held court….His options like his mind could here, he felt, endure without restriction.

A fleeting moment true enough, but generous was its soar unbound in flights of freedom, flashed release throughout his thoughts to closing darkly over all too soon again, forfeit on the shadowed spectre creeping from the east, thus causing wonderment its lapse to mourn in askance….How long until foreseen betrayal laid prosperous plans to snare him?

Surpressing answerless foreboding, Ishtaac drank heavily of the wine to pleasured ends, and satisfied, eventually found discomfiture as forcibly withdrawn…if not entirely forgotten, then arose disordered for to amble off and seek, above the stealth of villains, a hostel for the night, driven on the need to rest in full before assuming his inquiries at first light.

The room acquired, as expected was small and bare offering little more than doubtful sanctuary from the pry. A single, tiny window allowed for but the gentlest sighing breath of air to flow beneath the poor fit, fragility of wooden slatted door. Perhaps…at least he hoped, beforehand there would be some indication of a creaked intrusion to prepare, as he lay himself unsettled down upon the ache of his belongings to call on awkward, restless sleep.

Below and frequently around him shuffling footsteps accompanied by muffled, unclear voices could be vaguely heard above the honesty of dwindling acts outside but only the relentless demons of suspicion would approach him sinister, in truth, that night.

Morning arrived starkly uninvited on a stabbing ray of brilliant sunlight to pierce his dreams and wake him. Ishtaac squinted up at the minute portal, yawned and stretched then went about his business, in possession and himself relieved.

Down at the water's salted lap bargaining was underway, haggling full sail. The catches of the day corpsed dormant in the early haze on warming sand, some plump with rounded belly goodness others frightening as cold eyed, dead souled monsters, spiked or sleek and gaping evilly to menace their distasteful ranks of nasty teeth. Ishtaac preferred the view ahead and watched instead the traffic's distant prows approach as others turned and left. But dogging still the idea of that water teeming with such horrifying life-forms…suffice to reinforce deep reservations coursing through his bones would stir.

Tanned and weathered sailors eyed him optimistically at first only to assume a frowned disdain when he would pass them by unfavoured. Their sinewy, taut appearances suggested that the silvered wealth of fishing lives remained with unjust scales tipped biased on the land, beyond even the best net earnings of the most astute of far cast, drifted mariners.

He followed then with hunger as his guide, the luxuriant, luring trail of banquet's spicy scent and maidens' half remembered sweet perfume, on towards the jutted, groping piers and jetties built to hold the larger, longer distance vessels that sailed forever from and to where profit was the greatest, too big were these to drag ashore and lean their casual loiter. Where ample men of wealthy girth fought valiantly at close financial quarters.

Amphoras of wine and oils were hauled aboard, both as perishable and asset depending on the crew. Lashed together wooden crates containing poultry chattered under the careful eyes of would-be dealers who leant for talking amicably amongst themselves despite their obvious contention, whilst awaiting for the growing interest of the day. All unfolded on a stage of sand before a planished, tranquil sea of promised green as backdrop…and along the length of gull cried quay the warmth of life fulfilled his soul with buoyancy replenished.

Remaining there many bountiful days, Ishtaac learned to good advantage what he could of the ways and customs of the many visitors that put to port. In particular, fair-haired warriors of the cross he witnessed for the first as bearded as was he. Sun burnt, unaccustomed red, intolerant skin would pain whence salt and wind had dried and overlong exposed them. Barking guttural their demands they came for disembarking on religious grounds, or so was understood. Both heavily armed and heavily protected they rode away towards the southern lands from far flung northern corners and naturally were treated with suspicion but nonetheless their commerce was accepted, for great it was, their wealth possessed to yield.

Ishtaac found himself returned with frequency to the company of one particular family venture, comprising of a father and two sons who ferried goods of all description back and forth a distant island. They laboured quite contented in the scorched intensity of afternoon's baked heat whence others took their ease he saw, whilst readily preparing ground for day or nightly dealings. Ishtaac had, with knowledge of the language aided in the smooth offenceless transfer of a number of their wares. Quick to assume mock indignation and deep felt personal hurt he played the game successfully, rarely coming off the worst, proving the persuasive go between that poured good humoured oil on stiff and creaking elbow joints to hand shake's satisfaction. Gratefully they thanked him with such payment as they could and listened patient in return when Ishtaac told of his desire to travel with them when they left. Cristobal, the father, saw mutual benefit from the proposed arrangement and took gladly back the funding Ishtaac tendered. With ample space and unseen hazards stretching out before them, this wily vagabond might yet show himself to be of further worth to him, he thought. The homeward voyage might see the cargo change in content several times depending on what news would reach them on the way and in position as a carrier, if nothing more, Ishtaac might fulfil a useful role.

For now though, the returning load consisted, as Ishtaac was aware, mainly of the pungency's of Zafaran, Cassia and leaves of Tarkhun, Sana and of Bay. Jars of fragrant oils and balms with bundled silks laid over there were also, but concealed and snug within the stern beneath the heaps of bound up sacking lay, the stifled gleam of polished silver tableware and porcelains thought wisest to be wrapped in secret, stowed away. For further trade or newly bought, Ishtaac did not know and considered rightly not his business to inquire.

Cristobal requested his assistance while he toured the port that evening for to view the rows of merchandise on sale, resulting with their purchasing the basic needs of passage, enough for many days. Sacks of grain and nuts, stout breads, fruit, vegetables and meat with salt and olive oil to cook them, all of which were leisurely returned and neatly stored aboard the boat named Spruzzo destined for to sail the following dawn.

Their craft was a double-masted vessel converted several times throughout its working life thus far, sturdy and alive with the natural laden protest of its ligatures, their tongue lashed marriages to curse repentant build, on gently warping timber planked foundations. Wide and low, she wallowed heavy in the water to discontent the eye, but despite this obvious reservation, Ishtaac and his scant possessions forsook the land that night to sleep afloat, with nervous trepidation evident in unsure feet, for trial in case ill-suited.

The authorities' official master graciously received the necessary excise and permitted their withdrawal from land that morn' as overhead the crying of the gulls would herald in the jubilation of departure, to carry off with fairest omens on the very wind that gifts their wings with flight. Ishtaac tensely lounged as best as nonchalantly forced appearances allowed and watched the shore behind recede, knowing once again the growing doubts and fears long held ingrained from an unforgiven previous seaward voyage...although in fact and quite to his surprise, he found with every passing league the shifting of his apprehension would gradually subside to just the remnant of a lapsing frown, the only traced reminder.

The sea was calm and warm around them, the wind direct and favourable, they made good speed and for their time unneeded, idled on the deck. Ishtaac sat making notes to pass the day or sketched the near and changing southern coastline for distraction and to compensate amusement. Cristobal steered the boat without concern or taxing effort from the stern beside a hanging tiller loosely held one handed, languishing inside an added hut-like cabin built for shaded shelter and a lengthy while exposed on open water. The swinging lateen sails as now, in full, cast thin, their midday shadows over boredom without to cool the crew beneath or goods in hot and suffocating hold below.

In time, Ishtaac would, under the allocated supervision of both or either of the sons learn the skills for tending and repair of boats from land and underway. Leonardo, the eldest of the two though barely just a man he found as easy going and relaxed about his duties showing small regard for minor detail or the age old, seaman's rituals but acted rather with panache and added personal flair. His brother Louis, however, appeared buckled by the weight of owning fewer years and felt behind and lagging in his one man competition, seeking always the unnecessary reassurance of his father to wield as tokens of success. Retarding sourly, Ishtaac felt, the development of an otherwise more gentle disposition, and simply seemed to try too hard in his malignant battle for affection. Ishtaac ignored with embarrassed tact as much as possible the childish banter that passed between them, refusing to be drawn on sides or re-endorse each petty, puerile squabble. Otherwise all went remarkably well, the unaccustomed mariner even began to enjoy the effortlessness of seabound journeys. The good winds held their course and strength and the coast slipped smoothly by. They ate freely from the bountiful provisions, supplementing nonetheless their diet frequently with fresh caught fish to boil, collected lithe from trailing nets, and the stores of drinking water that they carried, washed down every meal with little indication of its ever drying out. The sky both day and night lay clear up unto the heavens and long were the occasions Ishtaac spent in peaceful contemplation with a changed, uplifting friendliness of spirit towards his new association with the sea.

The family slept with practised art upon the open deck, unmoved or rolled amid their slumber, times when Ishtaac would embrace those private moments now and then to inspect his guarded treasure and wonder at the meaning of design upon its surface, a muted inclination he presumed on grounds unsafe, conducive to reveal the whereabouts of a certain lock that might one day be opened. A gateway to the gods, the prize that turned cleansed hearts and minds to evil deeds....and thoughts, to passive lines of men and women, children also, waiting on a fate without redemption. To stem the tide though was his task assigned and nothing else besides, preventing floods of swollen human despoil and so thwart perhaps, a king along the way...if not his lordship, Rashkulcan. And often in these moods of self-possessed concern he would sigh devoid an inkling to solution but resolve himself as all the more determined to continue.

Little more than seldom other vessels sidled close at hand about their private errands, hailing news pertaining to events and life around the coastal regions, a worthwhile knowledge rendered inexpensively among the occupations bound upon the middle land's held sea. Tales of daring battles real or imagined, of natural disasters and of displeased gods and consequence. Of trends in different cargos where better deals might lie and of now unrested moorings long believed as safe, deemed wiser to avoid.

Several times Cristobal considered the advice to alter course and pursue a possible advantage but was forced on each, with some reluctance, to regard the whined objections of his offspring longing to be home. Under quiet sufferance then, the loving father maintained their westward heading to a port he knew as welcome, retaining thankfully from Ishtaac's point of view, a distant sight of land.

Regular, upon some predetermined prompting, Ishtaac would consult his guiding stone, suspended carefully under hand for over viewed inspection, generating thereupon as consequence, the interest of his fellow travellers, who stood absorbed but coy in bouts of silent staring. One such afternoon, bright and pleasant, having torn himself apart for quite some time restrained, Louis could contain his questioning no longer and succumbed to leering ever closer, engrossed until, with the untimely aid of a coercive, thrusting wave he nudged his intrigue's revelation to be known.

Legs crossed, sight concealed beneath the all consuming cowl he wore and lost in private thought, came felt abruptly, the disturbing presence of another at his foot. Squinting up directly into sunlight, where the brunt of a regretful, shocked apology was asking its acceptance Ishtaac nodded unconcerned, understood a fascination overwhelmed and bade the boy to sit beside him on the deck tapping with the flattened palm of invite's hand. Alarm extinguished, the young man's gaze froze undeterred and shiftless whilst he carried out the process, eying up intently the strangest of devices in so doing, wary of both heresy and tricksters. And aloofly now ignored by those who rather wished a secret glance, Ishtaac demonstrated privately to Louis the import of its purpose.

In gentle harmony with the rolling, outside waves the faceted, black and elongated object swayed a pendency without impedance towards its twisting movement on a strand of finest thread, held to perfect balancing about constriction's waisted middle. Whichever way the motion took, the ore would duly thus return reliant, so to face a natural bearing, always lengthways north and south. Self-propelled or steered by skilful hand or even artificial forces, Louis had no answer though clearly showed himself as doubtful and concerned.

Harbouring the inherent suspicions of a mariner, or any other whose fate is often decided by another's more important hand, the youngster slowly dared himself to touch and then manipulate for entertainment's sake the mysterious thing that conjured, swung and span before him. Then instantly, as if exposed as being vulnerable with over interest and without apparent reason he snatched away his hand, recoiled and eyed, aware, his family all too closely watching.

Louis rose to his feet with marked defensive pride and indicated angrily of the following winds, and then those lighter to the sides. He sniffed and wet his lips in show of serpent's tasting, pointed eager to the coast, his finger stopping with aggressive jolts to punctuate repeatedly at intervals then turned attention skyward, on to search complete a scanned rotation with accentuated, satisfying nods that bore the definition of finality and knowing. He had no need of toy or trumpery to reveal a course of travel, he knew enough already for to sail successfully his world.

Ishtaac replaced the lodestone to the bag before its attraction brought more the interest of unwelcome kind and sat again becalmed to hearken to the wind punch firmly at the dull, red faded sails. Louis paused a moment uncertain of offence before then striding haughtily away about some other matter nearer to his kindred and the fastness of unspoken solace only they could offer.

As the days passed they spoke increasingly little, and for a short time Ishtaac felt resented and intrusively confined to the inescapable family presence. The headway that they made, far outweighed however, any feeling of regret he might otherwise have had in assigning himself to overbearing company…and anything was better than trudging painful, long, sore leagues on either aching foot or atop a stubborn mount. He was, in fact, sincerely glad to be aboard and sensed that despite the atmosphere at present, soon enough each would come to accept the other once again with new found, forced acquaintance.

Cristobal approached one dawn for early fare and told the crew of his intentions. The town that he had spoken of lay now not far away, a place where dwelt an old acquaintance, long residing, blessed with influence and many friends who might take interest in their load. The deviation was minimal and so felt the loss of time to hold good value. His sons agreed and Ishtaac too, would especially take great pleasure in the simple act of treading land again, to wander freely on foundations of established kind.

As it was the small, inlet port they came across that evening appeared sparse and empty in the gloom, domestic in comparison to harbours previously slipped by. A mere haven in which to shelter out a closing storm or on better days, propose sublime embracement of a sweetheart's respite there within to spend a sun kissed afternoon.

Leonardo took the tiller and influenced to guide with ease, the commanding of his father captain calling out directions from his standing at the prow, keenly vigilant for rocks' hull breaching, ahead the swirling, eddied crests betraying bashful peril's upset part concealed beneath the breaking surf.

Towards the shimmered points of welcome's light, they ploughed through twilight's heaving spray, land bound, hearts raised with solid ground expectancy and the scent of bonus pickings hanging in the air. Ishtaac aided Louis tending sail to order whilst observing youth with awed respect displaying sound, a mastery of seamanship and agile strength beyond deception's innocence. Ducking, diving, holding fast to finally unleash, allowing then the flap of cloth to have its way, Louis thus permitted them to drift approach for grinding's reassurance that would grant a journey's pause upon a narrow shingle lay.

With suddenness and jolting, listed jar their wind blown voyage ceased upon a sharp, abruptly ending motion that only Ishtaac felt, it seemed, as Spruzzo crackled, scraped then came to stable, bedded resting, nestled for the night. A bloated mother bird upon a nest of many polished eggs she lay to brood, there undisturbed until the morning light.

Ishtaac's thoughts of idle roaming soon were quashed alas, as each was asked to stay close by…only Cristobal would disembark to stray upon that night. With worthy inclinations towards inspiring useful curiosity, he left them, reappearing satisfied much later, his coming long revealed in quiet song on wandered, pebble's crush, unsteady and fatigued but nonetheless apparently content.

Ishtaac listened testily to several feeble, scuffed attempts to climb aboard before offering his aid, relapsing whence the task accomplished to his draughty corner, self-condemned to stirring restlessly, the remaining darkness through.

Rising awkwardly upon the first cold paleness, parched and stiff he knew the sound of unrushed interest, as disciplined and measured marchers pace deliberately when counting every step and saw them bleary come, attired as he remembered cultured people, untainted, brilliant white, bearing linear resemblance to a ghostly scene played out, recalled from idle memory, so very long ago.

Leonardo yawned and blinked then roused his sleeping brother, their father wisely, he would leave to dead man's sleep, for each exchange they thought to make themselves and so arranged with haste the merchandise for optimism's prompt and beneficial business. Sample quantities of all they carried were laid upon the deck and beach without undue disturbance, on show for eyes to see and hands to touch and so embolden fancy's purchase.

Ishtaac mused upon the illustrations of but simple scent's imagine, when unveiled anew aromas issued forth from spices and perfumes reminding pleasantly once more of quayside scenes and haggled barter.

Decoratively painted crockery and effigies of varying worth and standard were bedded ceremoniously on spreads before the growing crowd to prosperous effect. Undaunted, the brothers spoke earnestly avoiding hesitation, encouraging with animated gesture, appealing to a willing generosity and an obvious local wealth. Sacks of grain and silks off loaded into servants' care brought solely for the carrying, with gold and silver paid in turn to ready, outstretched, enterprising hands, grasping avidly substantial profit before the morning's interest waned.

Ishtaac brought and stowed away as bidden resting only at the onset of an afternoon with heat sufficient to reduce their buying number to a knot, from whence they ebbed away completely. Cristobal chose his moment carefully, enduring with acquired patience the need to quench his arid tongue, until he knew the time arrived when naught remained but counting to be done, raising then his aching head on cue to pronounce his consciousness in full.

As pleased as Cristobal was to have been excused the morning's feverish duty, the day sat poor upon his muddled senses, hushed to probe relentless, throbbing eyes with goring fingers of contempt…and hence throughout the light to evening dusk was audibly bemoaned his sacrifice and strife, conveying honest pledges never to repeat such woeful sin again…at least until the next.

Soon after their day's first meal the balance of their cargo was cleared secure into storage, whereupon Ishtaac together with the family tugged and rocked then heaved to free the hull with the aid of off shore breezed assistance. Once back, sitting somewhat lighter in the freedom of the water, Leonardo turned the sail to windward and with leisured ease surpassed the holding grip, plunged in deeply and resumed their way again.

Homeward buoyed on spirits graced by fortune and in voices strained, returning songs to loved ones. With clearest eyes to see through keen edged, brittle stares, the brothers worked alert but needlessly to pass the time attended by inane and ancient sea songs both epic and of rhyme. Tales of stricken sailors put to verse for memory's sake, their timely warnings to impart. Of ill-matched, tragic love affairs doomed to failure from start. Of places thought mysterious and others far away and some of certain falsehood, upon scant credibility they played. Infectious, comic yarns of drinking bouts that ran 'till dawn both trivial and grand, though seaman's course without intention for to reach the soil of gentle maiden's ear resigned to dwell on land.

Ishtaac found himself belonging as a fellow crewman member, drawn unto a mariner's world of shared endeavour's wealth, cast upon the throes of fate and bound to stand together brave in hardships, nonetheless enduring through their stealth. Sanguine, bright adventure driven easily upon the succoured winds of prospect, or lost as dashed and broken on the rocky shorelines of remotest, hostile landscapes…never to return. Forged in unison by creed each dared to face and dance the jig and sail upon the rolling swell melodic, accompanied as always and forever by the fickle, unforgiving sea, for evening's hearken to alluring tunes where only fools would put their trust to be.

The course they'd long pursued, from here began to alter, and as a consequence the coastline gradually fell behind then disappeared totally from sight beneath the seascape's horizontal. Into the open blue and Ishtaac's growing consternation carried on a rasping gale that steadily increased and fuelled their speeding flight.

Wine was brought at mealtimes to accompany triumphant feelings of a successful journey's near ending. The bickering had melded into brotherly bonds of shared adventure whilst in fabrication of their far fetched stories to impress by, fully in the knowledge that each would need a confirmation's ally whence retelling.

Onward past the sunset's dipping off the port they raced and through the cloudless night. Surging ever nearer throughout the following day and so on through the next...until finally the yearned for signal came. Hence Louis' cry from perching grasp atop the creaking mast was soared aloft encouraged on the chorused cheers resounding from the little deck below....Their land at last, was coming forth to greet them.

Leonardo rushed responding with all the haste that he could muster to the fore and gazed ahead with high expectancy through shielded, eager eyes. And as the shore arose with slow and proper grandeur from the realms of deep azure, Ishtaac watched considering of the gusted implications sent upon the scenting of the breeze, storing much away for future contemplation.

Once Cristobal had recognised his mark, a closing natural feature that to him would whisper sight's informing of location, he steered the boat accordingly for rounding on the westward squall to sustain once more another coastal margin. Ishtaac noticed how the tiller changed its yaw direct in keeping with the headland as the sailspread then was trimmed conforming to a starboard tack assumed along, for some their homebound, known terrain. And all the while the brothers called aloud their pointed observations thinly veiling hitherto suppressed, heartfelt excitement, when not adjusting idle rope unnecessarily and fidgeting without direction.

Cristobal pleased and proud looked on and smiled, his crew were once again, to father's eyes, returned in full as innocent and mere children.

So it was in fading light their island home among the sprawling cliff top snag appeared into view, and turning then towards the rugged shore they made their final sea borne lunge together. With no aid to navigation other than his instinct, Cristobal bent sail across the last, grounding out to shouts of pleasure and relief upon their native soil, as there within a sheltered, windless, sheer walled cove, they found again retreat's front door step, readily accepting of its kin's deliverance safely from the sea.

Ishtaac stayed with Cristobal at the boat, Leonardo and Louis unable to contain their zeal much longer carried what they easily could, bounded off and raced for home. It was not long, barely enough time in fact, to unload the stock from hold down onto waiting shingle before the mariner's entire family came hurriedly to greet them. And exuding great elation they engaged once more united in embrace, the father with his daughters, his wife and parents also.

Old and uncertain in step, the ageing pair were willing nevertheless to help, however they were able. Ishtaac introduced himself although would spare through shyness his forthcoming, preferring rather more to occupy himself with the bearing of their load. Many times they crossed the beach that night to climb the crude worn, slip of steps laden with the cargo, until eventually but one lone sack remained, a previous oversight let languish in the bilge, whereupon Cristobal extended gratefully his hand in further friendship, offering hospitality as a thankful meal and sturdy bed to rest in.

Inside the family dwelling, a motherly concern for comfort shone through the wearing function of the house. Flowers perfumed well the large and open, lofty rooms where floors were swept and free from clutter. Overlong clearly, had she expected back her husband with the children…and thus from every cherished fluster, Cristobal redeemed each poignant fret reflected.

Soon enough, the wine was pouring its harmonious plunge to thirsty beaker, on then freely flowing from the flask to yarns of relished exploit. The meal was set and ate at long endured, absent, mournful table…and afterwards, amid rejoicing family's sweet encounter they would sing their gilded songs and drink 'till daylight's interruption.

Never had the glow in Ishtaac's eye been fired warmer than that evening, inspired by the merchant's dearest…and many times in places cold and dread thereafter, he would drift remembrance back inside his heart's salvation for to visit once again that homely refuge perched upon the clifftop reach of generosity and friendly welcome.

However, weighted was that cankerous charge about him and recalling aid received before from gentle hosts and the ill-fate that befell them, he believed his company as yet unsound, and ought therefore continue with his voyage.

Cristobal had much ahead to do, but for now was restlessly content to sit reluctant with his wife among their family for a day or two on stern instructions to defer all business dealings…just a short while longer. Upon this time Ishtaac spoke of these regretful wishes to be moving off, along his westward journey and on his part Cristobal listened well, with understanding interest giving reassurance of an ability to provide assistance in the matter. Many friends and associates he knew residing on the coast who, like himself, owed their living to the sea and as such would often travel west towards the fiefdom of the Franks or even to Hispania with reasons of extending trade or to fish the rich resources found among their waters.

Cristobal duly obliged and made inquiries into this concern on Ishtaac's behalf, eventually securing the means required, with some unexpected influence having to be exerted in this rather individual transaction, barely reaching his interpretation of a mutual satisfaction. However, the terms were struck and he, the west bound trader agreed with reservations plain in doubtful furrow, to take the stranger on good merit all returning leagues across the sea as far as their companionship was suffered, unto a place named Catalunya, where, at the completion of the deal they would simply part and he turn south for home.

He was a forthright man, impatient with advancing years apparent in the weathered grain of seaward life's erosion standing proudly out upon his face as dried and ageing, oak tree bark, cracked with rough frowned, ridges. Cristobal introduced him only as Fernandez, and informed that this was intended to be his final voyage so far distant from his homeland. His family having grown and dispersed to households of their own, meant that his wife awaiting in the south was left alone in ailing health and waning, which explained the root of his concerns and reason for the press. The outward leg of an anxious journey had taken its toll, leaving the man curt and angry at nothing in particular. He cursed his luck at slightest cause and paced himself with haste. The craft he sailed was old and tired also, undeserving of a name, small and fragile sitting light and skittish in the water with its single mast made good, as Ishtaac saw it, more than once too often. The food and wares he carried, some of which included Cristobal's perfumes, lay piled or thrown, exposed, inside the open hull to elements and view.

Seating was a benched affair, three in all, their purpose being twofold thus acting also as essential stiffening ribs across its narrow beam. A sadly tattered, patched redundant sail lay bunched and crumpled stiffly in the prow, promising poor protection were they to experience but the slightest hint of unfair weather.

Ishtaac looked on with seriousness and grave opinion, doubting either's worth, much to the mirthless amusement of the caustic mariner who sneered disrespectful jibes at his expense. It was a hardy sailor's vessel where only the bravest few that had survived worse transport or the desperate and the needy without a care might chance, he thought. But as it was he felt compelled from somewhere in between and starved of options with a yearning to be gone, he said farewell to Cristobal that day, came climbed aboard unsteadily and embarked upon his fate.

Holding tightly to the key and trusted blade within the folds about him in a lame attempt to overcome the flagging of residual confidence, he seated facing forward to meet head on, all likelihood, feigned unyielding and set scowled, his grin determined.

Wind buffeted an agitated send off as Cristobal hailed them from the shore. Glowering dismally around the head and shoulders of the ailing man Fernandez, Ishtaac daringly, had turned himself to watch the parting of brief friendship with a sense of doomed, dissatisfaction gnawing at his heart. Cristobal noted sympathetically the image of distress, gave loud a cheer to encourage, waved his arm, then walked away and thus was gone forever.

They sailed on quietly without a hindrance, the old man and repugnance, his companion, a stiff wind's brace of uneventful of days, passing by a land mass distant to the north, on…and isolated, into open sea once more.

The conversation being awkwardly curt between them at the off, dried soon enough to the occasional coughed command, usually with overdue, intentional delay whereby Fernandez swore and Ishtaac paid the price. As time progressed the old seafarer found a growing difficulty in mastering with any inspiring degree of ascendancy, the wayward draught and currents. Seaspray freshened then chilled and stung on Ishtaac's face. The little craft began to surge and drag as the whistling blasts blew louder, soared to dive in gaping troughs with increasing heavy wash, twisted, groaned and rolled along, sometimes even seeming for to stop complete with all their headway lost, then lifting high above the peaks would drop and plunge itself alarming, on and on again.

Doggedly no less, Fernandez wove to forge their weary way ahead throughout the following day and night, whence not a wave but tiredness it was, that finally overwhelmed to claim life's arduous battle with the sea, seizing cold its suddenness unkind, and callous there amid the plight.

The helmsman slumped away beyond all care and spent, thudding forward without one last complaint, to the indignity of lapping bilge stench, forcing Ishtaac's hand to take unsure, his fear's control and more, the thrashing tiller's arm and boom. Nervously about the fallen, stoic heap he climbed for lashing sail and rudder tight, yet bent in vain repeatedly, on one last try, to wrest assisstance from a man already dead.

Lamenting angrily his lot, each apprehension fully realised, Ishtaac looked up helpless to the fading light, but none there were alas, to offer comfort to a stricken fool as he…not as far as condemnation's eyes that bleakest night, could see. Nothing but the wind lashed, torrid rain's blind scour and the ceaseless outrage of a rising sea.

Several times immersed in ordeal's desperation, he would leave the boat untended to pursue erratic aims, to exorcise his temper, crying loud release of hateful demons and to curse consistency of luck. And so through venting wrathful impotence soon came sincere denouncements with proposed, devout allegiance to any other gods that paid attention to his call. Never would he venture forth to water from the sight of land again, he pledged, this would be his last. And the lifeless, ashen body slouching crooked at his feet would always there remain his loyal, wide eyed, staring witness to that fact.

The howling wind encouraged of itself to raging gale as the tempest sprung its fury, unconcerned for tiny vessels caught within its grasp.

Thrown and tossed beneath the gathered storm clouds closing overhead, Ishtaac held steadfast his tightened grip renewed and braced a snarled retaliation against damnation's thoughts to ride defiantly to bitter ends regardless, into the very heart of tortured darkness and his foulest, final nightmare. Long beyond intimidation, he blared his infidelity and challenge to the gods above, abusing them to take him. His futile battle all but lost, now truly he was, he felt, the victim cast aside as wretched and forsaken. Indeed at times he thought the boat already sunk but loll then list she would instinctively and shed herself of weighty burden for to rise once more above the jagged mountain's glaciated bite of ice capped, foaming crests merely then to claw him further back towards the abysmal pits of malice and the abandoned swirl of lonely hell's encounter.

Daring the roared, tumultuous fury, Ishtaac managed to free the nearest of the cargo and hurl it overboard. Fernandez, through respect, he left until the last and swore farewell with regards to meeting later before then heaving too his heavy burden to the savage boil of violent ferment snapping from beneath. Drowned in thunderous, crashing surf he never saw him go but shrunk instead relinquished, sagging down, exhausted there to jam his crouching cowardice against the pounded hull, trembling in his shame to blame and wish the full mistrusting of his misery away.

He never knew how long he lay as craven hearted, hidden from his terror nor did he see impending doom approach on thrusting blades of rocks' intent. Though woeful moans he heard aloud, of grinding protest ring like tuneless bells for tolling out his failure whence the wounded hull henceforth, could give no more and fractured brittle on the impact. One grim, portentous moment later the frailness of his sanctuary was smashed and stripped to bareness all about on fraying shards asunder, and came forthwith, the timber vessel as dissolved complete of shape, to worthless debris torn apart by ragged wave.

Exposed to the wild and pressing torrent of night's black, choking spray, Ishtaac floundered struggling for a purchase, groping stricken as the sudden sightless 'neath the enveloping of stampede's utter rending cascade. Swamped to gagged convulsions, dogged by crushing lungs he fought for air against the surety of drowning before a tidal rush of odious, flooding sea...where then the bitter taste of salted fate consumed his eyes and omens whispered taunting from the deafness.

Dark-edged, deathly, monstrous forms marched out their wicked stamp on Ishtaac senseless, the Devil's shadowed host themselves had come at last to claim him, torturous and pure, unfit for granting clemency or respite they would goad upon the spears of hope...for prior to assuming souls as charged, and for naught else but amusement's sake, their joy's malevolence would spite him. He blurred and swooned then came around again still trapped within a whirling, turmoil's vortex, caught as stranded and alone, yet nowhere but within a timeless void succumbing helpless to eternally endure it seemed, the evil laughter of surreal surroundings...and thus cocooned inside a fisted madness inescapable, bereft the reason of awareness, he noticed not the strangled hold which suddenly released him.

The robe that bound him fixed in ignorance against the surging swell had ripped, the contents of his pouch spewed forth and all was dashed as lost within a single issue's vomit, gone, cast unbeknown to any or to where.

Roused once more yet not perceived, the tragedy befallen, Ishtaac battled bravely on, near faltering on the brink of life considered almost over, and pressed to face blind fury on the rocks that earlier had failed, but now with scornful irony, might save him. And so it was, beyond the very threshold of despair whence scratching forth on blighted feel alone his numbness came across a cramping tear, suffice to thrust his hand up to the palm and thence make painful, twisted anchorage, from where his striving further to locate, allowed himself a reach towards another into which he forced some fingers. With little thought of their retrieval, he hung there crucified, near dead as creeping vine secured in locking grips tenacious, then dropped his head to bury deep within the shelter of his chest and rasped for air whilst calling out in private whimpers, scoffing at the personality of storm itself to rip him from his mooring...as if it even cared. Long dispelled were any feelings in his limbs when ultimately the ire subsided, long absent too was the delicate grip on consciousness that Ishtaac once possessed.

The cloud streaked, wind-washed dawn glowed purple pale and faintly hopeful along the drab horizon when Ishtaac woke and looked across a new found calm restored, although with broken heart through tear, strained eyes of anger and regret it turned to one of mockery whence known in full the true contempt bestowed upon his toil, for there within the stunted clutch of land, ensnared in grimaced island's backwash gape he had met debased, affliction and its downfall.

A well-shot arrow's flight might carry on fair breeze to strike ashore where pine clad hillsides crumbled sharply to the sea, shorn curtly from their inland march to oversee a sweep of crescent, sandy bay. Thus salvation was again conferred in hallmarks of another cruel jest perhaps, assumption sneered before it spat the wilful sourness of unappeasable and vengeful gods from the unsavoury tasting of his mouth. Only the necklace of high office and the banded stones about his forehead remained as permanent reminder to a former life he regretted ever having left.

A struggled search, improbable and pointless was stretching out to overwhelming. Must he be forever shackled to this hardship's bane and sentence? Ishtaac wondered sullen and was brought induced to swearing with a snap of surly venom cast not only out towards the absent, ill willed charge but also to the envious, short lived lives of men.

Stiffly he freed his rigid grip, releasing knotted fingers to unfolding and then looked about the world with heavy sadness frowned from weary eyes. Waves lapped solace gently around his knees as with a sigh he realised himself upon a ledge whose serrated pinnacles now stabbed him painful through the remnants of his sandals, but still they held, he scathed....unlike his errant garnish from the realms of minor gods, they would endure yet.

Dawn crept fast to light the upper reaches of the steeply inclined crag above where the gulls sat damply on their ravaged nests to eye. There showed itself a simple climbing to the summit, but if he fell then so be it, he truly had surpassed such caring of life to live or die.

Dragging spiritless then up the rugged face he partook the tired ascent for dryness, bent upon a vantage point from which to view the completeness of his woe, where despite their fractured, scraping yield to tear his flesh relentless the rocks held mostly firm conceding him a passage to the top, and from here he let proclaimed a heartfelt vow be known, affecting no-one but himself. That if ever, the part of his damnation, sentenced ever to protect, should see the light of day whilst yet he lived, he would without delay or deviation, at whatever was the costing, find the means, or meet his end in trying, as deceitful fate permits, to return his undertaking back unto the rightful care of those he now despised, the Quauchen Holy Order, thenceforth being done with the whole affair and discharged of any further interest in the matter. This would be his renewed and lasting obligation. Out, he forced such caustic wisdom spat with words that came from solemn depth, caring naught for consequence or favour.

The dismembered wreckage lay washed up, strewn upon the mainland's beach in small fragmented form, offering little sign of useful jetsam…and as regards his lost belongings, promised even less for inspiration's sake.

Ishtaac shrugged, sat cross legged windswept, cold and hungry. The discomfort of the latter eventually spurring forth to cause his scour among deformed and haggard trees, although would there locate but few suspicious, unknown plants and tasteless, wooden seeds.

Returning downcast to the promontory graced above his climb he espied again the treacherous landscape to the north where broken cliffs plunged starkly into virile, turquoise sea. He viewed them from his severed island finger's reach flung out to beleaguered isolation half a league or less in distance, observing of their inland contours rising west as mountain ridges steepling out of sight, to cater shelter at its southern, arcing hemline for a small and tightly clustered village, part concealed by night's remaining shadow.

Slumped fishing boats, their web of nets at rest before him for to dry expectant of the sun, occupied the nearest corner of an open, flatland bay that yawned from tired revelation's slumber off towards the south, obscured of distant features by a shroud of early morning mist, where finally above, arose however, another stride of lofty, darkened spined terrain curtailing further sight. True, the village with its austere walls of whitewashed clay thrived closely from the storms inside the haven of the mountain's keep, protected from unfriendly, seaward winds, but its right and proper guardian lay beyond, inland to clearest view and greeting of arrivals with a dubiousness, suffice to self-impose inquiry.

A majestic single, solid, granite outcrop thrust up bared and bold, to catch and hold imagination and a cloud raced, sullen sky, where dawn's first crowning buzzards hung to trim its kingly mantle…and on all sides and to the fore a cape of verdant pine flowed on, serenely there to drape in regal, biscuit green. Stately bluffs in thoughtful, pensive gaze, stared nobly out across the bay implying cautious, reservations tinged within its welcome. Ever-present, was its sentinel stern observance, considering well internal, withheld judgements of its own untold conceiving.

Such a sight must surely be entitled, Ishtaac claimed in quiet whisper to himself whence now reminded of the far off places near his home displaced by hardship's press but not, he knew, forgotten…recalled enough perhaps, to be the reason for his wrestle with a yearning creep of fondness.

Unable to remain, coerced by twisted stomach's cramping, Ishtaac decided on an attempt to make the crossing and so commenced a scan for quick descent, whereupon, beneath the smiling dupe of fortune he was blessed to see some boxes floating trapped in eddied swirls, remnants of their stock, beset by almost patronising currents. Large enough to bear his weight and sit astride, to paddle even, if one had the means, and there on close inspection, with begrudging luck, its fickle presence holding, discovered further usable debris. Some rope he saw as torn from flapping sail and frayed edged strips of planking that would serve as oars requiring only small invention.

With careful deliberation and nigh rejuvenated spirit, he managed then to shape a raft of sorts, unstable but with unforeseen fortuity to bolster shattered faith, it adequately suited…thus the strangest craft of fine aroma set its maiden course, pungent from some perished phials inside, releasing content high to herald proclamation's powerful scent, it bore expensive change to that of squally sea salt and the stalest smell of fish.

With fought success, he broke the watery clasp to bob his way across the gusty strait, and soon, having ridden the surf triumphantly, was beached upon the soft sand's gentle shore. Where, with crates then dragged to fastness on firm ground beside him, Ishtaac set about examining the horde, thinking first and foremost of a trade for food and lodging, although later it would dawn that he might even gain enough to build himself a boat, henceforth enabling him to search again for his belongings.

Ishtaac was beginning, somehow and despite himself to feel the gentle warmth of optimism's rise, unexpectedly finding a relief of sorts in this, his overdue release from fealty. There was nothing to be done about the loss, that blow having already been delivered, but still he saw a chance, albeit small, remote and indistinct, an opportunity if nothing else, to look for his possessions, and on that resignation he would simply have to base condolence...besides the surroundings seemed agreeable enough, regardless of his having yet to meet the townsfolk. Ishtaac knew then that his only recourse was to try, but if the key preferred concealment under waves than in his hand...well, he decided, that was some success in measure also. Tomakal-Zaqual's imperial arm was long indeed but never would it stretch to such a quiet corner, surely not, he thought. And after having had quite enough of travelling for the present anyway, found these musings easily endorsed.

Save for a modest number of breakages, a dozen of the fifty or so bottles housed in just one case, the remainder of the contents were in tact, as evidential testament to skilled and ample packaging. It was a worthy inheritance by any standard without the slightest chance of restoration to a rightful owner....But such a prize as this would be in need of guarding well, dawned dour his deduction, and therefore looked around instinctively for all unwarranted attention noting as he did so, a lowly figure wandering under the mantle of presumed incrimination along the outskirts of the village without, his aberration deemed, defining purpose to the gait. Ishtaac watched him tensely for a while with suspecting in his eye until poor realisation fully grasped the expense of many years upon the form whereby his will relaxed, invoking self-rebuke. Nevertheless and somewhat inevitably, it soon became apparent that the stranger too, had gained awareness of the wash up from the storm, as straightening slightly from a gangling, natural stoop he began to hasten an approach.

He was an elderly man of rustic, soiled appearance with stubbled beard and a matt of unkempt straggled, bleached white hair sapped deathly dry of life, dressed in sturdy fashion, stitched of hard worn, robust fabrics oft repaired. Sackcloth for a tunic, once white now dirty grey, with patchwork poorman's trousers that barely met his ankles, falling short of limp and grass-made, stricken sandals.

The sprightly figure hailed arrival with a forthright honesty that swiftly peaked to an alert expression of acutest intrigue etched upon an age deflated face, whence inquisitive, one beady eye scoured Ishtaac's features closely and attentive, lacking previous recognition or any cultural placement. Ishtaac forced a mindful smile of small embarrassment and watched him with reserve returned, instead, as the old man further wrinkled the defining of his nose and loosely mobile, bristled chin, to sniff the breeze with beaming pleasure and to smile delightful knowing after stealing nothing more than just a glimpse into the nearest of salvaged crates.

Tightening his posture once again, Ishtaac soon became aware of wanting better manners, and so daring his suspicions to unfold, extended wiped clean hands in show of open friendship. Willingly, the trusting stranger advanced to the embrace for Ishtaac's holding firmly about his bone felt, rigid shoulders, and hesitantly was it rendered, but also with a private humour scarce reserved, the villager's returning of an unfamiliar gesture.

When first he spoke the speech and subtle melody, to Ishtaac's ears, were not entirely uncommon, thus was struck a broken conversation with words and indications, where Ishtaac told of his adventure, riding through the tempest to eventual deliverance, whereupon, within conclusion's timely pause the old man introduced himself and gave the name Joaquin. Pointing to a milky, blinded eye he laughed a hard-gummed, toothless chuckle and held both hands before him in a feigned display of blind man's groping to amuse.

Savouring the moment's naive banter, Ishtaac dislodged one of the unspoilt phials from the open case beside him as a gifted token of his greeting. Joaquin on the other hand, although enjoying of the scent immensely refused to take the offer, provoking thus a humbled self-reproach for initially distrusting. Grinning wide his credit to inspire, he then bade his new acquaintance stay upon a promise of return, and hurried off towards the village at an oddly quick and spindly, virile lope, to emerge a short while later toiling stubbornly before him, a cumbersome and crudely timbered barrow-cart supported on two spokeless, wooden wheels. This he was forced to leave on firmer ground however, where compacted sand was more secured by root, returning eagerly dishevelled nevertheless to offer his assistance in the removal from the beach by hand, of the heavy load that Ishtaac brought.

It took considerable time and effort to carry, sometimes drag the clumsy haul across the deeply giving underfoot, but eventually both were raised to sit precarious their discomfort on the straining of the carriage. Ishtaac lacked foundation for his certainty but invested nonetheless, his full approving, heartfelt trust believing to have found himself a hard won, simple friend…and together side by side they pushed the cart to where the lonely hermit guided it, directly into town.

With the motion of the sea invaded still inside his head for causing slight unease and nausea, they trundled awkwardly their mastery of the wayward track, passing by the little fleet of fishing boats that lined in languished incline's sloth, their route along the beach, painted brightly for the coming spring with coats of greens and reds and yellow ochre, pastel fresh in storm's musk aftermath and cleared air's crystal sunlight.

Ishtaac sneezed and shielded his eyes from the reverberating glare that issued blinding off the whitewash, laid on homes beyond to wall complete, the deserted maze of narrow, coarse, uneven streets…and with care and often failed attempt negotiated corners to his suddenly making the surprised discovery of a neatly tucked, reclusive square.

Wheeless carts as makeshift stalls remained behind from recent market day, their place and usage now mere lifeless stored against a small and plainly ordered church, but otherwise, here as elsewhere too, the village showed up well an emptiness that lay abundant all around. The sun's gloss glinted nevertheless, intrusions bright and clear to piercing from labour's years of dedicated polishing, inflicted on the brass stud, timber doors, at present firmly closed, and shut with rituality imposed. Atop, a single tarnished bell, marked silently, the hanging slumber for permitting dreams to pass untolled, whence, as now, the respectful shy community would lay itself in dormant Sabbath's resting behind its straw or wooden slatted blinds, shuttered tight to ward away an outside world concealing sound each torpid, inner presence, wherein contained, their secrecy ought thrive.

A cockerel crowed and unseen dogs responded in a timeless morning call to stir the pulse of life's arousal. This tranquil fishing village was indeed quite different then from its relations far more easterly, with their fervent marketplaces and a diverse wealth of goods to trade. Where dealers haggled endlessly and commerce seldom slept...and yet, the link was there...somewhere. Perhaps a similar savoured salty warmth upon the air, drying textured crisp against the skin or in the shades and hue of land on sea combining...or something in the natural charm of easy disposition adopted by its people. Elusive, fetching qualities inherited by both so far apart, but present nonetheless and ideally courteous with discretion to delight him...but more, these sensations' first attachments really were he felt, in some unclear way, calling him on breeze scent whispers to adjourn harsh judgement of the world a while, repose himself and indulge seduction's sway.

Momentarily they stopped at Ishtaac's bidding and watched the yawning stretch of life begin. A bulky, bent black figure shuffled by about her waddled business on ancient feet unseen beneath her trailing cloth, crossed the square and disappeared behind the far side of the church. Once again a dog barked close at hand with geese and chickens stirred upon this time, declaring also noisy intervention. Next an ageing gentleman came crumpled and unsteady, hobbled, coughed and wound his way upon a stick as gnarled as he. Joaquin offered morning's greeting and was answered with the heartless, tired wave of all too frequent gesture, but on spotting Ishtaac there would render thoughtful pause a time before then following in the bustled footsteps of his presumed good lady wife, around the church soon lost to sight.

The two new friends continued their meandered course between the single storey dwellings, onward through the stone strewn streets worn deep to viscous troughing with the frequent weight of varied bygone passage. Slithering clumsily along the gradients either side until their turning sudden and severely for to climb a torturous, steep, long incline.

Heaving by a shallow lying wall in parts dismembered to their left, Ishtaac oversaw with interest the gardens of the residents below. Fruit trees, growing here and there, enshrouded poultry pens within, whose plots of ill-defining border, suggested friendliness of neighbours…alas but a moment's contemplation spent to ease, before their deviating on an upward snaked ascent once more beneath the shadow of the looming hillside. And as they rose his view improved whence cast above the rooftops to an unimpaired perception along the length of arcing bay.

The track diminished now to the poor repair of seldom usage, overgrown excessively and difficult to pass…but just ahead before them when the path could reach no further, at first concealed by overhanging boughs, a cave mouth gaped its wide intent to greet them. Protected from intrusion, should any venture up that way, by a door that hung in simple fashion as a clutch of dried out brittle driftwood splinters, set a stride within its throat, creating thus a welcome porchway. Joaquin proudly announced his home and opened up the flotsam threshold offering invitation with a carefree, jaunty flourish.

Following to the darkened gloom beyond, Ishtaac assumed his lean upon a central, makeshift table whilst the old man went about the pointless task of realigning things in customary house proud fashion. Ishtaac tried politely not to notice the flurry of tidying activity, holding instead his curious gaze cast downward until the hermit's doubt was overcome or else had been forgotten. Joaquin clearly lived alone and had done so for a time, but there were obvious signs informing that the natural confines of the dwelling had in the past, seen alterations with a purpose to accommodate…adapted several times in fact, throughout its homely usage. The probability being by generations of his forebearers who had dwelt there also, but among their large and needy families.

The chamber's entrance cell which gave itself for one to live quite comfortably within, led to scraped and cleared out hollows, scooped deeply from the side walls at a great expense of labour, producing extra rooms of sorts, for an age it seemed, disused. A cornered ledge, gouged crib-like at the furthest point, smoothed kind with love surpassing any real need, where infancy's mementoes lay arranged aplenty still, jutted over yet another scene of dusty, undisturbed, forgotten order, but here, relating moreso to the designation of a child's importance. In one of the side alcoves a pile of wooden planks and slats he also eyed, collected from the yielding shore they rose as neatly stacked for ready use…ample likely, to construct himself a boat he mused, then pondered on the doorway.

It was not to be long though before Joaquin called his exploration to a halt and bade him to the table where lay awaiting now, an array of large, clay pots around an even larger jug of water. They ate and drank and became firm friends, the hermit and the stranger and talked extensively of things both high and low…but took enjoyment also from the pleasure of their silence.

Ishtaac got to build the boat desired, aided by his often, odd companion. A triumphant masterpiece of unskilled hands against the demandings of the sea, it proved to be a curious marvel for the locals. He settled easily into the cave and came to understand and breathe the ebb and flow of village life dependant on the waves. The usual vibrancy of early morning's cast off and sun drenched, drowsy afternoons, of collecting in the idyllic evening air for naught but drink and song, and at times the hearty celebrations of religious feasts to cleanse for some, both tainted soul and senses. Together they watched and heard them all from comfort's private introversion…and yet even paradise he came to find, had spawned its title, rooted in repulsion. A fitting irony imposed perhaps, but one that Ishtaac nonetheless, was finally at terms with.

And so it was, that sadly far too soon Ishtaac came to own the cave, inheriting alone…but lasting found his measured solace in the simple company of captivated children when only they would pay him visit.

Choosing to remain in nearby seclusion he watched them grow and told them yarns of sea borne, high pursuits to lands and people far away, inspiring there with dreams of romance brought to life, sufficient for to stoke the spirit's smoulder for adventure.

The children came and passed away to manhood's serious business as others took enthralled, their places at the storyteller's feet...and through acquaintance with the years, fantastic tales and rumours of a new-found world, he knew at once as home, came issued forth in naive youngsters' words to find his mountain lair like plague.

Despite predestination's binding contact with the past though, Ishtaac would mature unmolested to assume himself, the look of one in later age. He greyed contrasting to his raiment and when climbing to his door was more inclined to crook with once known easy burdens, overtaxing...nevertheless his fruitless search continued along both shore and island's debris margin, coursed upon endeavours to endure each day...and futile, ponder much alone. A solitary figure, small and black upon the sawing waves that played their tricks on old men's minds. A single lost and fallen crow, long strayed adrift from bearing by a vast forgotten storm, his isolation bobbed and steered its forlorn way hereafter into local tomes and lore.

Then one day it surfaced in the news of anxious neighbours, that the cave above their little town was realised inhabited no longer. Not pot, nor cloth, nor trace remained, nothing did betray the melancholy stranger's visit, nor told them of his passing. Some said his fate had been recalled and taken from the land, beset by the same and sudden, springing squall that brought him. Others, that the old crow chose his time and simply flew away returned from whence he'd come, forever cursed to search in vain for lost love dearly cherished.

In its course the cave relapsed beneath consuming thorny blankets and all was gone except the unseen feeling of regretful presence fractured to a residue of stories for endorsing well the mystery of "el corb home," the placid crowman that had once lived high above their village.

It too, was often later said with sage like nod, that one day, in the wake of foulest weather, he would come restored again to claim his rightful place and perch his bones outside the cave anew. To cast his knowing eyes and oversee them all with wisdom's watchful gaze for time protectively eternal, as was his residential wont...and when such looked for morning did arrive, prevailing winds of fortune would then also fall on each once more, and gift to them the blessing of his surety.

Thus it was become in time, the place for young and hopeful love to turn whence suffering for a mate, or even merely chancing on some favoured outcome, optimistic heads would turn expectantly in solemn veneration, toward their absent guest upon his mountain roost and say their words of grace.

Chapter 4
Denials for a Messenger's Deliverance

But livelihoods of humble fishermen however worthwhile and fulfilled, do not alas, suit all. Some indeed, must fare as blown aside on different courses, towards their finding other compass points far reaching. Rodriguez Maria Gonzalez was one such individual destined to events of worldly consequence. He had grown he felt, to full capacity within the little town of L'Estartit and longed for high adventure beyond the prosperous sea. Cared for by his mother single handed, his father lost in stormy water whilst still young, he hoped one day to bring returned a wealthy status buoyed upon ambitious dreams accomplished. And so enlisted in the expansive Spanish fleet, donating services at first, to his highness Charles I, Holy Roman Emperor, aboard a swift converted, square rigged caravel, among a small flotilla, west bound to explore the new found world thus riding fortune's call upon the ocean's whim. To la Isla Espanola and the promised riches there, awaiting, or so the stories ran, for any loyal son of Spain to come and claim his own.

Many weeks they sometimes sailed or drifted robbed of breeze, besieged by numbing boredom where the wail of mournful sickness reared its contrast grim beneath a blue and pleasant sky. A slow and painful way to end one's days then, falling to unchallenged hand, lacked in sense of glory with no saving option but to merely entertain a time dragged tortured torment waiting for demise, whilst all about looked on with apathy expectant. Endurance also, soon would force itself to fracturing the lesser souls, obscenely stealing dignities denied, amid the common spectacle of pendulating madness and a garbled, blind eyed death of mind, from which, even some of those that simply witnessed, never full recovered.

Nevertheless it came at last one day, elation's crying to proclaim the sighted port of Santo Domingo, much relieved, with celebration and rejoicing. Whereupon the feel of solid ground once more beneath his feet would offer to Rodriguez fundamental pleasures unbeknown as missed.

Fresh supplies were brought from shore steepled on the toiling backs of natives now enslaved. Men, with women also laboured through the throng to bear the heavy burdens of their stores, hauled from dockside's growing merchant houses, expanding here unhindered as did too, peripheral trades that flourished at their sides.

Sugar cane from the vast plantations that were springing up contentiously inland and maize, the alchemy of different gold, tobacco leaves and fruits of wondrous shape and size. The port was fashioned in the newest image of an ideal Spain, with style and prestige in abundance despite the pressing need for each day's mundane function.

Rodriguez imbibed both deep and wholesome of its scented, prosperous air awash with fine achievements, and also yearned to make his mark of merit recognised on this, their new unfounded land. Burning was there a desire to strike and quickly at the draw of hidden riches on the mainland, to find elusive treasures yet concealed and consequence but dreamt of. To emancipate the heathen Indian from possession and his strange, imagined gods, their gold to then deliver with impassioned pride back unto his country, God's only true religion, and so escape himself perhaps, along the way the poverty that haunted all his life.

They remained the day aboard before sailing off again upon the tide, a shortened trip around the isle to Cuba and the call of Santiago with new, enriched supplies. Arriving at the protected valley port and stronghold of Hernando Cortez, both revered soldier and the town's enduring mayor, a position held as granted by the island's overall governor, one Diego Velasquez for his aiding with its capture in the prosperous decade previous. Here, the scene before him teemed in the midst of chaotic, hasty preparation for an excursion planned to gain the Indian's coastal homelands. As inspiring news had reached their eager listening, through the declarations of a local slave raider named Juan de Grijalva, that wonderous cities, the likes of which had never been before encountered, were finally revealed with promise and in number. Sited inland from certain known locations, they arose unoccupied, apparently abandoned to the strangling vines of jungle's creep and the lowly chattering sensibilities of monkey's guidance.

Originally Cortez was assigned the task of exploring only its potential worth to future expeditions but rumour ran as often does, to quiet contradiction. He stood now proud as Spanish noble, trimmed, neat beard and splendidly attired with flare and style uncompromised, to overseeing his entire operation in fine distinguished person. A tangible impatience cloaked the man, however, that showed starkly manifest in the frequent flurries of barked commands and condemnations when naught but mishap was to blame. He struck as being a master hard to please, Rodriguez thought, whence noting how a vein of urgency would surge through those affected by his zealous ire to ripple on engulfing all in fact, who worked at his disposal.

Backed by steel-edged will and warlike means, this was clearly an exploration with determination and secure intent. That of piercing the defenses of a stout withholding and achieve success felt overdue to Spain. There harvesting by sword in place of tempered scythe and honest dealing.

Rodriguez stepped amid amassed commotion driven on the tide of disembarking and met the nobleman's stare by accident or fate-provoking interruption.

"You!" Cortez called above the passing heads. Standing tall astride a pair of lined up, re-conscripted cannon. "To me!" and made gesture as if beckoning the wayward hound.

Rodriguez looked around for any other, bemused by his attention, then straightened boldly upright, considering himself above all else a Spaniard and a soldier, to walk as do those of self-assured prominence, with patient, idle gait upon a clear bearing.

"Has my memory failed your name, young...?" But the initial interest Cortez showed had waned once Rodriguez made approach, turned instead towards the needy business of another now who stood below, hands wrung with bothering questions to distract whence clutching papers flustered to impress of their importance...perhaps he knew his answer.

Waiting overlong and somewhat foolishly at first expecting some renewed interrogation, Rodriguez then gave coughed, a clearance to his throat and introduced himself, now disregarding with intrusive confidence the effect of intervention.

The conversation with the other ceased upon this instant as those nearby stopped also, adherent for a brief, excited moment...although soon afterwards such declaration would itself, show preference for to carry on in case they too, fell sorely on unwelcome inclinations.

"Rodriguez Maria Gonzalez," he supplied, concealing any waver in his tone. "And no, I do not believe we have met before this day."

Hernando Cortez, who, from the southern lands of Spain, held well the sharp, honed features characteristic of an ancestry among the Moors, glowered directly at him with angered consternation. His glare, Rodriguez bore with some polite discomfort and awaited for the storm to break, shifting uneasily within his retrospective silence. Cortez's mood at length altered though, and thankfully to pensive. He stroked his beard and enjoyed the pause with an unhurried air of self-importance, to impose his will and hold a little further for the sake of his amusement.

The clerk dismissed, another took his place, disturbed in different ways, less troubled and more troubling.

"Your first time in Sandiago, I am to assume." He was not looking for responses ."Newly arrived and fresh from old Espana by way of Santo Domingo, I can see. How are these places in my absence?" Cortez mused aloud, appealing to the crowd. "Been you yet to Havana?

I doubt it. Know you of anything that occurs upon this day or in the hesitant mind of Velasquez? I think not. Trust you a new king's wishes before an old one, perhaps? And would you place a service to your country before the requirements of the present throne?" Cortez searched Rodriguez's inner measure.

Rodriguez waited for a prompted contribution to proceedings. Beside him the soldier, resonant in a polished breast plate of Toledo steel, glowered beneath a dented helm of previous action, poised mid-sentence waiting tensely for an order.

Cortez's eyes slid slow with accusation down towards Rodriguez's sword. "Have you an affinity with that, or do I behold a mere peacock's plume for the wearing and attraction of young ladies? Or have you something else unseen, worthy of reliance?"

Rodriguez felt his mocking painfully. In place of making good impression, he was being held to ridicule instead but furthermore endured it, and willingly it seemed. He despised himself a moment then rallied to collect, to defend his self-possession and regain his lost respect. "You are correct to question loyalties, sir, for rightly you may have need of my assistance, of which I freely gift, but…"

"Assistance!" Cortez crowed a haughty laugh possessed of little humour for everyone to hear. "Glad of you to come, we are. I am assured," he scoffed, performing further to his subject crowd.

Rodriguez burned his pride affronted, thinking of how best to make amends or halt if nothing else, the accumulation of deep insult.

The soldier, hand on hilt, watched closely as his master toyed, mindful of a group of high-ranked officers that herded on the fringe of sight, uncertain and beleaguered by mistrustings of their own, concerning their Alcalde. Harbouring ill conspiracy between them, it was known their private ways were gaining loyalties unsure…although for the present time at least, ungauged reaction to these sentiments in such environment would stay their public tongues, if not their look, as guarded sinister and secret.

"I say only that I am here to serve. As regards my ordering of priorities.…Then I would add that for a man as am I, of little worldly status, to distinguish easily between kings or queens at such great distance lies beyond my privilege. I must be content therefore, to serve through chains of office and cannot do their bidding unless it drains alas, through lesser men," he paused, allowing words with weight to linger. "Thus my country must remain as upmost in my heart. But must you not also, and forgive I pray, uncourtly rudeness, serve through lesser men?" he remarked with due intent, strengthening the importance of repeated words.

"You have wit and a perception, and indeed a voice above your station," Cortez replied carefully, noticing the collected attention of untrustworthy men.

Those upon the sidelines waited for incriminating answers, keen with memories alerted.

"But in Spain all men are of equal value are they not?" Cortez played.

"We are no longer in Spain, sir. I am arrived here newly, if not fresh from Santo Domingo as you have surmised," Rodriguez countered bravely.

The officers whispered concealing their responses to the conversation.

Cortez laughed genuinely. "Quite so and there are many lesser men between myself and his majesty." He emphasised the lesser also, with delight. "Some gather reports…" Cortez found himself curtailed but allowed the indiscretion.

"And others gather to report…" Rodriguez glanced around at eavesdropped prying curiosity and returned a meaningful expression of allegiance intended to portray revulsion at such cowardly a practice.

"You will sail with me. Fret not upon arrangement…it is made. There is possibly more interest to be found in you as yet, Rodriguez." Cortez looked down on the soldier at Rodriguez's side, "Teach the man to use a weapon, Pedro. To cut as sharply as this tongue of his." He frowned at Rodriguez's sword. "A soldier's blade…and not this pauper's illustration." And then waved them both away.

Pedro's void came instantly refilled by the clerk now armed with quill and starched inventory brandishing again dishevelled persecution implored through haunted eyes.

Whilst acquiring for Rodriguez a new and worthy weapon, Pedro introduced himself as Pedro de Alvarado from Badajoz, a town that flourished near the border in south eastern Spain. He had enjoyed a long association with Cortez despite the numerous hardships and implied Rodriguez count himself as fortunate to receive this opportunity to join them in such a short unproven time, advising him to use the moment wisely, but further…not to disappoint.

Carracks and Caravels, eleven in all, were loaded and prepared for rapid cast off and the mastery of treacherous undercurrents that gossiped discontent their swirl around the port. Some had heard the expedition cancelled and considered their departing now a provocation of insulting merit from Cortez to Velasquez, who Cortez without much feigning pretence, suggested envious of his growing strength and fearful of perceived ambitious nature. Therefore could do nothing other than presume himself from Velazquez' sight as someone who undoubtedly would use the occasion to further endorse positioning…and justly so, with whatever he may find. For these reasons, Cortez had realised the shortest while ago that Velasquez would prevent his ever leaving and so was hastening events accordingly, before requested word could reach official interference from those northern regions of the island.

Cortez knew the moment far too good to let slip by and thus resolved, would set his sails regardless.

Their number totalled little more than half a thousand bearing crossbow, sword and musket with cannon also for their usage. Rodriguez observed the nervousness sweated from the small accompaniment of horses as they too were taken skittishly aboard. Then when all was settled each directed hearts and sights upon discovery, drawing eagerly from tales of latent treasure soon to be forthcoming and were quickly underway.

Hernando Cortez, proudly arrogant shielded by his self-belief, led the expedition from the front, keenly optimistic…for the realm of God, for Spain, for destiny but more deservedly, himself. His intention was to strike the peninsula and follow the coast to beyond the limits of reliable exploration then cut a forthright, cleansing swathe through the very heartland of this naive and childlike world. It was more than just a quest for riches he often told his men. They were bringing the highest qualities of Spanish civilisation and tradition to the heathen ways of savages that they might turn their heads away from courting with the Devil's favour and so become enlightened as were they. It was, in truth, a high crusade professed as duty bound to execute, where natives ought to come to know themselves in time, esteemed no less that it was they who had arrived there first and not the uncouth likes of some other, vulgar nation. Those then, under his authority must too, therefore consider themselves as proud to take their part in this, God's glorious application.

Rodriguez was comfortably swept along on the crystal clarity of shallow seas and like ideas for pairing, entranced and easy led from sight of land. Fleeing on towards whatever was to be and away from all they knew. To his first previewing of a new world's shore, and thence participation in the haut parading of their landing.

Cortez came ashore with flags unfurled declaring his intentions and walked upon the blanched, sand beaches with an air and stature undenied. Short lived, however, was that feeling of accomplishment whence but meagre showed the benefits of interacting with such humble people. In fact, woefully shy of expectation were demandings met, with there little progress being made either, as regards their discovering the exact locations of those fabled cities that had gifted them the inspiration for departure. So driven before the despair of yet another failed expedition and unable to return, Cortez tightened his grip for information, though tempered with a measurement of caution, his firmness on an increasingly resentful and uncooperative populace. Nevertheless hostile resistance did break out on numerous occasions to fall severely upon those of their number that foolishly strayed away on private quests and other matters, despite the threat of consequence. Finally Hernando's limited patience thus gave way to snapping fury, under duress he felt, to seize control. He turned his men with sword in hand, unleashing on their foe a keen-edged rage of retribution, subsequently finding all the same, that when at last complete dominion was attained, submission only was the single, hollow triumph there on offer.

Taking thereafter the favour of a dark-eyed princess girl, Malinche, as his justified reward, Cortez then changed her name accordingly to suit his way, renaming her Marina, of the sea, as testament and proclamation to the route of scant achievement.

Her halting tongue engaged adept by thoughtful mind would through association, bring salvation to the remnants of her folk...but for that purchase, she must bear the cost alone Malinche felt, compelling to prepare herself, reluctantly at first, as Cortez came henceforth each time to court her.

Blessed arresting beauty in delicate abundance, her eyes, her skin and hair so dark and soft, shone pure at heart and gentle but possessed of wily spirit also. A slender youthful form, as flowers the womanhood in springtime's sunkissed forest glade, her worship for to bloom, and flawless as in perfect yearning's crystal dream. Wearing wove beneath the mantle of enjoyment, the company and fragrance of desire itself as fresh as high sierra's glistened stream...closely wrapped about for gleeful pleasure's mutual acquaintance. Unattainable, she graced beyond all means and art that seemed to him improper or might indeed lend harm to soil her worth and yet with copious charms she frequent smiled...unknown to her the poignancy instilled instead by mirth.

Harmoniously at odds with this, dilemma's confrontation, she stood a suitor's prospect, Cortez could not, would not shame with hastened undue force nor underhand coercion. He proposed then for to spread the word of God, to pacify the nation and agreed on terms to tame another's vanquishing suppressor also, to enhance his individual questing for to know and feel her genuine love returned.

Rodriguez had played his part in the subduing of the Indians with pride, and honour hung on sternest backbone, words he gladly called unto himself, but when he looked upon the beauty of Cortez's treasure there he knew instead emotion stirred and lustful, passions of the beast denied.

Bereft alleviation thus he sought distraction, spurred to stallion's flight and flew away one morn' bewitched by such intriguing and uncomplicated innocence, until a time of thwarted mastery came forged on self-rebuke, to haunt forever true, but with finally a respite's solace in its place...of sorts. Though doomed now was his fate perceived, to know but consolation's love in dimmer pastures new. For he too, wished a share of this particular prize and was despite himself, ashamed.

Malinche told in a way, relating graphic detail the devilry which ruled the land, that left not even hardened men without some pity for her cause whence tears were let to roll unchecked on tender, blushing cheek. Where all who listened, though some laid claim to deafness, would henceforth resolve themselves to aid her. She spoke with an accomplished flare for her new adopted tongue and revealed to them with reason, the whereabouts of Tenochtitlan, the strongest foothold of the Mexica, beyond the mountains, King Moctezuma's island lair. Hernando pledged in turn, unto Marina, with a mind's encouragement towards her love, of their assistance there that night and declared his leadership to any Indian also who would follow, to rid the land of evil men extinguishing their tyranny....But it was soon understood that not all under the banner of Cortez rippled on a similar breeze. Some murmured quietly against proceeding, considering sufficient the advantage earned thus far to have at least regained a partiality with Velasquez. To further add their insult by suggesting for appeasement sake a wanting to return one day with greater number and the fullest will behind them...and likely Cortez thought, beneath a different standard also.

Being thereafter no longer convinced entirely of several misplaced loyalties and becoming increasingly less tolerant and angry, as was revealed in disrespectful slighting at every opportunity, Cortez finally ordered those that doubted in his cause to be forthwith installed upon their vessels with the merest of condolence, and forced whenever the occasion found it necessary.

So was continued beneath the billowed temperament of a growing unease, their voyage northward along the palm lined coast, that hemmed within, the steeply rising mountain peaks, slate greying to the west. Navigating around and through the coral reefs with care, passing by alluring, uncut turquoise gem lagoons and refreshing shaded inlets to the place from where Marina knew to travel overland to

Moctezuma's palace. Whereupon Cortez demanded of the ships that bore them, forth and ride the waves towards the beach for grounding. And when eventually darkness lay itself to blanket stillness nigh complete, and all required stores were deemed to be unloaded, Cortez and his men stood somberly on pledge and promise for to watch as silhouettes against Hell's furnaced background, the finality of wrecks' abandonment to charred remains was cast, retreating thoughts and inescapably...their homeward passage.

Each with hearts divided shook their mournful heads and bit sour words to silence, committed now regardless, stranded to the service of Cortez. Who, in ordering such an irreversible violation had sewed the seeds for later consternation, though would for now ignore those stifled murmurings of trivial consequences and reprisal and commence upon the spot, the town of Veracruz. Proclaiming in uplifted voice to bolster, that from 'here we cross the border to a new country' where reservations and a cautious hand be damned.

The initial foothold of their spirited adventure was thus established and Cortez, with due success and sword in hand, promoted himself to Captain-General of his private, land-bound army. However, whence driven on desire's advance once more, left only those who could be spared and trusted not to flee, in order to prepare with means and trade the flourishing of this, his first and crucial outpost. Rodriguez Maria Gonzalez was rewarded for unwavering devotion and a likened mind and hoisted to the closest ranks ahead the due receival of most others, providing room for jealous discontent to prosper, although as disregarded would it flounder in his wake.

The arrival of the Spanish, an occasion previously foretold it later came to light, was not for long, to be maintained a secret. Word of the shining gods aboard their strange-winged craft, gusted on the squalls that blew unrest throughout the land, reaching shortly, the attentive ears of Moctezuma enthroned inside his golden valley city many leagues inland, who in his wisdom acted on the news by sending out persuasive token gifts to find them with his warnings of retaliation should they dare to venture further on his realm. Which in place of fear's creation aroused but keen attention, tempting the allure of greedy men to hold suspicions of vast riches rather wished concealed.

Cortez and his men marched overland courageously without a thought now for discretion, casting down before their will with ease the resistance offered in futility and mere gesture, where native warriors, unprotected and poorly armed presented themselves in great attendance to the slaughter. Heroically, Cortez and his men butchered their way across the land against an overwhelming, under dogged opposition. Rodriguez earned the respect of the noblest and most common soldier alike along that irksome route. Protective of both horseback rider and the lowliest of ragged low, he waded through the choking sea of frenzied, bloodied faces, but still would find the time though none knew how, to aid those fallen, left behind, consumed beneath the heaving crush of onward surging infamy and lust.

Savagely relentless, the bare-skinned foe would throw themselves upon those disciplined formations with their torrid steel in hand, attempting to suffice on sheer numbering alone whence feathered spirit failed them, but at each occasion, deprived of conflict's unrealistic mercy they were hacked or lanced away and parried downward where from then their only further intervention was providing hindrance underfoot. The road to Moctezuma's gold was indeed paved deeply with the dead and dying for unsheathed steel is seldom dulled on skin or spent too much to want to slay again.

Battle followed battle until at last, ahead an awful rout of countless, Cortez stood as proud, defiant and above all else, victorious. Alongside, on either shoulder, sharing in the triumph were Rodriguez Maria Gonzalez and Pedro de Alvarado worn and wounded but joyous also to receive yet more the cowed, defeating of surrender. Marina came upon this time and took up converse with the broken, kneeling leader, there making known to him restriction's offer clear, to be claimed outright the lives of his remaining, or continue on against a common foe together, henceforth within the higher service of Cortez...and a dwindling, ever distant Spain.

When agreed, the gods on horseback returned from over sea, charged to cleanse the land of Aztec rule, received them willingly among their swelling masses, spreading moreso now the front of stormed rebellion along their westward march...but at that time and unbeknown another spread made rampant its minute but grim, diseased appearance...although for now would wait with patience, as clandestine in their shadows for the best deployment of its deadly charge.

Nevertheless, victory seldom finds itself without a price and this was no exception. For here then as they faced the lull returned, though briefly it might be, they took the time and buried fallen comrades not forgotten, to place both dead and living thus amid the bosom of God's ease. But as is likewise, frequently the nature of a loss, a gain is oft presented lain along another's path, so it was that one such benefit befell Rodriguez, no less the fortune of to ride straight course beside his Captain-General at the forefront of their conquering forces.

From this lofty positioning, he grasped the opportunity to air his thoughts whence gazing out together on the wondrous smoking mount of Popacatapetl upon the hour they skirted closely by, and also when at last they stopped in sudden awe, to view before them spread below, the valley of the Mexica stretched far unto the distant lake of Texcoco, and afloat within, the island heartbeat of the Aztec nation, Tenochtitlan.

An arachnid shimmering of sun-drenched burnished gold, whose beaming rays splayed cautious out upon its web to touch with pensive feel, the surrounding, lowland shoreline, and soundless steal intent along a mass of causeways interspersed with buoyant gardens, dominated by the growth of maize...chinampas, Marina, Cortez heard, entitled them, reflecting light back to the very heavens themselves for illumination of the farm land all around. Cortez and his men now deemed themselves as duly compensated for their faith...God had indeed delivered to their hand the wealthiest of heathen habitations for the funding of his work.

Unopposed, Cortez led his wary army inside the city confines, filing past the silent, curious lines of bowed, averted, downcast stares where clearly it was seen that word of their arrival had preceded them.

The previously unguessed might and skill of the Mexica people arose in splendour and magnificence from every pave walked street and avenue, rich and vast enough to equally compare with any cluttered city, even in the noble realm of Spain.

Temples, palaces, the many houses of the rich, stepped up with robust styling to confront an azure sky's temptation, soaring sheer from wide and tall tree shaded routes and promenades. With schools to teach the growing offspring fully of their ways and there instill in them their culture's knowledge, dreams and aspirations. Where ornately carved reliefs of complex fretwork would adorn facades with images both strange and wonderous, and yet adversely gruesome to behold.

Immovable and resolute, with order and with history, the natural features of a stable land sprung forth, allowed. Ripened orchards and divine the luscious gardens flowed away on scented glee beyond inquiry's eyesight...though too, and unashamedly this aromatic pleasure masked to incomplete, another odour quite dissimilar...somewhat cloying in suggestion, with faint its nausea, stalking pungence, undefined.

Following Tenochtitlan's course towards the tensely nervous focus of the complex, they would find immersion pressed among the collected horde of grave expectancy afoot King Moctezuma's pyramidal greatness, where stood the dignitaries diffident, as painted from a deep and common font of diverse colour...feathers boldly scarlet, virgin forest greens and winter's frozen whites. Each awaited their approach absorbed abnormal with a naive, unbefitting reverence that invoked the sentiment of just obedience in some but which others found disturbing.

Moctezuma, enthroned aloft a royal bier, came borne processional on the shoulders of entrusted household staff beneath a shaded canopy of pearls and jewels for each to see respectful, would that any dared to look in his direction...but for those in armour none would witness this arrival.

Courtiers blindly tried to line the way as best they could by laying down luxurious cloth to spoil and flowers for destroying, fearful of his countenance at touching common ground, until released the labour only whence his resting came affront Cortez and his bewildered, dumbstruck men.

Rodriguez looked out disdainfully over the humbling submission of those subjected to their staring meekly at the floor and turned away the higher worth of his attentions to the temple sides nearby, where a myriad skull formations grinned a greeting, carved to catch the eye. Meticulously set in thousands, row upon macabre row, the sight provoked a will to raise the hackles and impose upon fainthearted....But then a chilling light of understanding opened further wide, this seasoned soldier's eyes whence dawned the perfect truth behind such sculpturing formed not through substitution but in fact of bleached white, cobbled bone.

Disgusted almost to convulsing, Rodriguez cast his sight elsewhere from trophies of the dead to then espy another, keenly watching he.

High above the city interest, atop the temple tiers, one stood unbowed at odds, a phantom robed in sacred black, unmoved, distinct from humble view. Reeked ominous beneath a covering hood poured out, conveyed through probing eyes, a dread that no less made itself amid the shadows known...chill potency concealed within unsettled brooding malice.

Moctezuma spoke and in so doing he was echoed by Marina. He welcomed them and granted freedom of his city. They talked at length with neither discord nor with humour interrupting....and all the while the heads stayed cowed apart from one alone who muted, would observe intently from the distance...thus did the day pass contradictions, stopped both sinister and peaceful. Their host provided food and residence without requesting recompense, before, as sun went down behind their mountain realm, returning to his business.

Throughout the days that followed, the Spanish found themselves increasingly appalled to sickened stomachs by the depravities that endless played for entertainment's sake disguised within the foulest rituals performed in name of them and thankless gods. An insatiable thirst was sought to quench in payment for their world, where human life when not consumed fell sacrificed undaunted on a thought defying scale. Where too the stench of decomposing flesh and content clung now recognised about a city's rancid fester on the entrails of its evil scented filth.

The abhorrent nature of this new found place was proving hardship to abide where only lust for wealth could keep them compromised to stay against the need to breathe fresh air again. And so the stealthy guile adopted first soon crept without due caution unremorsefully to hastened greed spurred virile on returning thoughts of yearned for Spain, as Cortez led, flanked ever by Marina, in the press for gold himself, abetted with the feverish, oft uncompromising aid of his companions to wherever dallied promise.

The reward was deemed, however, insufficient for their number, rising to the issue of requests in time, for granting private audience in the palace to discuss arrangements further. Demands nevertheless that floundered undeservedly, or so was felt on all the impropriety of rebuffed delay, infuriating the Captain-General to the point of future leniency's consideration, though in truth despite his disposition he kept curt patience well.

Having climbed the many steps above the central plaza at the eventual hour of appointment, they came upon a feast of honour to assuage as compensation laid for splendour in abundance.

The royal household flickered warm and private gloomy from the scented lamps that flared along the heavy stone blocked walls, empty but for servants in attendance of his lordship, Moctezuma seated grandiose upon a carved and fearsome throne, whose upper workings styled in pouncing jaguar form would awe recall in those, not merely the displeasure of their personal audience but more distressingly, cold notions of them being rightly seen as prey….His counsel though, lived not for vanity's attention and remained discreet, unseen by most through choice within its murky umbra.

The king motioned each to find their seats as befitted either status or their friendships and gave misleading his impression of a solace found amid strained new association whilst encouraging also of his guests, enjoyment from the fare provided.

Long were the restless moments that ensued hung silent in the lapping flames of mistrust where nobody wished the pleasure of consuming first and each instead would watch of his companion daring to begin. Rodriguez, henceforth Rodriguez 'el osado' when named in jest, was inspired then to take the lead and gorge with careless, wild abandon. Boastful of his fearlessness, he clambered proudly onto the stone slab table spread before him to the goading chants of 'atrevido,' grabbed an unknown cut of meat, kicked aside the rest to punctuate his arrogance and publicly assumed the daring title from more feeble minded friends. Suddenly the hall erupted likewise to the unbridled bravado of excited feasting, each inwardly now feeling cowardly usurped by the young Rodriguez and therefore frothing with desire to amend.

Gradually as stomachs filled, the merriment becalmed itself to murmured conversation, where the occasional wine-induced forgotten song stained mere backdrop as a jaded tapestry to hang befuddled, bloodshot plastered in the corners.

"Sir," Rodriguez whispered to Cortez, "the gentleman behind the throne." He glanced up quickly and indicative.

Cortez managed a sly flicker of his eyes returning his gaze without attention drawn, back to the remnants of his food before him. "An old minister or courtier perhaps." Indifference guessed. "What of him?"

"Well," Rodriguez began thoughtfully, "this may sound foolish but... I shall say it anyway."

"What man? Spit it out!" Cortez hissed.

"I could not help but notice the manner in which his necklace so reflects lime zest to bite the light...so, so keenly....and yet. It drew my full attention reminding me of something...or someone...I was unsure as regards to which, but now when I look again with eyes alerted and specific my mind finds clarity anew and there I see distinguishing similarities bearing more than mere resemblance to an old recluse that once lived near my village, whom I used to visit as a child. Leave apart those eyes...the forehead, nose and chin may not be much to speak of individually perhaps...but when all these traits are bound together...it has...well...fascinated me." Rodriguez was resisting his urge to stare whilst sensing too his conversation's failure to impress with naught but mounting disregard. "Would you not also find it strange then that such a fine and unique piece of jewelry, whose manufacture was so assuredly inspired, fall as victim to the accident of mere random duplication or that similarities of birth are manifested in another so acutely half the world away from here?" he pressed.

"An accident of birth, nothing more. Each of us, even I, am assumed to have a likeness somewhere. This association you have conjured up I deem, belongs unwittingly to a weathered statue that we passed some time ago, near the outskirts whence along our route of entry." Expressing dwindled his small interest in the subject, Cortez spoke as one in condescending tone for making light instead upon another's dour affliction.

"I have no recollection of seeing such a thing," snapped Rodriguez.

"Nevertheless," he dismissed, "let us drain this slop that masquerades as wine and turn attentions on to where they serve us better. To unearthing the fruitful source of this exported jade of yours? Or perhaps even to our finding lowly gold. Both expenses and expectancy run high, Rodriguez. You are aware of feelings in the ranks, are you not? The need is great for our success if we wish ever to return to Spain." Hernando Cortez was feeling the cold draught of whispered rumour drying on his neck again, a chill that only sunshine could relieve…Spanish Golden sunshine. "Besides, as already you have said, your last sighting of the man came through the eyes of infancy. Am I not correct? What other memory have you that assures lucidity its credit over equal years to any accurate degree?" Cortez played with the food, prodding it suspiciously with his knife.

"The eyes are alone sufficient in themselves to stir remembrance. And those years may not be as remote for some as doubtless they appear to others," he barbed.

Cortez felt the prong and laughed. "Does the young pup seek to sire the bitch himself?" Although the jest fell humourless upon a frown of ill-receipt as he continued, "Do you believe then that your friend, the hermit, flew to Spain from here, or rather that this furtive individual is indeed the self same traveller with whom you had acquaintance? Surely not? Only childlike minds would dress such nonsense with belief…" The trailing of that final jibe however, revealed a curiosity aroused to more than mildest interest as yet sceptical, he gauged his trusted with due merit.

"Odd that you should suggest he flew."

"I was mocking."

"Regardless....He was named the Crowman...and not only by the children. His attire is, or was the same as this you see before you, but I restate the fact that there is a great deal identical and much of it unique to these particular two alone, among all those not in stone carved form that I have ever seen outside of multiple birthing."

Rodriguez's insistence prompted Cortez to view again the man concealed behind the king. "I concede there are strained features that might remain with me, had I little else to concern myself with. Owed I expect to the tightness of that headband. But again, I place no measure of importance on the matter."

"There lies another curiosity," Rodriguez blurted, betraying his unseemly excitement. "They both are, or were apt to wear these headbands, with the stones in them."

"Stones?" A looked of tired puzzlement sat upon Cortez's face.

"Indeed. I'll wager all the gold we haven't found yet, if one were to remove the band, though in this I doubt he would comply, one would find stones of lode stitched across the banding. There...those pieces..." Rodriguez indicated with his finger and nodded with conviction. "I guarantee it."

"What are you saying, man? Come on out with it." Cortez's impatience rose above his intrigue. "Is there to be conclusion to your idle banter?"

"I'm not sure, but I feel that these coincidences are entwined too closely to be dismissed as mere chance. Your leadership alone has shown me that to be a failing. However strange or insignificant things may on the surface seem, this man and the hermit whom I knew as a child are kindred. Of this I am sincere and certain. Incidentally, as but curious reflection, nobody ever made assumption as to where the crow man hailed from, though it was rumoured his arrival chanced among our lineage on the back of some tempestuous storm one night, but from which direction...." Rodriguez shrugged, raising the open palms of baffled ignorance.

"From the north, are you not?" Cortez asked with the trace of a forspent sigh.

"Catalonia, sir," Rodriguez answered proudly .

Cortez rubbed his eyes and slumped his elbow on the table to assist in propping up his weary head. "Are you and yours truly inclined to believe in fairy stories as much as rumour has it? How would the hermit have come to Catalonia from here or hereabouts? For I think we can dispense with the idea that this king's counsellor has his origins in Spain."

"We alone have proven, have we not, sir, that the world rolls as a sphere?"

"Precisely we alone. No other. Not the English nor the French nor Dutchmen. Did none think to ask the man from whence he came? A simple task…"

"Evidently not," Rodriguez responded curtly.

"You Catalonians, I'm sure I've said before, are far too trusting ever to achieve upon your insulated wisdom." Cortez sensed the need to sniff a jocular awareness.

Rodriguez stood up, to the surprise of the hall. Conversation ceased immediately with entertaining expectations running high around their finest youthful upstart. And looking directly at the figure now attempting to melt his drift discreetly coy imbibed within the folds of hide that hung around the throne, beckoned him directly to emerge forth to the light.

Throughout the meal thus far the advocate had, in clandestine guise turned whisper many times towards his king to frequently effect the shifting of his regal posture. A communication which had not passed by Rodriguez' notice. Now however, it was justly felt the time that he, the humble Catalonian should have his say on matters also. When he spoke, Marina got dutifully to her feet and instrumentally interpreted converse.

"What function do you perform, sir, that finds its practice disadvantaged out among us in the light? Are you fearful of our presence or so prideful of your own that it forbids for you to walk and talk around the likes of us fool strangers sullying your midst?" Rodriguez quizzed with all his recently acquired disrespect.

The old man glared, exposed to the pry of foreign eyes providing them with overlong discomfort in the moment. Rodriguez felt the tension rise and began to wish he had perhaps, observed a little longer. "Well?" He pushed. "Have you no words of counsel for the rest of us? Or speak you only to the dignity of kingship? If that be so, then I feel obliged to inform you of my royal station through descent forthwith and announce my kingdom Catalonia, one glorious realm across the sea."

The soldiers laughed their insolence at such a proclamation, deriding too his elevation's sombre silence and whatever else the figure might have stood for.

Knowing not the honesty of words at first intent was plain to see…and thus intolerable was spawned each further moment to endure, unredeemed. Hence the blighted contours shuffled forward to the torch-lit room seen heavily reliant on the staff that bore its crouching weight. Writhing as a snake in torment yet contrasted strong, unyielding was the wood that wrought its length to suffocate with pensive click approach across the stone paved, callous floor…and atop with polished lustre at the level of the eye, the striking snake's head shone, a menace deep with essence forged inside.

Age-corroded caustically on rigid, sharpened features but beneath, slack draped across delusion's buckled frame. "I am Rashtak-oatl." The presence stated clearly and sufficient.

Rodriguez looked around at his companions expressing feigned his disbelief conceited in the farce, raising there derision's laughter once again though now was tinged with nervousness denied. Uncertainly, Marina looked to Cortez for reassurance, knowing full the gravity of circumstance and position held to ridicule. Cortez smiled and nodded openly sanctioning her actions, raised himself also, to his feet alongside Rodriguez, halted briefly, to snatch the hall's attention, then neared the scowling dignitary and began encircling ponderously his intimidation to impress, stroking through both judgement and his beard, to deliberate effect. Eventually he stopped and stood before the twisted knot of ancient manhood, peering intensely at the curious headdress regarding it perhaps as true, the suggestion of Rodriguez. Rashtak-oatl exchanged with ease the glare the conquistador inflicted and maintained his silent self-assured stare of resolution without the need of costing.

"My impulsive colleague here," Cortez indicated to Rodriguez vaguely, unwilling to release his eye, "believes that there exists uncanny likeness between yourself and another in his homeland oversea. A kinsman...or a brother perhaps? Have you insight to impart?"

Rashtak-oatl's stony visage flickered for to mark the slightest of abruptness with unexpected, pleasurable surprise. A sentiment betrayed to Cortez's close perception only. "I see the circumstance provokes arousal in your bearing, despite all efforts to the contrary. I myself, have not gauged the substance of this other man's acquaintance but entrust that I have measured yours. Have I not? So please, humour me if you will and disclose your interest in this counterpart, so very far away."

Cortez was answered with a quiet, passive withdrawal as Rashtak-oatl became distracted by a long-enduring and more personal concern.

"Trust in this, old man. If you do not respond, I will cut the tongue from your clam-like, wizened head, henceforth to flap adornment at my neck as heathen charm!" Cortez was not to be refused his answer.

Moctezuma leant forward and with daring hesitation lightly prompted his advisor with regards to revelations. Rashtak-oatl sighed testily impatient returning to the present, his skeletal frame arising pointedly beneath the heavy folds conveying physical frailties previously but guessed at.

"I am Rashtak-oatl," Unaccustomed repetition coldly re-informed, whilst translated duly by Malinche's echo. "I know nothing of another's semblance to my own. Just as I know nothing of the land from which you hail, although it is now I muse, my purpose to learn more of it, but also, from you too I must take a satisfaction." His intentions fell upon Rodriguez with that hanging utterance and delayed there for a momentary measure before turning back to Cortez. "As for my position...I merely advise his majesty on simple, mundane matters that occur within this realm as I have been at liberty to do beyond his reckoning." The response was curt but delivered with intentional consideration.

"Yet, you alone consult this night upon occasion of

importance....Or judge us simple and mundane? I think not. Rather, I believe you sell your titles lightly and that the mere old man's wisdom which clearly you possess conceals a worth of far more import than your pretences would have me otherwise accredit."

Rashtak-oatl saw the implications mounting. The searching questions that were certainly to follow, tiredly under threat of death no doubt, would seek out deeper answers, and the further his retreat towards the hidden corners of completed lies and half-truths, then the greater would responses be required to alleviate inquiry, and so carefully professed, apparently relenting. "My people," he began, "are now but few and distant flung, seldom do we meet. We dress this way," Rashtak-oatl had loathed Cortez's close examination of his robe and saw he needed explanation. "...out of a traditional loyalty and nothing more. We were and some may yet still be, a nomadic people. I, as you see, am not. The kinship with my brethren dwells only in a memory...as frail indeed as I...and equally as vague. With surety until this day, I was aware of no others, and so concede am rightly glad, to understand that you know more, more in truth than I."

"By what name are your people known?" Cortez's tone became more genial having drawn presumed advantage from submissive issue.

"When young, we walked with Itar the ancient one," Rashtak-oatl paused for thought, "but our name was lost. We have since been distinguished with many titles, although I prefer the higher nomination Itzamancha." He continued evenly, defying either challenge or doubtful contradiction....which in itself sufficed to alter rash opinion, for the immediate time at least.

"Then there was no reason to allow your previous silence to be misconstrued as shame. None that I can see. You should be proud of your lineage, senor Rashtak," Cortez encouraged condescendingly.

"Rashtak-oatl." But was corrected with a firm solemnity.

Cortez took the lunge and held a while regarding well the context of correction before finally permitting the remark to fall unanswered. He turned to Rodriguez, feigning further questions but instead sensing it unnecessary to pursue the subject at this juncture, requested solely with a private glance, obedience in his leaving things aside.

"We have much to speak of, Rashtak," Cortez persisted with imposition, undeterred.

"Much," Rashtak-oatl replied unto himself. Slighted and annoyed at lack of due respect, he turned his penetrative gaze upon Rodriguez and searched his mind for more unguarded revelations. Rodriguez returned the cold, dark stare and reflected on the purpose of withholdings, regarding overmuch unsaid. They remained in glanced exchange a time before the loss of interest and the call of wine brought slow, the soldier to be seated. The rest of the evening passed without event, suffered in forced brevity, each awkwardly aware of the discomfort felt within the other's presence. Mistrust held the drinkers hand and a cautious distancing prevailed until with excess courtesy Cortez relieved his comrades of their tolerance and ordered them to quarters.

Descending the palace steps the Captain-General dallied long enough for Rodriguez to reach his side with a mind to hold discussion on the way.

"Tell me more of this hermit," Cortez spoke softly, barely above the whisper for expected overhearing's sake.

Rodriguez, shrugged and taxed the recall of his childhood. "He was likewise, an old man whose estimated age was equally unfathomable, again extending beyond the limits of a tired body's natural span. Never have I nor any other that I know of, witnessed such an age on one who clings so handsomely to life…and yet as I envisage him again he appeared to exist forever pressed…haunted even and therefore as a consequence more among the living than this Rashtak-oatl."

"Hunted perhaps?"

"Maybe…but I saw nothing to substantiate this most hindsighted of impressions."

Cortez nodded. "As for this one, if he had been dead and resurrected some years later I doubt he would make more wholesome spectacle and probably smell the better for it, but neither do I doubt that the pantomime of his shuffling demeanour is as much purposeful as it is a falsehood."

"Nor I," Rodriguez continued. "He too attired himself in black though. Not the strain of costly darkest grey fit only for a royal son's investment, but as you see, a shade akin to long dead cat's eye blackness, a privilege to behold with that richness unseen prior to his coming, courting not however, the maintenance afforded this particular advocate. He spoke of distant lands, also over sea. Relating yarns in which we found our entertainment often on a long, warm summer's eve.

Far reaching travel as we know, bestows a certain depth of wisdom and he held his volumes in great store. He could cure ailments in the beast, adult and child alike, predict the seasons also but more importantly the variance of impending winds precisely using sun and stars to guide him."

"You speak of heresy," Cortez remarked matter of factly.

"I know not, sir. We found no harm within the man and gladly kept his secret, for on no occasion did he err or seek to gain advantage. Quite unto the contrary in fact, for frequently we felt that his obliging us ran only to his detriment, whence cursing afterwards with bouts of deepest melancholy to a point some saw as reaching madness. A sense of regretful loss or suffered guilt perhaps, that drove him off to search each early day, a little island out across the bay. Why? No one understood and few dared ask. More than that I cannot say, but for the lodestone headband as I have already spoken, the necklace and the tricks he used to play. We were children and respectfully in awe." Rodriguez shrugged away his lack of further detailed knowledge.

"And now?" Cortez asked.

"Now, what, sir?" Rodriguez answered bluntly.

"Are you not now transfixed in similar awe despite your age and travel? This Rashtak-oatl commands an inconceivable respect, does he not? And I deem it through some device or art and not singularly from the phenomenon of living to endure the erosion of his statue's gaze…for now I sense that each are more than likely linked."

"I find it curious that two seeds from a similar, if not exactly the same tree should be blown so far apart in a lifetime, even one that breaches generation's boundaries.…but as to the natural root of their origins and what could possibly be gained from acquiring such information.…My thoughts are not precise."

"Have you not felt the inner strength residing? I was close to him, it reached out, I could feel it. This quiet self-consumption is born of an arrogance which surpasses physical stature…but not I think concealed ability….Beyond his years or supposed lowly status? Such audacious nerve, affronting all for any reason?" Cortez shook his head perplexed, "I am caused to give it wonder." And was largely ignoring Rodriguez, preferring instead to ponder the scarred impression Rashtak-oatl had left behind.

"What is it that you imply, sir? Are you bewitched? Do you believe there to be sorcery at work here? What next, that the women's talk of youth bestowing springs and magic waters…are they to be pursued henceforth as credible? Who now has been drawn on curious tales and flights of fancy?" Cortez glowered at Rodriguez who respectfully softened his tone before continuing. "You cannot expect me to entrust importance to such nonsense. Nonsense at best, my lord. For now I think it is you that speak of devilry and heresy, or at least those with looser tongues might call it so."

"And you…how would you have it then titled?"

"My sword, sir, as well you know, is yours. I am a soldier, and that will be the only title I assume."

"This is a strange land. There is much here that we do not know," Cortez spoke distantly, quite prepared to believe in anything that might bring even partial triumph to his thankless undertakings.

"I agree." Rodriguez nodded. "I agree that there is much that this old man will tell us, now that we have wriggled him toward the light and made fast his will as ours, but as for…"

Cortez's voice raised unpredictably. "You think that you can own this man's will? If so, then you misjudge him at your peril. He has parried us off with half-truths, silence and disinterest and you believe that you have the measure of him? I assure you that any compensation or insightful lore acquired from this individual may well prove itself a worthy prize but will all the more be hard to win. His mind is strong, the people here are his. Even the king, it seems to me, follows at his bidding…though whether or not in this he is compliant…." Cortez paused to reassure himself that the conversation stayed as private.

"….we may have time enough to see. He does not fear us regardless of our weapons or achievements. Be wary and alert for he will seek to find his gains at your expense, Rodriguez. I see it in his manner. You have awakened something that has hitherto lain dormant, and placed a dark desire stirring now within his heart. Whatever that entails. I refuse to make assumption…but I know that he is dangerous and requires as such, the most careful of approaches."

"I believe….May I speak freely?"

"I have always permitted your doing so before," snapped Cortez.

"I believe you show a greater respect of this old man than is truly necessary. I think coincidences can and do occur. I regard this Rashtak." He dismissed the power behind the throne with a flurry of his hand. "To enshroud himself in mystery for protection and feigns an inner worth not lurking there in fact, which by my reckoning makes him fearful and therefore weak. You have the reckoning of him, sir. Of that I am convinced."

Cortez appeared dubious but was torn between a massaged ego and his instinct. "Maybe so, but fear can also be a valuable and dangerous ally. Whatever the reason for it. As yet though I disagree and believe him unafraid, so would see it kept that way, for the present time at least. To that end then, I order that you neither corner nor restrict him. I shall allow his freedom to practice however he must for now, but shall inevitably speak with him again, when the occasion so demands it," Cortez concluded.

"Indeed, sir." Rodriguez found his position painfully reasserted and retreated to the seclusion of his chamber.

He was housed, as were most others, in a complex vast and plush, expensively adorned with ornate furnishings and hanging tapestries of varied, clever woven colouring and intricate design. Where too even the diligent sculpturing of simple household wares betrayed to mock the whereabouts of thus far undetected, promised riches. Hastily cleared of all its guests immediately upon their arrival, Hernando had set their operations centre there, surrounded constantly by speculation from his closest and most trusted.

Marina entered softly on hearing Rodriguez's receding footsteps stamping angrily along the empty, flagstone hallway, and crossing the brooding solitude of deep concern in which Cortez had put himself to lay, she chose to ease her lover's mind and aid to his fulfillment, firm desires of the flesh.

Inquiry into the city's hidden affluence had met throughout, with at best, a peaceful obstinacy. Each discourteous access and appropriation finding in their path, a certain cordiality that often turned attempts aside resisted, only for to fuel alas, frustration's escalation in accordance on both sides where tensions once were stifling, hereafter simmered at their highest edge, towards the copious overflowing of destruction's boil. Then came one day as Cortez and his men had reached the straining note of tether's end, foul news returned from messengers long previously sent out, that Veracruz was overrun and mercilessly sacked. Set upon by a frenzied host of native warriors intent on slaying everyone who dwelt there she succumbed complete and in her fall would mark the graves of many. Those obedient who stayed behind awaiting on Cortez's proud return and were not slain were forced to hiding or were driven to their seaward succoured ends beneath the unforgiving waves.

Whilst Cortez's back was turned, the knife had struck thus easily and deep with an implication so enraging with its sense of treason that it twisted features far beyond the recognition, even of familiars for his mind became as dark and cold as ocean's depths with bloody thoughts of swift revenge. Immediate was his return then forced, to Moctezuma wistfully indulging in his palace.

Incensed with spitting fury, he ascended to demanding recompense from those involved and furthermore divulgence of their whereabouts. Rodriguez was on hand to watch as Cortez sharp applied his fearsome malice unrestrained, seeing too upon that regal face the likely truth of innocence and ignorance toward events revealed…thus it was he caught suspicion of another's hand involved. But from cowering, names were tendered all the same whence Moctezuma gave his dubious issue regardless of impending fates, exchanging rather, for the promise of his own dear life and exclusion from affairs.

So must be the only option for ungodly men, to seek and barter then postponement from their judgement day, Rodriguez thought. Eager to exempt himself whilst settling scores of old perhaps, through manipulating Cortez as a necessary weapon....Either way the sins continued mounting.

Moctezuma's selected victims were rounded up and herded like the bovine for parading to the central plaza, baiting every skirmished confrontation that inevitably broke out to find its opportunity come scythed abruptly with the flash of cleansing Spanish steel. Public execution was to follow endorsing Cortez's cruel intolerance to those he deemed as traitors, whereupon the entire city down to the most evasive child was forced to stand and watch. Only the king and palace staff escaped their sordid plight, Cortez having declared it beneficial that they squat as penned for now, secured hostages from sight.

Hearts and minds were hardened on that day, there turning a collective fear to seething, silent rage, whilst justice was again renamed the sword of vengeance, felling each at little cost. The final, hate-filled taunts however, thought veracious for consistent was their number, foretold of doom to come avenging. Of others, conquistadores, similar to they, arrived and long since charged with bringing Cortez to his downfall...his corpse to feed the glut of crows and thence remove whatever failed digestion as example back to Cuba. Cortez stepped among the bodies putting halt to hear proceedings in his stylish boots of finest leather, from Spain to blood of foreign land and heresy to soil.

The wicked interrogation of the remaining few produced reports of an innumerable force of soldiers that exceeded his by thousands, on a march determining to end their quest and seize all meagre plunder.

Cortez glared with deepest loathing to the palace where hid king craven Moctezuma shamed and shrunk amid the fuming spoil of cowardice and spat upon the nearest of the last to fall deriding. In league with Velasquez, he deemed, and doubtless harbouring smirked preference towards the thought of throwing each of them as carrion to the dogs and vermin thereabouts...and on that count gave airing to assumption.

No matter, he was after all, Hernando Cortez, his achievements equalled those of the great Alexander himself. He would not be quite so easily consumed by any.

Pedro de Alvarado, Rodriguez Maria Gonzalez and the other faithful, came when bidden to his side and together strode as loftily uncaring through atrocities that spewed about to dampen naught but studded heel, and climbed the steep stepped incline of the palace for a second time that day to come forthwith to where the lowly Moctezuma lay.

"What manner of treachery do you practice in these halls?" Cortez demanded with death's intention gravely etched upon his face.

The king in turn, confused at first, recoiled as terror filled his eyes, shifted dangerously at knife-point but maintained a while, his trembled silence to the hostile storm that crushed on hand besieging. And when eventually Moctezuma offered up a mumbled utterance in response, Marina's tongue translated but Cortez neither cared nor listened for his answer. He had made his move for better or for worse, events were underway, so called more men to reinforce the guard upon the hall allowing none to gain their entry whilst reiterating none must find escape. While he held the king entombed and while the situation lasted, he would continue to gather whatever frugal wealth he could attain and govern the city as his own, which for now it truly was. The onslaught of Velasquez' soldiers he opted to encounter soon enough…but on the terms of his own choosing.

With palace residents amassed, and every breach within the stronghold sealed secure, Cortez turned at pace and haughty out onto the terrace overlooking his dominion. Pedro and Rodriguez assumed their now accustomed positions on either shoulder and put their gazes also to the coast, preparing for to face the coming tempest.

"A good day's work." Seemingly unaffected by events, Cortez's tone was light, his banter trolling well the shallows of facetiousness. "We now have control of the city. What shall we do with it? I wonder."

Rodriguez sniffed deep, prideful lungs of great achievement from the air and oversaw the littered, blood-soaked butchery that stained afresh their square. "When time enough allows, good conscience ought to strive for severing of these people utterly from vile and nauseous ways. Foremost, I regard that to be our duty as fair men of clarity whose light extends from higher birth." And then he stated noble aspirations.

Pedro concurred, "The many demons that exist with welcome in this place must indeed be cast aside. Only-then will we have purchased the required control of hearts and minds to mould anew and cleanse. Even if it costs them all, their tortured lives to purge."

"Quite, and yet our first priority lies in stemming the advancing tide of our own brotherhood. Velasquez will want whatever we have earned however wanting our accounts may be. It is his nature to usurp another's victory, Pedro this you know from past events, Rodriguez, you must trust me. But believe this also, I shall not permit such thievery to befall again. Therefore the. strength we have attained since our valiant arrival here must now be turned, I fear upon our own. Pedro…" He looked respectfully into the unwavering eyes of his loyal consort. "You will have to remain during our absence and hold firm order in my stead. This palace is now beyond the reach of all but Spanish blood, on pain of death. Maintain the life of Moctezuma until my return and continue to seek the tribute. God's work too, has its price, far better that the Devil pays. Do you fully understand the demandings of your charge and office?"

Pedro nodded and stood erect with honoured salutation, displaying fine his thrust of breastplate proudly. "Rodriguez Maria Gonzalez. My friend. I know now that I have no need to ask whether you will assist in aiding myself and God, before your country…"

"Lesser men, sir," Rodriguez corrected. Maintaining his outward stare, unmoving and as resolute as ever he was in past commitments made.

"Yes, lesser men…of course," Cortez mused half-smiling. "The palace is summarily declared the private residence of King Moctezuma and his Spanish administration." He returned his attention to Pedro de Alvarado and made his proclamations. "A new order is decreed today, by Moctezuma. Make known my wishes as his own. Pedro, you have sole authority now. Hold your station well until my return. Spain and God himself gain in wealth and prominence each moment by our actions. Can you not feel the depth and meaning of these deeds? It is no accident I say, that such important times have fallen unto our redeeming hands. It is but God's glorious application of design at work. Do you now recognise as clear as I, the relevance of our being here? Damnation! I can almost taste it!" He enthused with passion to behold.

Both nodded solemnly. "And of the gold, sir?" Pedro inquired conspiratorially. "Are you now enlightened as regards its whereabouts that I may concentrate my efforts better...or should I question the minister Rashtak-oatl on the matter?"

"No. He is not to be disturbed or inconvenienced in any way unless it is absolutely necessary. I have other intentions for that one."

"Very well. I pray for your swift return. God's speed!" Bowing low, Pedro ended the conversation and retired inside striding purposefully away to execute his duties.

Cortez and Rodriguez made their way together back down to the plaza, where the city breathed and pulsed collective heartbeats in restraint.

As frustrated as the assemblage were, they would through lack of prominent leadership, albeit from behind the resulting veil of fragile impotence that situation so imposed, do Cortez's bidding, at the behest of Pedro de Alvarado....and furthermore, supposedly endorsed now by the strength of royal command must surely turn at last, possessions over to the unknown cause, Hernando Cortez felt.

Leaving only those who could be spared, Cortez left the capital Tenochtitlan ahead of his followers with a purpose to annul complete the contemptuous ill of misdirected retribution. Being experienced and fully trained in all concerns of conflict likewise devious and noble, Cortez deployed his force with guile to sound advantage and surprised the soldiers sent to win his capture, cutting short an unprepared advancement on a sad and grief filled day when countrymen fought countrymen and personal friendship also, oft confused itself, suffice to die as foe. Those not of the fallen who declined to turn and flee found invitation to unite with kindred and increase the might still further of Cortez's outlawed army. Pledging loyalty and services renewed there on the promised draw of gold, old oaths were rendered into two beneath the wielded axe of greed. Where too, allegiances became exchanged across the drink of avarice and speculation's makeshift gaming tables, blind to aught else but perspectives on good fortune.

Cortez returned attentions towards the sacred valley of the Mexica. Though he would come to empty fields, abandoned in the listless, tempered air, hungover with defining anxiousness that stressed dissension's brittle calm.

Disturbing then the allied multitude came thundered over silent causeways on into the tautness of a brooding city grim expecting their arrival. To the heart of Tenochtitlan where the royal plaza's confine throbbed and confrontation once again embraced its grisly scene of routine execution.

Pedro de Alvarado stood his ground at fault for driving hard against resistance with intolerant and unleashed hand whilst baying crowds encircled palpitating on the edge of his demands unwilling to continue yielding more of their requested assets...and from aloft his temple's high enclosure Rashtak-oatl watched today, the deeds unfold, impassive and unblinking.

Welcome shone relief from Pedro's brow at last, on seeing sympathetic timed approach, victorious and in number...as, to the contrary the Mexica saw only their demise at his receiving and prepared themselves a final, desperate stance.

From command or signal of some other sort, an issue understood though neither seen nor heard, the dammed adversity released itself erupting on all sides. Hence urging forth to remedy ignited failure underway, the brightly coloured, feathered High priestess exclaimed aloud her frenzied invocations from the sanctuary of distance. Assuming leadership in place of those now known less suited to the task, she fuelled and stoked the bloody outpour of revolt to overwhelm, declaring open warfare...and with spear and rock and ritual blade inspired subjects carried keenly now her wanton bidding to the foe and to its ends.

The pressing throng crashed driven down on Pedro's guard to suffocate in but an instant, whereupon all trace of him seemed lost. Rodriguez though, resolving through the cries of such infringement, cut a swathe to aid protection slashing flesh and bone, and struggled on subduing furor's will ferociously before him, seized his ally from the scavenged talon's raking of cessation's dyeing shades and fought with hope renewed to reach the high ground of the palace. Behind him in the swirling boil of savage chaos, small and personal battles formed their isolating pockets of an acrid bloodshed's spill amid the wake, where too, opposing, lurked the cautiously respectful stand offs, stalking death's digestion to devour...sampling flavours ere engagement.

For their part, besieged and separated in the seething melee, Cortez and his men came also almost overrun...however, spurred to near shame behind Rodriguez's lead he nevertheless made clearance of their valiant way for each exhaustive step toward the top and earned the slightest of advantage, there uniting with his protégé once more, who, aided in the striving by any other Spanish hand that could, defended scant position ably, claiming footholds as a resource that the others might adhere to.

Reaching the summit by grace or chance unscathed, Cortez plunged his anger past companions through the palace doors beyond dissolving forfeit to the gloom, where emergence blood spent terminations later saw his urging out before, the wretched and defeated form of plaintive kingship, for his throwing down before a people once regarded as his own.

Laid bare that day besieged contrition's glare, the Mexica knew clearly exposed the conquering intentions of those forevermore considered as invaders. For forced with sword at neck to ground upon his knees, Moctezuma begged conclusion to events and wholly uncontested, their abeyance, creating stunned, the uneasy fleeting interval of order that descended there again upon the delicate wings of fragile promises and lies. And as a nation watched in shame the travesty brought forth to greet them far beyond all comprehension of such devastating downfall, their sadness forged as rivulets in stone, where culmination pooled and found itself despising soon enough whatever was remaining of their great and glorious leader.

Those of Cortez's faithful, unable until now, to reach the haven of the highest terrace, took the battle lull as opportunity and joined his side apace...but alas, the stretched and murmured hush of hesitant appraisal endured no longer than the shortest while and presently became as dashed as was the king himself, against the rocks of tidal outrage, purging irreclaimable its kindling flotsam at the dawn. Unrepentant and with fierce brutality were rained all things to hand upon a wanting and discarded monarchy erasing from collective memory each painful sight and sense of its betrayal. Pitiful would his ailing, cries have been should any have dared or cared to stop and listen but with thought and hope in disarray, preceding stature was it known beyond the saving, and so was quickly cast bereft to face alone, the questioning of fate.

Rallying his men, Cortez pushed a hasty retreat into the safety of the palace and barred the heavy doors above an island city drowning in its discord as the fury of ignited vengeance crashed without, relentlessly to halter. Hammering its echoes chill through core, entombed in revolution, their prison walls though held as fast and gave the chance of respite, safely there ensnared inside a trap of their own making.

Rodriguez sat head bowed beneath the heavy weight of wounds in bouts of quiet solace listening introspectively whilst Cortez paced the hall to dredge the reaches of his mind in quest to find solution. Insufficient was the food within to sustain a lengthy siege he knew and less of water even for to quench the parchness left by conflict…and yet somewhere nearby not wholly so confined as he to bearing saddened thoughts of valiant men whose search for glory faltered, ripped apart by rasping demon hands, Pedro de Alvarado struck the air, a tormented, cheated figure, his restless spirit filled with raging mood now venting proclamation to the vow that severed heads of Indians would adorn his belt that day with many more to follow.

Cortez seized a courtier who had mistakenly remained on hearing battle's clamour raise and applied his knife to throat benumbed in search of answers to escape the clutch he found himself within. Marina, loyal to the end, neared and put herself of service.

"Who alone, out there would constitute our greatest foe?" he snarled.

The young man answered incoherently afraid to the very marrow of his bones, conveying shame as limp enough to soak, though soon collected whence presumed already dead to find the strangest tranquil peace inside, resigned despite himself, uniquely stayed in one clear moment's undeterring to the inquisition of cold steel, and furthermore could oddly, somehow feel his skin relinquished of its pressure.

"Tell me of the feathered witch who, as I speak, incites outside, a will amassed against me, far exceeding that habitually required to spawn impromptu insurrections, one which I further say, ought surely spell an end a thousand times to each misfortunate enough to have their oafish part in ponderous deeds today…but inform me also of the reason why I entertain no recollection of her vile acquaintance prior to this sorry date," Cortez demanded, intimidated by a gnawing sense of his being made to play the fool.

"She, my lord, is High priestess Chetroquilla revered servant of the mighty Huitzilopochtli…as are we all, though less directly than her ladyship of course. She is guardian and tutor also of Cuauhtemoc who must follow in Moctezuma's illustrious wake. Chetroquilla commands highly and sees much that others cannot. Tonatiuh's divinity flows through her and as such she falls at no one's feet but Moctezuma's…and naturally, Rashtak-oatl himself, within whose sacred walls she dwells."

"Rashtak-oatl," Cortez repeated testily. "You see, Rodriguez, he is a curious player as already I have said." He spoke considering the reality of horrors to be faced, whilst yet deeply intrigued by a chosen inconspicuousness, where should have been to his mind, great distinction. "What true office does this old man Rashtak hold? And I warn, speak not to me in falsehood or your life's short journey will assuredly find its end this very afternoon."

"He holds no office, lord. About him all things move as they have, and always will. He is Rashtak-oatl." The courtier spoke plainly in an obvious factual manner suggesting even ignorance personified would know the answer to that particular question.

"….and what of likely tales that tell from whence this royal slyness came?" sneered Cortez, realising perhaps too late, that their time there might well have been better spent enquiring deeper of their hosts than on misguided quests for hidden quantities of gold which may or may not even at the last, exist.

"It is said that northward ever was his course, a scorching swept afore the blighted squall destroying all resistance to his cruel determined need, in prosecution of the one whose blackened heart betrayed him long ago. To no avail he searched, a lost embittered soul, until Quetzalcoatl granted Tenoch unto him to lead and change his heart with purpose, so to scour instead for peaceful lands where we, the Mexica might grow and hopeful, prosper…unmolested." Objection's dour glint gave Cortez meaning to reflect undaunted before it too carried on regardless. "Here then, it was upon the very ground on which we stand they laid our roots where long ago the eagle and the serpent strove, a welcome contest thus defining true an omen sent to look for. And sufficient was the serpent's number on this isle to provide our bearers food aplenty, lending freely of itself until the harvests could be gathered and repayment duly made. Ever since, Rashtak-oatl has ordered our lives, from time beyond the long count and spread our borders widely. For is it not so that far across the land the dominion of our people holds from shore to distant shore?" Intended pause allowed for recognition unbestowed so did collapse to hasten on ahead frustrated sigh. "Undisturbed his residency bides above the temple with the priestess and boy prince Cuauhtemoc therein for tutelage in the privileged ways…and from such point of vantage watches over us, seldom taking ventures forth…but even more infrequent suffering our distraction further in the drudge of mundane audience."

"But, if you will forgive my intervention, sir, this is an absurdity, is it not?" Pedro interrupted. "These are mortal men who live in fear and superstition given over to the Devil's hand. The Lord has judged it time to shine his beacon on their handiwork's depravity and brought us here to rectify that ill. Pure and simple! Therefore, I state readily, and in the face of all who stand opposed, that we must neither deviate nor waver in our duty to impose the justified correction, so that one day, if not even seen ourselves, then some at least might win deliverance through example, for this vast perverted realm."

His comments were met with general approval around the hall on a rumble of support to punctuation as he finished, with a subdued and stifled cheer for the closure. Cortez seemed lightened by their reaction released of heavy burden. Despite the seriousness of the predicament their courage found itself not dulled but honed instead by scorn and pride whence pressed before such overbearing challenge.

"What say you, Rodriguez?" Cortez had witnessed many times duress where men could shine or fail according to the nature of beliefs, but was asking now this trusted counsel on a worth already proven.

"We cannot stay here, that much is clear. Whether we choose to remain a time and leave in weakened, famished state to better chance an organised entrapment having lived a little longer, or whether we strike out swiftly while the chaos still persists inflicting what we may whilst battle still becomes us are sole matters for good leadership's concern. I, indeed as should be known, will follow where you take me, sir…but you were correct when you implied that fear retains its value as a dangerous ally, for I believe myself to be in receipt of a shortened measure now, and for the first, albeit from the most stingy bodegeuro….and if I, then others here will feel it also, of that I have no hesitation to make mention. Perhaps even you, the mighty Hernando Cortez, might confess to this rarest disposition, which can only serve to forge us each in truth, as all the more formidable opponents. Can it not?"

Reluctant nods cascaded sad, upon reflective sighs of grim acceptance as he gazed around with presence bold enough for lending every soldier present a relief from individual shame concealed, and focus from self-doubting.

"Very well, then we shall leave to whatever destiny awaits us, ere our stomachs make complaint," Cortez began, "and regardless of the outcome that awaits this stand we make together, always shall my words resound with earnest pride of those of us still here, we sons of Spain and new world's recent friendship….that never before was rivalled deed requested.

"For the cause, you have endured long beyond your call throughout each cursed occasion and suffered only detriment thus far as scant reward returned in service of our king and country. Distinguished you have borne yourselves with backs of steel on all accounts commendably, and likewise have our fallen brothers also. This would suffice, and well you know, for any of a mongrel breed, the English or the French whose fickle terms, of old are lore, but for us of legend's worth who straddled first this globe of ours in God's true name and application we must steadfast, seize the greater charge. Fully, we are aware of the accumulated foe that loiters for our end outside this heathen refuge. We hear their cries of anguish and foresee the pagan savagery in store, but to all distinct ancestral mark accounted for today I say take comfort in the knowledge that the chore we have assumed is holy work and therefore of the highest order. Think yourselves then not as mere men but as extensions of a righteous will. Understand this also to the fullest, that a fierce and mighty hand descends in wrath before our chosen selves to rid this land entirely of the wicked craft that dwells herein.

"United then, we march perhaps a final time, forth and proudly from the Devil's hall with issue from these very gates towards the baring teeth of hell itself, to quench the raging demon fire on this defining hour of our accomplishment and reckoning. Heaven's arms are open to embrace and wait attendance if we must, but first we have redemption's work to do. So I ask you now prepare within, stern consciences to satisfy the soul, for this historic, glorious confrontation, for God through men of Spain, for fallen brethren undiminished nevermore denied and for a task we cannot fail!"

Cortez turned in haste his fire burning bright for all to see and follow, drew his sword to wield aloft then striding led the way to quell the pounding at the door.

"Remove the bar," he called upon approach, "that I may pass! Strike down the feathered demon-slut and let us cleanse triumphant foulest realms of Satan's lust! May God have mercy on infernal souls this eve for retribution stalks the dust with menace to perform. Come! The call is now for destiny at hand, to claim the hour and staunch an end on rancid deeds hereafter to confess in noble voice aloft, that we still hear damnation's final echo fall resounding from the steps of Spanish judgement day!"

The bar was lifted, the doors fell open and flooding in on twilight's havoc the Mexica came unprepared on brandished steel. There issued forth a charge of reckless loyal men unto an unsuspecting world. Drenched in timeless acts of fear-inspired and dreadful honour in the making. Reaping all that stood defiant with a shocked, astonished ease. Brutal minds remorseless, pure and clear scythed themselves a bloody path with polished blades to freedom, surging on the upturned, frightened faces lending neither thought to carefulness nor wasting precious skill on mercy.

Rodriguez caught a glimpse of desperation shrieking orders from within the crazed, fanatic horde. Bright in effervescent colour, she revealed herself and gave an odious mark for single-mindedness incensed, to make direct, its plunge towards her. Cortez saw the move and pursued the target also. Pedro filled the space behind instinctually protective of their backs, defending bravely on his own he fought for friends and countrymen alike.

Ever closer, Rodriguez struggled through the angry, lashing crowd. Disorganised and packed too closely to inflict intention's clearest strike, he forced his way upon the stricken priestess close surrounded at her sides and as such trapped within the overbearance of amassed companionship, restricting all about.

The silver gods among that heathen number preyed religiously with relish on uncertainty, loosed chaos and the glory reigning from war's regimented discipline when came they bearing arms against her…and so it came to be that Chetroquilla's influence succumbed to deafened fate, dispersed beneath Toledo's slashing fury.

Hacked and flailed, her body rent and further crushed, the Mexica now found themselves once more without a leader. Overcome to reel with smarting shock indignance had insightful watched her taken from them, impotent and slain in shame amidst their naive, vain protection. The gods of old, they once believed, would harbour them, instead had cast their servants down forsaken, as condemned and worthless where resistive efforts languished only to prolong the surety of futile.

Chetroquilla was no longer, her remains clogged scatter underfoot, the resolve for revolution had, upon such soil shrunk withered to remove itself again…and broken, a bewildered people drifted aimlessly about forlorn and tortured by regretful woe and sudden disbelief.

The conquistadores took gladly of the battle's unexpected, eerie calm and made their cautious exit, filching eager from the spoils there piled on hand for ready counting at the edges of the plaza. Foolishly some sacrificed the trusty weapons that they bore exchanging steel for gold. Some indeed accrued themselves too heavily of both and suffered overtaxed, their inability to run, whilst others argued pettily of baubles fit for naught but gift or fancy. Almost all delayed escape on sight of easy wealth to some degree or other….But not forever would such lull remain before short-lived described in truth, that opening provided.

For so it was another grasped the reigns of orchestration, turning downcast heads to lifted once again. Beholding from their swung obedience, along the strongest draw of wills, a sight opposing every eye to stir the heart's incline or stain the temple summit with its poise outstretched and shaven head thrust back, against the leaden death of evening sky, the Devil's pride himself enflamed, aroused to wreak dominion over all.

Billowing of raiment, struck to swoop it seemed and slay from high, he spread the vileness of his malice reigning down upon them. Stationed thus the Raven's cry of challenge plundered through the city streets below, its echo haunting through relentless from containment's walls disturbed, with dread enough to shatter and an awe to summon forth dejected spirits with a single gathered purpose…that to hurl and nothing less, all dead intruders from its realm.

Cortez saw the tide of conflict rise renewed against them and issued therefore, orders for a swift and guarded flight. Through the streets he strode with dignity alone sufficed to staunch the wounded urge to flee, though overtaken was his march on either side by others not so noble, whence then pitiful the discipline of shape, and form of rank, fragmented delicate about him as dissolves the crisp morn' frost to naught when harried by dawn's light.

Those laden with their greed or bound on dreams of better lives for them and for their loved ones simply slipped to lag behind, slow falling woefully as victims to the vast stampede of trampling feet, there being little opportunity to aid from drowning in the following flood which now began to clash against their trailing flanks with threat to overrun.

Face glared twisted into snarling face, jagged spears thrust wildly to harass retreat along its outer edges. Shards of clay and heavy objects cast from high above by women and their tender offspring crashed a fierce intensity to fracture perilous amongst them. Ordered rigidity and sterile pace deep forged in other places, brittle cracked now through the main though barely held sufficient for the final lunge to make the outer causeways…but close beyond the binding of the city's walls the conquistadores saw their fate however, sealed, whence forced to separate in isolated bunches, becoming overtaken with despair at first though soon surrounded utterly, would perish, crushed indeed among those dismal, harrowed spaces.

Many fell that night and never gained their footing, committed blindly to their unknown courses seeking passage through a darkened, unfamiliar landscape. Taking routes that suddenly ended at the water's edge or worse, returned on themselves and led back only to possessive arms of ready ill intent. Some were forced in cruel mockery to swim as best they could to rich men's deaths beneath the cold of inkwell blackness clutching still their hard fought gold to light up ways on murky paths to afterlives befitting. But some survived and told the tale of sorrow, repeating with a hope to ease their troubled minds and justify remembrance of 'El noche triste.' The saddest night when men betrayed themselves with preferential loyalties to dreams and thus were found forsaken by their god.

Hernando Cortez regrouped in time to further strengthen his diminished army, swearing keen reprisal on the Indian nations for his loss, returning cold of mind for razing Tenochtitlan and its memories to the earth, severing retribution from the land at its infected heart to cauterise a festered wound inflicted on himself as best he was able. He took then Cuauhtemoc's surrender and assumed control of all the Aztec empire putting finally an end to pagan rule, installing in due course no less, Pedro de Alvarado as the city's governor for a while. However, owing to the shortfall of appeasable wealth recovered there, Cortez in his wisdom chose to make those people mine and grub the soil for he, and for the good of Spain as supplement to recompense. A decision that, in the early days, drove many to their deaths through overwork and famine, before his heart was eventually softened by a dreamer's disillusioned eyes so slow to find their waking.

Rashtak-oatl disappeared without a trace or rumour of direction, and so would prompt Cortez before that moment of enlightenment, to order soldiers searching far and wide across the region holding he alone accountable as the architect of downfall. Pedro de Alvarado, when he deemed the moment right, ventured south converting all beneath a vengeful hand whence wiping clean the landscape of its many tribes and colonies, ever scouring also for the whereabouts of one elusive demon and the secrets he might hold…. As for Rodriguez Maria Gonzalez, he remained many loyal years at Cortez' side permitting wounds to heal whilst overseeing expeditions with control of vast returning shipments, and when Cortez received renewed and welcome favour, he too was given blessing to return to Spain and his beloved Catalonia.

So early it was one summer's cloudless sunny morn' he said farewell a final time to his friends Hernando and Malinche, turned his face into the eastern wind and looked towards the coast. Alone on horseback, he rode the arduous trail to Veracruz, passing by the rocky mountains over ground once trodden long ago with conquering intent and unsheathed sword in hand. Through the open, gentle countryside and on towards the gloomy shades of woven bough, there putting down to rest the night, upon the fringes of a wide leafed, star encrusted clearing, where he watched the embers glowing for a time then drifted off to wrestled sleep and stirring.

Shortly after such descent to fickle slumber, Rodriguez lurched with dreadful insight, there for naught and much too late he knew the blackest blade of evil's dagger firm against his throat and hence discounted was he let with no more than a sickened savour's relish, for to turn enough and see the noxious staring pierce cold from lifeless eyes. Long ago consumed the ashen, deathly face that grimaced from beyond the pale, enveloped wry a stench that was by definition, Rashtak-oatl.

"Mock me now," the sneering hissed, taunting venom in clear but broken Spanish.

Rodriguez did not move.

"Tell me of Ishtaac Maluk and where this land that you have shared exists, and I may make some use of you."

"Que se joda!" Rodriguez Maria Gonzalez spat, his own salvation to refute, and never spoke again.

Printed in the United Kingdom
by Lightning Source UK Ltd.
107259UKS00001B/82-84